T0006234

THE
NIGHT WIRE

and Other Tales
of Weird Media

THE
NIGHT WIRE

and Other Tales of Weird Media

Edited by
AARON WORTH

This collection first published in 2022 by
The British Library
96 Euston Road
London NW1 2DB

Cataloguing in Publication Data
A catalogue record for this publication is available from the British Library

ISBN 978 0 7123 5411 0
e-ISBN 978 0 7123 6754 7

Frontispiece illustration by Mauricio Villamayor and Sandra Gómez
Cover design by Mauricio Villamayor with illustration by Sandra Gómez
Text design and typesetting by Tetragon, London
Printed in England by CPI Group (UK) Ltd, Croydon, CR0 4YY

Contents

INTRODUCTION

Some 250 years ago, a grim, spectral figure stepped out of a picture frame and descended to the ground, to the horror of his awestruck descendant (to say nothing of a legion of terrified readers). Much more recently, millions of moviegoers found their hearts beating faster as they watched (those who *were* still watching) a grainy video on a TV screen depicting an old stone well, from which a drowned thing emerged—all tangled black hair and twisted pale limbs—and crept slowly towards the viewer, *out* of the TV screen, and into the "world" of the movie itself.

Our media have been frightening us for a long time.

There is, in fact, a very good case to be made that the entire category of Gothic, horror, the weird—whatever you want to call it—is the offspring of new, non-literary media technologies. The famous animated-portrait scene in Horace Walpole's *The Castle of Otranto*—by common agreement the first Gothic novel—was most likely influenced by its author's exposure to the magic lantern shows which were then metamorphosising into the terrifying Phantasmagoria, a wildly popular pre-cinematic horror show that would leave its mark upon such Romantic-era Gothic masterpieces as Matthew Lewis's *The Monk* (1796), Mary Shelley's *Frankenstein* (1818, 1831), Charles Maturin's *Melmoth the Wanderer* (1820), and James Hogg's *Confessions of a Justified Sinner* (1824). These novels were written in a world of lantern shows and other optical entertainments, of new and improved postal systems, and of the first telegraphs—not electric but visual in nature, networks of hilltop towers that waved jointed arms or flashed signals at each other. It was the faintly glimmering dawn of the modern media age.

Then the sun came up. First, a pair of astonishing inventions, born in the late 1830s and coming into widespread use in the 1840s, forever changed the way people thought about time and space. Photography, first perfected by Louis Daguerre, captures the fleeting moment, preserves the past and brings it, unchanging, into the ever-changing present. The electric telegraph, invented on both sides of the Atlantic at the same time, harnessed the newly understood principles of electromagnetism to achieve the ancient fantasy of instantaneous communication across vast distances. After these, the deluge: in the decades to come, a virtual cascade of new technologies spilled from the workshops of inventors largely building on this dual foundation—the submarine cables which allowed for the wiring of the entire globe; the radio which did away with the need for wires altogether; the telephone and phonograph which enabled the human voice to be transmitted or stored; the cinema which captured not only images from life but, seemingly, life itself, inspiring such coinages as "Bioscope" and "Vitascope". (This is not even to mention the first steps towards modern information processing technology taken by Charles Babbage and Ada Lovelace, those retroactively canonised patron saints of our own computer age.) By the end of Queen Victoria's reign, a dynamic new media ecology was in full flower.

As in the early days of the Internet, this brave new technological world spawned plenty of optimistic, even ecstatic, predictions about the future of humanity. In Nathaniel Hawthorne's Gothic novel *The House of the Seven Gables* (1851), the Rip Van Winkle-like Clifford Pyncheon, emerging from prison after thirty years into a world of daguerreotypes and electric telegraphs, promptly goes into raptures over the possibility of a wired planet, part global village and part love-in, where even death is no barrier to communication. But, then as now, each new technology brought with it anxieties as well; and media, with their seemingly preternatural ability to enhance our powers of perception and communication, are particularly *intimate* technologies—they become, as Marshall McLuhan put it (and as every owner of a smartphone knows), extensions of ourselves. And just as—coincidence or not—the classic Gothic novel had emerged in the age of the Phantasmagoria, it was during these heady decades of media multiplication that horror fiction evolved into its modern form, with much of this evolution being driven by weird writers' engagement with new media.

For a famous example of this engagement, one need look no further than that landmark novel of modern horror, Bram Stoker's *Dracula*. Here is a text purportedly made up of a myriad of state-of-the-art technologies and practices (Dr. Seward's phonograph cylinders, Jonathan Harker's shorthand journal and Kodak snapshots, newspaper clippings, Mina Harker's all-transcribing typewriter), while its archetypal monster is a telepath resembling nothing so much as the centre of a far-flung broadcasting network. It is surely no accident that the novel appeared soon after Guglielmo Marconi arrived in Britain with his early wireless-telegraph machine. (It is worth noting that H. G. Wells imagined a race of telepathic vampires, in *The War of the Worlds*, that same year.) Interesting, too, is Stoker's conception of his famous creation in relation to technologies of representation. Count Dracula, as everyone knows, casts no reflection in a mirror. But Stoker's notes for the novel indicate that the vampire lord's resistance to media capture went beyond this; he wrote that one "Could not codak [sic] him—come out black or like skeleton corpse". Could not Kodak him! Stoker cannot quite seem to decide whether the vampire would not appear at all on film (the photo would "come out black") or would be shown more truly, as his (un)dead self ("like skeleton corpse"), but either way, the camera's vision is uncanny, revealing something undetectable to the human eye. For a modern analogue, we might fast-forward, again, to the movie *The Ring*, in which snapshots of cursed teenagers show blurred, distorted faces. The spooky augmentation of the senses; the opening of new channels of communication with the dead (or worse than dead); the ambiguous boundary between representation and reality; the uncanny telephonic or phonographic detachment of the human voice from its body of origin: these are only some of the abiding terror-tropes of what we might term "media horror," a genre with its roots in the past that is very much still with us today.

In preparing this collection of shorter fiction haunted by weird media, I wanted not only to select good stories—of course!—but also to include depictions of a range of information technologies, to give as full a sense as possible of the rich media systems in which these writers lived and worked—and found fodder for their readers' nightmares. Within these pages you will encounter telegraphs and telephones, phonographs and radios, cinema and typewriting and television, as well as more obscure technologies. Quite a range of authors, too, are represented here, from the justly famous to the unjustly forgotten. These writers are introduced in the headnotes to the stories, which I have also tried to contextualise by saying a little bit about the technologies that feature in them. Those not in the mood for a history lesson are, of course, free to skip on ahead. But my hope is that they may enrich the reader's understanding and enjoyment of the stories by providing some historical background to the technologies and networks of a lost media age—one which is both strange to us and, at the same time, strangely familiar.

AARON WORTH

A NOTE FROM THE PUBLISHER

The original short stories reprinted in the British Library Tales of the Weird series were written and published in a period ranging across the nineteenth and twentieth centuries. There are many elements of these stories which continue to entertain modern readers, however in some cases there are also uses of language, instances of stereotyping and some attitudes expressed by narrators or characters which may not be endorsed by the publishing standards of today. We acknowledge therefore that some elements in the stories selected for reprinting may continue to make uncomfortable reading for some of our audience. With this series British Library Publishing aims to offer a new readership a chance to read some of the rare material of the British Library's collections in an affordable paperback format, to enjoy their merits and to look back into the worlds of the past two centuries as portrayed by their writers. It is not possible to separate these stories from the history of their writing and as such the following stories are presented as they were originally published with the inclusion of minor edits made for consistency of style and sense, and with pejorative terms of an extremely offensive nature partly obscured. We welcome feedback from our readers, which can be sent to the following address:

British Library Publishing
The British Library
96 Euston Road
London, NW1 2DB
United Kingdom

THE EIDOLOSCOPE

Robert Duncan Milne

A highly original writer of speculative fiction, Robert Duncan Milne (1844–1899) was born in Scotland and attended Oxford University before more or less vanishing, only to rematerialise in California. During the last quarter of the nineteenth century, Milne's ingenious tales of planetary cataclysm, time travel, cryogenic preservation, and remote-controlled aircraft (among other things) appeared in the pages of *The Argonaut*, a periodical best remembered for its association with Ambrose Bierce, whom Milne likely influenced.

As the subject matter of his fiction would indicate, Milne was fascinated by technology, especially technologies of transportation and communication (it is a grim irony that he was crushed to death by one of San Francisco's new electric streetcars). In his stories he imagined, among other then-impossible-seeming media systems, global satellite networks, while two of his tales, "The Palaeoscopic Camera" and "The Eidoloscope", reflect his keen interest in the experiments in motion photography conducted by a fellow English transplant in San Francisco, Eadweard Muybridge (1830–1904). In 1878 Muybridge, fresh from his acquittal for the murder of his wife's lover, set up a chain of triggered cameras to prove that a horse's four hooves do, in fact, all leave the ground at the same time. A crucial precursor to cinema proper, Muybridge's chronophotographic studies added a temporal dimension to photography which clearly influenced Milne. (Interestingly, a real, if non-fantastic, "Eidoloscope" was developed in the 1890s, but there is no good reason to assume the inventor was influenced by Milne's story: there had been "Eidoscopes" and "Eidotropes" as far back as the 1860s.) In the story's somewhat prolix opening, Milne paints a useful picture of the state of media invention near the end of the century, with a cameo appearance by Thomas Edison and a nod to Alexander Graham Bell.

"The Eidoloscope" appeared in the January 27, 1890 number of *The Argonaut*. It does not appear to have been reprinted since.

will premise by saying that my narrative deals with the correlation of forces and the production of ghosts.

My narrative will have the effect of removing all doubt about the reality of that class of spectral manifestations which has ever been a subject for jest to professors of positive science, who, where they admit their existence at all, refer them to a diseased or abnormal condition of the brain. This question, however, will now happily be set at rest, as the distinguished scientists referred to will have an opportunity of producing these spectral manifestations almost at will, and have the pleasure of knowing that the spectres they produce are the result of an invariable and ordinary natural law and merely constitute another example of the universality and harmony of the great law of cause and effect which pervades nature, acting alike upon the atom and the nebula. Many ghost stories, which now appear to be the maunderings of superstitious or half-witted idiots, will henceforth be known to have originated not in a series of diseased imaginations, but in the workings of an obscure but unerring natural law. It must not be supposed, however, that the class of spectral manifestations which can thus be produced are of the same nature, or have the same origin, as the phantasmagoria of the mediaeval necromancer or modern charlatan. The spectres which these invoke are independent of time and place, while those to which I allude are purely local in their character and depend for their very being upon surrounding conditions.

What old residence in any of the old countries of Europe, England, Scotland, Ireland, or Germany, or even in the older States of America itself, does not boast of some particular ghostly legend connected with its grey old walls, antiquated galleries, and dilapidated chambers? Not to possess some family spectre associated with such a residence, would be evidence against its claim to the honours of antiquity or romance. What would the old castles of Germany be without the spectres of their mail-clad barons, their clanking chains, and their pale ladies in white? What the old halls or abbeys of the British Isles without the nocturnal visitations of the ghostly Sir Marmaduke or the gliding figure of the stately Lady Clare? Have not the spectral apparitions of these renowned personages been attested to and vouched for from time immemorial by grey-bearded seneschals and grave waiting-men and women, whose very gravity and sincerity proclaim them as innocent as they would be incapable of deception on so serious a subject?

To what then are we to attribute the faith and veneration with which these visions and legends are received on the one side, and the scepticism and ridicule with which they are met upon the other? Is it possible that traditions so exact in their character regarding the appearance of particular spectres in particular places should be absolutely baseless, and if not absolutely baseless, whence came the substratum of truth which developed into the substantial entity in which most of them are found? These and similar speculations must frequently have arisen in thinking minds when discussing this curious psychical problem, and it is with the object of affording some assistance toward its rational solution that I now, for the first time, make public the following experience.

Last summer, while visiting the Paris Exposition, I chanced to meet, in that portion of the building devoted to the science and applied mechanics of electricity, a gentleman with whom I had become acquainted in the city of San Francisco a few months before. He had been then introduced to me as a man of science and an inventor of some note, though his inventions, I had been told, were of a tentatory and theoretical rather than of a practical nature; in other words, though his ideas were valuable and often grand in their character, to the ordinary mind he would have seemed to be aiming at too much, and, while endeavouring to grasp the unattainable, he would miss the practical results which he might, with less imagination, have secured. For instance, in the domain of electrical science, to which he had lately been applying himself, he had sketched out the theory of several novel applications of that wonderful medium. One was telegraphy without wires, by means of an electric diaphragm or envelope, which he conceived encircled the globe at a certain height, and being tapped at any locality by a small captive balloon, up whose anchoring cord ran a conducting wire terminating in a recording instrument, would furnish a suitable medium of communication with any other instrument similarly connected with the diaphragm and keyed to the same electric pitch. Another was the transmutation of metals by means of the transmission of a powerful electric current through their masses, thus changing their densities and consequently their volumes and their colours, by merely altering the collocation of their atoms through this mysterious and all-potent agency.

These instances will serve to give some idea of the brilliant though visionary character of my friend, and it was accordingly without the least surprise that I found him ensconced in the electrical department of the exposition, still less that he had had only the modest space of some six feet square allotted to him, while his more practical, though not more ingenious, collaborators in the same sphere of discovery had ten or more times the area.

It was while I was sauntering leisurely down one of the aisles that my eye fell upon the familiar figure of Mr. Espy, of whose presence in Paris I had not previously been aware. He was seated at a little table, upon which were set some instruments, or models, connected with his art, and upon one of which his attention seemed to be particularly concentrated. This was a highly polished globe, or sphere, either of metal or silvered glass, I could not tell which, about six inches in diameter and raised upon a slender pedestal to about the same height above the table.

Presently Mr. Espy awoke from the fit of abstraction with which he had been regarding this sphere, and turned his eyes critically upon a curious piece of mechanism which stood on the table beside it. This bore no resemblance to anything I had ever seen before, and I can only describe what it looked like by a simile. Imagine for yourself two hollow hemispheres, hinged together at a point upon their peripheries, and set flat upon the table so that they stood side by side. From the surfaces of these hemispheres radiated, in every direction, from a point which would have been their common centre had they been shut close together so as to form a perfect globe, a series of slender rods like the bristles on a porcupine, each terminating in a little bulb at a distance of some ten or twelve inches from the surface of the globe.

Preoccupied as he was Mr. Espy took no notice of my presence, but seemed to be revolving some problem in his mind, with one hand on the curious appliance I have just described, his long black hair hanging down so as almost to conceal his sallow face. After a moment or two, he raised the bristling hemispheres from the table till they were over the polished globe, round which he clasped them together like a cover, the outer hollow sphere, as I could see, fitting very closely to the inner one. This was evident for the reason that the outer sphere, or envelope, was, I could now see, composed of some extremely diaphanous substance, so transparent as only to intercept with a gauze-like film the reflection from the spherical mirror within. Neither did the slender rods that radiated from the centre materially affect the field of vision, as they were only about one-sixteenth of an inch in thickness, and closely serried as they seemed when viewed laterally, they formed scarcely any visual obstruction when pointing directly toward the eye.

When Mr. Espy had effected this arrangement, he looked up.

"Glad to see you," he said, rising and shaking me by the hand; "I did not know you were in Paris."

I told him that I was equally unconscious of his own presence, and made a remark regarding the queer instrument upon the table.

"Yes," he said, "that is the practical embodiment of an idea I have lately evolved, and though it is, in some respects, crude as yet, I see great possibilities in it for the future. My friend Edison over there," with a gesture in the direction of that distinguished inventor's department, "or if not Edison, Bell, or whoever else may lay claim to the original discovery, ascertained that sound vibrations could be conveyed along a wire by an electrical current and reproduced at the other end in precisely the same manner—pitch, tone, and expression—as they had been originally delivered. Edison has since gone a step further, and by a very simple mechanical means has caused these sound vibrations to transcribe their own equivalents upon a wax cylinder, which, by an inverse process, can be made to give forth the same identical vibrations when required. The phonograph is simply an adaptation of the principle of the telephone, storing up for future reference, just as in a book, the sounds—be they words, harmonies, or discords, simple or composite—which have been committed to its keeping."

"I understand the principle perfectly," I assented, as Mr. Espy mused for an instant in abstraction.

"Now," he continued, "this little instrument here is also a receiver and transmitter of vibrations, not on the principle of the phonograph, for it has no means of storing what it receives, but reproduces the vibrations instantly after the manner of the telephone. It is, in one respect, less serviceable than the telephone, as it is not susceptible to ordinary sound-vibrations in the accepted sense of the term; in another respect, it is infinitely more delicate and more potent. What would you say," he went on, earnestly, and looking me keenly in the eye, "if I were to tell you that that little, simple, and insignificant instrument is capable of recording and reproducing luminous pulsations, or light-vibrations, call them what you will, so delicate in their nature that it would fill you and the scientific world at large with incredulity and amazement were I at present to even hint at or suggest what they are competent to reveal?"

I replied that scarcely any new discovery in the mysterious domain of electric science would surprise me, after the results we had witnessed during the past few years.

"I do not know," went on Mr. Espy, "whether I can make myself intelligible, without ocular demonstration, on the scope of my discovery. Briefly and simply stated, this little instrument, which I have christened the eidoloscope, is capable of becoming susceptible to the action of the luminous waves emanating from objects exposed to the impact of similar waves at some period of the past."

"I confess I do not quite catch your meaning," I remarked, somewhat mystified by the generality of the description.

"I perfectly appreciate your position," returned Mr. Espy, smiling; "the results I obtained were astounding and inexplicable to myself the first time I realised their true purport, and it was only after much hard and careful thought that I succeeded at last in reducing them to the very simple and beautiful law under which they are produced. Let us see whether I can not explain the matter by a specific illustration. You see this polished globular mirror here. It is made of glass, backed with quicksilver, and does not differ in any respect from hundreds of others of the same fashion, save, perhaps, in a more accurate sphericity. The hollow diaphanous envelope which surrounds it is made of an elastic preparation, into the composition of which I will say that celluloid largely enters. This is blown into spherical shape, on the principle of an ordinary soap-bubble or glass-bulb, while in a fluid or viscous state, and subsequently hardens into the transparent sphere you see before you. This spherical envelope, or diaphragm, is of such extreme elasticity and tenuity that the most infinitesimal pulsations of sound or light, even those of the violet rays of the spectrum—the number of distinct pulsations of which have been estimated at many millions to the inch—exert the most marked effect upon it, as I have proved to my complete satisfaction. The vibrations of this elastic diaphragm are, of course, transmitted to the sphere within, which is distant only about one-sixteenth of an inch. Here you see you have at once the principle of the telephone, have you not?"

I assented, and Mr. Espy went on:

"Very good. Now, how do we excite this sensitive diaphragm? Any vibrations, whether of light, or sound, or heat, will, of course, do so. The sound of our voices do so violently at this moment, but the receiver will not transmit the faintest echo of a response in answer. Why? Because such vibrations are too coarse for the delicately sensitive instrument before us. It might, it is true, reproduce sounds, but they would be of such exquisite tone as to be imperceptible to our gross auricular organisation. To what, then, is this instrument sensitive? Only to light-waves, to luminous pulsations conveyed to it under certain conditions, and, moreover, not in the ordinary manner by direct light-rays, but by their electric correlatives. It is to effect this end that these tiny rods radiate from and impinge upon the elastic diaphragm. *Now* do you comprehend the scope and purpose of the eidoloscope?" concluded Mr. Espy, in a triumphant manner.

"Partially so," I replied, hesitatingly; "but you have not yet explained whence these rays emanate."

"They emanate," returned Mr. Espy, "from surrounding objects within a certain distance, and this distance must not be great enough to preclude free electric transmission from the object to the receiver. An inclosed space of moderate size—a room, or apartment, of say twenty or thirty feet square—affords the best conditions for the successful operation of the process."

"And then what happens?" I queried.

"Scenes and occurrences of any and every nature that have ever transpired within a room in which the eidoloscope is placed, are vividly reproduced and acted over again upon the spherical mirror."

"You say 'any and every scene' is thus reproduced. Then why should any one particular scene enacted in the past be thus reproduced in preference to any other scene?" I asked.

"That also follows the subtle law which governs the manifestation," replied Mr. Espy; "heat is, as we know, a mechanical equivalent of light, light of electricity, electricity of both. Either force can be converted into any other, and this is the solution of the question you ask. It is *temperature* that governs the electrical emanations which cause the elastic sphere to vibrate, and thus reproduce the scenes enacted in a certain place in the past."

"But," I objected, "take the instance of a room which has been inhabited for centuries, as many rooms in old mansions have been, in what order or sequence would these scenes be reproduced?"

"They would appear upon the mirror," returned Mr. Espy, "in a reversed order of sequence—the last first, and so on to the earliest in point of time. Scenes would begin to appear upon the mirror as soon as the temperature of the room was sufficiently high to liberate the electrical energy stored away in the walls, ceiling, and furniture of the room, and cause that electrical energy to become charged with the light-rays which had once conveyed a message from every object within that room to every other object, and made each object the involuntary but silent repository of the history of every other object."

"But, my dear sir," said I, "this is a most startling theory which you suggest. How can you, as a reasonable man, account rationally for such an absurdity as that which you now advance?"

"Very simply," responded Mr. Espy, gravely, but without any sign of offence at my somewhat intemperate language; "you are enough of a man of science to admit these two propositions: First, that no force is ever lost in nature; and, second, that every form of force or energy is convertible into every other form. My eidoloscope simply reduces this formula to practice. The circles caused by the dropping of a pebble into a limpid pool, and which widen every moment as they recede, are not lost when they reach the shore; their splash may wash down a certain quantity of sand, or it may be thrown back as a reflux wave to meet a successor, but its initial force is not lost—it has merely changed its mode of action. The atmospheric vibrations caused by the sound of the words we now speak will continue to roll for limitless aeons through the limitless ether—light-rays in the same manner. What then happens when light-rays are stayed from their onward course—intercepted by the walls and furniture of a room, for instance? Are they therefore lost? I say no. The energy expended upon the material obstacles they encountered has effected a change in the collocation of the atoms of these objects, a change, it is true, imperceptible to any of our ordinary organs of sense, or ideas of measurement; but yet a change as real as that which would have been produced by the impact of a ball from a hundred-ton gun, the difference being not one of kind, but of degree. Yes, sir; the walls, ceilings, and furniture of a room represent the wax cylinder of the phonograph, and under proper treatment may be made to yield the electrical correlative of the light-rays which were once intercepted by them. I have discovered that proper treatment—and have I deserved badly of the scientific world, and must I be held up to ridicule because I am the first who has succeeded in doing so?" Mr. Espy concluded, with a certain degree of asperity and heat.

"And you have really ascertained, in a manner to convince yourself, that this appliance here is capable of reproducing the past as you have stated?" I asked.

"Yes," returned Mr. Espy, "my eidoloscope has passed the experimental stage and may now be classed with the scientific novelties of the age. Time alone will demonstrate to what uses it may be put. It may take the form merely of a scientific toy and become a source of amusement in households, while demonstrating a new law of optics, or it may be of benefit to the police authorities in locating crime and securing evidence against criminals. There are many uses to which the eidoloscope can be advantageously put. I may, hereafter, make adaptations and improvements in its structure, as has been done in the case of the telegraph, phonograph, and most other scientific inventions. But the *principle* is there, my dear sir; the *principle* is there. What you see here is only a model. I am here to explain its mechanism, just as I have now done to you, and to take orders from parties who would like to be supplied with it. There is one great advantage about it, too, and that is its simplicity. It does not require an expert to handle it. There is a small but very powerful battery concealed in the pedestal, and by simply pressing this button the circuit is completed and electrical connection established through these metallic rods, which, as you see, radiate in every direction, with all parts of a room. I am sorry it is so near the end of the season, or I am sure I should have received numerous orders for the eidoloscope. This is the first time, indeed, that I have been able to put even the model on exhibition, and you are the first person who has had the curiosity to put questions to me about it."

"You say you are prepared to supply orders for the instrument," I remarked; "is it expensive, may I ask?"

"Intrinsically, no," returned Mr. Espy; "the mechanism, as you see, is simplicity itself, and the first cost of the materials is not great. The adjustment of the elastic diaphragm to the spherical mirror at the proper distance is, however, a matter of much nicety. The packing of the instrument, too, for transport requires great care and entails considerable expense. Good results can not be secured with anything less than a three-foot globe, and when that is made of hollow glass, you can readily see the difficulty of packing it securely."

"I should very much like to see the instrument work," I said.

Mr. Espy told me he would let me know when he had one completed, and after leaving my address I departed.

The foregoing incident occurred about a week before the exposition closed, and the next and only subsequent time I saw Mr. Espy there, he told me he had received several orders for his instrument from English people, and purposed going to the great glass-blowing works of Newcastle-on-Tyne to execute them.

After leaving Paris, I went to London, where I ran across an old college friend, who invited me to spend a week or two at his country-seat in one of the northern counties during the Christmas season. Branthwaite Castle, my friend's place, was one of those typical old English homes which have existed, been repaired, and added to for the past two or three hundred years. Romantically situated upon the banks of the upper Tyne, its old ivy-covered walls and rambling wings were suggestive of legend as well as comfort. There are few, indeed, of the ancient mansions of that "borderland of old romance" which have not some weird, mysterious story associated with their walls and halls. Branthwaite Castle was not behindhand in this particular, and could boast of a goodly assortment of stories, more or less ghostly and mythical, associated with the family name of Haldane, which had figured in the old border wars for centuries back.

The winter season at an English country-house, when there is snow upon the ground and outdoor amusements are necessarily curtailed, can not fail to be somewhat dull. The billiard-room for the gentlemen and the drawing-room for the ladies do not afford so many resources as to cause almost any new mode of recreation to be despised. Even private theatricals and dancing will pall upon the appetite if unrelieved by anything else, and so it was with something of the feeling of the mediaeval discoverer of unknown lands that I bethought me one morning of my friend, Mr. Espy, and the curious instrument he was exhibiting at the Paris Exposition.

Here were possibilities, indeed! Though I confess I did not repose much confidence in Mr. Espy's discovery, to the extent, at any rate, of the extravagant claims he made for it, I thought that, in any case, the mystery surrounding it and the occult problems with which it dealt, would serve to excite the imagination of the guests and provide a *divertissement* which might, for a time at least, banish ennui. Besides, could anything be handier? Mr. Espy was engaged in getting his glass globes manufactured at Newcastle-on-Tyne, and Newcastle was not forty miles distant from Branthwaite. I immediately communicated my plan, together with my Paris experience, to my host, who was delighted with the suggestion. Accordingly, the very same afternoon, I was driven to Cholorton Station, on the North British line, and two hours afterward found me in close consultation with Mr. Espy at his workshop in Newcastle.

After explaining the object of my visit, that gentleman gladly agreed to furnish me with an eidoloscope of even larger proportions than it had been his original intention to construct.

"For," he said, "I foresee the business benefit which will result from a successful introduction of the instrument at such a gathering as there is now at your friend's house. I will not only take especial pains upon its construction, but I will make a point of accompanying it to its destination, when completed, in person, and will personally superintend everything connected with its first exhibition, so as to leave no room for imperfect results. You can leave the matter in my hands, and meet me in a week at your station with the easiest wagon you can get."

During the week, it became noised about at the castle that some peculiar surprise had been planned by our host and myself for the gratification of his guests, and that its production had been reserved · for Christmas eve. Meantime, I received a letter from Mr. Espy, in accordance with which I met him on the morning of the day before Christmas at Cholorton Station, where the north-bound train deposited him with a number of gigantic boxes, the largest of which was a cube of some six feet in diameter. These we conveyed with all possible care to the castle, where their appearance created quite a sensation among such of the visitors as had chanced to see them carried in at one of the back entrances, and proportionately increased the expectation of all.

Now came the important point of all to settle. In what particular apartment or chamber of the castle should the eidoloscope be set up and the test of its powers made? A committee of three ladies were let into the secret and selected by our host to decide this important question, in conjunction with Mr. Espy, Haldane, and myself. The ladies were all, more or less, connected with the family, and it was decided to give the matter the benefit of the quick, feminine intuition in the selection of a suitable place.

"Is there no room in the castle," asked Mr. Espy, when the committee had met, "which is associated above all others with some stirring incident, or series of incidents, which it would be interesting for your company to see reproduced as in actual life?"

"The difficulty is the other way," rejoined our host; "there are far too many such—quite an *embarras de richesses*, I assure you, in that respect."

"There is the state banqueting-chamber, where Queen Elizabeth dined," volunteered Miss Chantrey, a cousin of Haldane's, a lady apparently about sixty years of age, whose expression struck me as sinister and furtive in the extreme, despite the conventional smile and liberal application of cosmetics with which she strove to conceal it.

"Oh! yes," exclaimed another member of the committee, one of Haldane's sisters, gleefully; "how nice it would be to see Queen Bess sitting prim and stuck up, with all her starched ruffles, at the head of the mahogany table, and Leicester on one knee before her holding a cup of wine."

"The best place of all," said Mr. Espy, "would be a room in which the furniture has not been moved of late. The best results are, of course, secured where there are the most surrounding objects to gather the light-waves from."

"There is the blue room in the east wing where poor Aunt Margaret died," remarked Miss Jennie, another of Haldane's sisters; "I don't think a thing has been moved from its original place of forty years ago, except for an occasional dusting. Nobody seems to like to enter that room. There is a superstition connected with it, too. The old servants say—"

"Bravo, Jennie!" exclaimed Haldane; "I never thought of that. That is just the very kind of room Mr. Espy wants—isn't it, Mr. Espy?"

Here my eye happened to fall upon Miss Chantrey. Her face had become absolutely livid, her features drawn and pinched, and it was with a very forced attempt at calmness that she spoke:

"I am surprised at you, girls!" she said in a set voice; "the idea of selecting a place like that for such an exhibition! I am sure the banqueting-chamber would be infinitely more interesting."

"I am afraid," said Mr. Espy, "we should have to view hundreds of scenes before getting back to those of three hundred years ago. I am in favour of the blue room this lady spoke about. Forty years is not so long a time to be bridged over as three hundred. Besides the furniture, if I understand aright, has not been moved much during that time. That is a very favourable condition of things. By the way, did you not say there was some superstition connected with it?"

"The servants say they have seen a ghost—" began Miss Jennie.

"It all amounts to this," put in Haldane, laughingly; "my aunt Margaret, who I believe was a most beautiful girl—I was a child then and can not remember her—died there. There was some love affair—I don't know what it was—about it, and she got jilted or died of a broken heart or something. You ought to know all about it, Cousin Gertrude. You were about her age and staying here at that time, weren't you?"

"Yes," returned Miss Chantrey, with what I thought strained solemnity. "Poor Margaret! Hugh Wilmot is accused of playing with her affections and—"

"It is false!" cried Miss Jennie, her eyes blazing with indignation; "I have heard all about it, and I happen to know that Mr. Wilmot grew tired of life after poor Aunt Margaret's untimely death, and that was the reason of his going to California, where he died. It was *you* who were responsible for Aunt Margaret's death, if any one was, Cousin Gertrude. Old Jane Selby has told me how jealous you were of Aunt Margaret, and how you tried to catch Mr. Wilmot, and how he would have nothing to say to you," went on the girl, carried away by the heat of her emotions. "Old Jane was Aunt Margaret's nurse when she died, and she told me how careless you were whether she died or not, never even going near the sick room once during her illness."

If Miss Chantrey's face was livid and sardonic in expression before, it was now ashy pale, and there was a vindictive gleam in her little black eyes, as she listened to the impassioned tirade of her cousin, which boded no good to that young lady if it ever was in her power to do her an ill turn.

"Come, come, ladies!" said Haldane; "let by-gones be by-gones. I'm ashamed of you, Jennie! Mr. Espy, I think we had better select the blue room for your exhibition. It will be out of the way, and won't interfere so much with existing domestic arrangements. You'll help him, won't you, Robert?" he added, turning to me as he went out.

I accompanied Mr. Espy to the room in question, whither the boxes had preceded us, and stood open on the floor ready to be unpacked. The room was lofty and spacious, even for the Elizabethan period, to which that part of the castle belonged. It plainly showed the marks of disuse, the high-backed chairs, settees, tables, escritoires, and book-cases, all of antique pattern, having evidently made the acquaintance of the house-maid's duster only shortly before our arrival. Three mullioned windows opened on the lawn—it was on the second storey—and there was a large antique four-poster bed in one corner on the side nearest the fire.

"Just the place!" murmured Mr. Espy approvingly, as he glanced at the surroundings. "Stop!" he added, addressing the servant, who was just about to set light to the fire. "That would spoil everything," he explained, turning to me. "*Temperature*, you will remember, is the one necessary factor in securing our results. Heat is the one and only element which causes the atoms of these walls and articles of furniture to change their collocation and to disgorge the electrical equivalent of the light-waves which impinged upon them in the past. That heat must not be applied till we are ready to begin."

We then began the work of preparation. A pedestal about four feet high, the top of which Mr. Espy said was insulated, and in the interior of which was a battery, was placed in the centre of the apartment. On this was set the polished globular mirror, five feet in diameter, and around this again was set the diaphanous elastic envelope, studded with the radiating rods. This took up a space some twelve feet in diameter, but as the area of the chamber was about double that, there was still room for thirty or forty persons to stand comfortably around—a number greater than that of the entire company at the castle.

About nine o'clock in the evening, when the gentlemen had joined the ladies in the drawing-room, our host made a brief address, explaining the nature of the surprise in store for them, and ending by inviting them to accompany him upstairs to witness the mysterious exhibition. As the company filed into the room, Mr. Espy ranged them round the walls and proceeded to light the fire, which, independently of its scientific value, was also a physical necessity, as the night was bitterly cold. This done, he placed a metal screen, which he had prepared for the purpose, before the fire, excluding as much as possible the light from the blazing coals, remarking that artificial light was detrimental to the success of the exhibition. The few rays that struggled round the edges of the screen only made the darkness visible. None of the guests could distinguish the features of his nearest neighbour.

All was silent, even whispering having been, at Mr. Espy's request, forbidden. Gradually the chill began to disappear and something like warmth to pervade the air, and at the same time a faint, bluish, phosphorescent light seemed to emanate from the central globe. In a minute after, its outline became defined, and then, as the room became warmer, the light from the globe became clearer, but more tremulous, changing in rapid gradations from grey to violet, from violet to pink, from pink to orange, and finally from orange to clear white. It reminded me exactly of dawn breaking, on a clear morning, in the east. But all this time it was not a clear white surface which the polished globe presented to our gaze. Just in proportion as its surface became bright, did the scene depicted upon it become more clear and vivid. It was an exact representation of the room in which we stood, and, had it been reflected from the globe by outside light, it could not, in some respects, have been mirrored more faithfully.

But there was no outside light to produce such a reflection. The light evidently proceeded from the globe, and by it we could now easily distinguish the faces and figures of the assembled company. There was another circumstance in the picture which at once precluded the idea of its being a reflection from the outside; had it been so, our own figures would have formed a prominent feature of the foreground, but they did not appear. Neither was the position of the different articles of furniture precisely the same as that which they now occupied. They were, indeed, all there. The mullioned windows, the book-cases, the bed, all the fixtures were just as we saw them then. But there was no sign of life. No human figure lent interest to the silent surroundings.

But while we gazed, the door, as seen upon the globe, opened, and a woman, evidently a servant, entered with a broom, backward. Swiftly and noiselessly this figure went through the motions of dusting furniture. Never did house-maid work with one-hundredth part the celerity as did this phantom then. In a few seconds she was gone, again moving backward through the door.

Mr. Espy now explained, in a low voice, that the scenes were reproduced in backward sequence, and that consequently the figures must appear to do backward all that they had done in the past.

Again did that and other figures appear and retire at intervals, all acting similarly in the matter of retrogression. The spectators became spell-bound. It seemed as if time were forgotten in the absorption with which they viewed the passing spectacle. It seemed also as if every one there nursed an indefinable expectation of something about to happen, they knew not what.

At length, a bevy of servants entered and busied themselves about the bed. They were followed swiftly by two men who entered backward, bearing a coffin, which they set beside the bed. From it they lifted the corpse of a young lady, which they proceeded to set upon the bed. Then they left the room, backwards, and were succeeded by some men and women, who knelt beside the bed. Presently the corpse of the young lady opened its eyes. There was now a table beside the bed and on the table some medicine-phials and glasses. Next, a young lady entered backwards and backed up to the bed.

"Gertrude Chantrey, by God!" was the suppressed exclamation I heard issue from the lips of an old gentleman standing by my side. "Gertrude Chantrey, as I knew her forty years ago when her cousin Margaret died!"

This young lady swiftly and noiselessly changed some medicine-phials upon the table.

Just then I thought I heard a faint sound, as of a stifled groan, proceeding from an obscure quarter of the room, but so intent was every one upon what was transpiring, that it failed to attract any notice.

Countless other scenes were depicted upon the spherical mirror, but so swiftly and in such incongruous order that the mind failed to grasp their relevancy, as there was no sequence, their sequence itself being inverted, and cause, so to speak, following effect.

The last scene that I remember was the figure of a beautiful young lady seated at one of the mullioned windows. A young gentleman entered and approached her backward, fell on his knees before her, rose up, and acted generally as lovers do.

"My God!" whispered heavily the same old gentleman; "Hugh Wilmot and Margaret Haldane to the life! Just as they were forty years ago."

How long this strange exhibition might have lasted I know not. Every one, as I have said, seemed spell-bound by the extraordinary scenes there witnessed. Suddenly the deep tones of the tower clock struck twelve. Was it possible, I asked myself, that we had been there three hours? We had entered the apartment at nine; but a few minutes seemed to have passed; now it was twelve!

The thought seemed to recall the company to itself. Another incident likewise helped to do so. From a settee, in the embrasure of a window, the figure of a female slipped noiselessly forward and fell prone upon the floor. I instantly recollected that this was the quarter from which had proceeded the low moan I had thought I heard some time before. A general rush was made to the spot, and tender arms raised the flaccid figure of the lady. I pressed forward among the number. It was the figure of Miss Gertrude Chantrey. The features were rigid and the body was fast assuming the chill of death.

ROBERT DUNCAN MILNE.

SAN FRANCISCO, January, 1890.

THE TALKING MACHINE

Marcel Schwob

One of the outstanding practitioners of the macabre short story during the *fin-de-siècle* period, Marcel Schwob (1867–1905) remains little known to Anglophone readers. He was heavily influenced by English-language writers, however, particularly Edgar Allan Poe as well as his friends Robert Louis Stevenson and Oscar Wilde (whose French play *Salome* Schwob helped to revise and correct). "La Machine à Parler" was first published (possibly after an untraced appearance in the review *L'Echo de Paris*) in Schwob's 1892 superb, unsettling collection of short stories, *Le Roi au Masque d'Or* (*The King in the Golden Mask*)—a collection which I suspect may have partly inspired that landmark weird volume, *The King in Yellow* (1895), by the American Robert W. Chambers, who was studying art in Paris at the time. Schwob's story begins with a discussion of the phonograph, invented by Thomas Edison in 1877 (Emile Berliner had patented his disc-based "Gramophone" in 1887, but here "a spinning cylinder" is still the mechanism described); Schwob's uncanny "talking machine", however—a "monster" of simulated throat, lips, lung, and tongue which does not merely record but speaks, even blasphemes—owes more to mechanical speech synthesisers built by such inventors as Wolfgang von Kempelen (1734–1804) (better remembered today for his hoax automaton, the chess-playing "Turk") and Charles Wheatstone (1802–1875) (one of the co-inventors of the electric telegraph). In the 1860s, a teenaged Alexander Graham

Bell and his brother built a machine much like Schwob's unhinged inventor's:

> [W]e attempted to make an exact copy of the vocal organs, and work the artificial lips, tongue, and soft palate by means of levers controlled by a keyboard. While I was working at this apparatus my brother Melville succeeded in making an artificial larynx, or throat, of tin, with a flexible tube attached as windpipe. My brother found, upon blowing through the windpipe, that the rubber vocal chords [sic] were thrown into vibration, producing a musical sound... When this stage had been reached we were, of course, anxious to put the throat and the mouth together to see what the effect would be. We could not wait for the completion of the tongue; we could not wait for the arrival of the organ bellows. My brother simply fastened his tin larynx to my gutta-percha mouth and blew through the windpipe provided.

They used it to scare the neighbours. (Did I mention they were teenagers?)

he man who walked in, holding a newspaper in his hand, had lively features and a fixed gaze; I recall that he was pale and wizened, that I never once saw him smile, and that the manner in which he rested his finger on his lips was full of mystery. But what first caught my attention was the smothered and rushed sound of his voice. When his speech was slow and deep, one heard the gravelly tones of this voice, with sudden silences of vibrations, as if distant harmonies were shivering in unison; but almost always the words, gathering against his lips, burst out, muted, clipped, and discordant, much like the sound of something cracking. It seemed there were cables endlessly snapping inside him. And from this voice every intonation had disappeared; it no longer possessed any dynamics, as if it were prodigiously old and worn.

And now this visitor, whom I had never seen before, came forth and said: "You wrote these lines, isn't that so?"

And he read: "The voice which is the aerial indication of thought, by way of the soul, which instructs, preaches, exhorts, prays, praises, loves, through which being is manifested in life, almost palpable for the blind, impossible to describe for it is too undulatory and various, indeed too lively, and incarnated in too many sonorous forms, the voice which Théophile Gautier renounced speaking in words, for it is neither sweet nor sharp, hot nor cold, colourless nor colourful, but something of all that in another realm, this voice which one cannot touch, which one cannot see, the most immaterial of things terrestrial, the one which most closely resembles the spirit, science

37

pricks it in passing with a needle and buries it in little holes around a spinning cylinder."

Once he had finished, his tumultuous speech carrying no more than a muffled sound to my ears, this man began to dance on one leg, then on the other, and without opening his lips let out a dry, crackling snicker.

"Science," he said, "the voice... Further still you wrote, 'A great poet has taught that speech cannot be lost, being movement, that it is powerful and creative, and that perhaps, at the far reaches of the world, its vibrations give birth to other universes, to aqueous, volcanic stars, to new, combusting suns.' And we both know, don't we, that Plato predicted the power of speech well before Poe: Οὐχ ἁπλῶς πληγὴ ἀέρος ἔστιν ἡ φωνή. 'The voice is not merely a stroke of the air: for the finger, in its wagging, may strike the air and yet shall never itself possess a voice.' And we also know that one day in the month of December 1890, on the anniversary of Robert Browning's death, one heard the poet's living voice rising from the grave of the phonograph at the Edison House, and that the sound waves of the air can resuscitate it for all time.

"You are scientists and poets; you know how to imagine, preserve, even resuscitate: creation, however, is unknown to you."

I watched the man with pity. A deep crease cut down his brow from his widow's peak to the bridge of his nose. Madness seemed to stand his hair on end and light up his eyeballs. His facial expression was triumphant, as of those who fancy themselves emperors, popes, or God, and despise the ignorant from on high.

"Yes," this man resumed—and his voice grew smothered insofar as he attempted to raise it—"you have written everything that others know and the better part of what they may dream; but I am superior. I can, as Poe would have it, create revolving worlds and fiery, howling spheres, with the sound of a material dispossessed of a soul; and with this I have surpassed even Lucifer, for I can force disorganised things to blaspheme. Night and day, at my will, skins which were once alive and metals perhaps only not yet so, proclaim inanimate words; and if it is true that the voice creates universes in space, the ones I have it create are worlds which die before having lived. In my house dwells a Behemoth who bellows at the wave of my hand; *I have invented a talking machine*."

I followed the man as he made his way to the door. We passed down bustling lanes, unruly streets; then we arrived at the outskirts of the city, while the gaslights lit up one by one behind us. Before the short postern of a blackened wall, the man stopped and slid open a deadbolt. We entered a courtyard, quiet and dark. And there, my heart was filled with dread: for I heard groaning, grating cries, and syllabified speech, which seemed to roar from a gaping throat. And just like those spoken by my guide, these words possessed no dynamics, and in this inordinate swell of vocal sounds, I recognised nothing human.

The man invited me into a room I could hardly countenance, so terrible did it seem for the monster which stood there. Rising to the ceiling was a giant throat, distended and patchy, with hanging flaps of black swelling leather, the breath of a subterranean storm, and two enormous lips trembling on top. And amid the grinding of its wheels and the screeching of its metal cables, these heaps of leather shook, and its gigantic lips hesitantly parted; then, at the red bottom of the pit which opened below, an immense fleshy lobe jolted, stood on end, wriggled around, struggled up and down, right and left; a gust of wind exploded inside the machine, and articulate words began flooding out, spurred on by a superhuman voice. The explosions of the consonants were terrifying; for its *p*'s and *b*'s, along with its *v*'s, escaped directly from the swollen and black labial rims: they appeared to be born before our very eyes; its *d*'s and *t*'s rushed forth under the belligerent upper flap of snarling leather; and the *r*, readied at length, rolled sinisterly. Its vowels, modifying abruptly, poured from its giant mouth like the blasts of a trumpet. The stammering of its *s*'s and *ch*'s surpassed even the horror of significant mutilation.

"Behold," the man said, resting his hand on the shoulder of a meagre little woman, deformed and nervous, "the soul who makes the keyboard of my machine move. She performs opuses of human speech on my piano. I have trained her in admiration of my will: her notes are stutters, her scales and exercises the *ba be bi bo bu* of grade school, her fugues my lyric works and poetry, her symphonies my blasphemous philosophy. You see the keys which bear, in their syllabic alphabet, along their three rows, every miserable sign of human thought. I produce all at once, and without damnation intervening, the thesis and antithesis of the truths of man and his God."

He placed the short woman at the keyboard, behind the machine. "Listen," he said in his smothered voice.

And the bellows began to churn beneath the pedals; the flaps hanging from the throat swelled; the monstrous lips shuddered and yawned apart; the tongue worked, and the roar of articulate speech exploded:

IN THE BE-GIN-NING WAS THE WORD

howled the machine.

"This is a lie," said the man. "It's the lie of the books they call sacred. I studied for years and years; I opened throats in the dissection rooms; I listened to voices, cries, sobs, weeping, and preaching; and I measured each mathematically; I drew them out of myself and out of others; I broke my own voice in my efforts; and so long have I lived with my machine that I speak *without dynamics*, just as it speaks; for dynamics belong to the soul, and I have suppressed mine. Behold the truth and the new word." And he cried, at the top of his lungs—but the sentence resounded like a raspy murmur: "The Machine shall say:

I CREATED THE WORD."

And the bellows began to churn beneath the pedals; the flaps hanging from the throat swelled; the monstrous lips shuddered and yawned apart; the tongue worked, and speech exploded in a monstrous stammer:

WO-RD WO-RD WO-RD.

There was an extraordinary snapping among the cables, a grinding of the gears, a collapse of the throat, a universal sagging of the leather, a stream of air which swept away the syllabic keys in debris; and I had no way of knowing if the machine itself was refusing to blaspheme, or if the performer of speech had introduced into the mechanism a principle of destruction: for the deformed little woman had disappeared, and the man, whose wrinkles cut across his absolutely strained face, wagged his finger with fury before his mute mouth, having definitively lost his voice.

RÖNTGEN'S CURSE

Charles Crosthwaite

The Dublin-born, Oxford-educated Sir Charles Crosthwaite (1835–1915) entered the Indian civil service in 1857, becoming chief commissioner of Burma in 1887. Crosthwaite drew upon his long administrative career in the Raj in a pair of later books: a memoir, *The Pacification of Burma*, and a collection of stories, *Thakur Bertáb Singh and Other Tales*, from which "Röntgen's Curse" has been taken. First published in *Longman's Magazine* in 1896, this is one of the earliest stories to exploit the Gothic possibilities of the uncanny photography made possible by German engineer Wilhelm Röntgen's discovery of "a new kind of ray" the previous year. The first to realise the X-ray photograph's potential as a memento mori, revealing the skull beneath the skin, was Röntgen's wife, who upon seeing the bones of her own hand exclaimed, "I have seen my death!" No doubt this episode was the inspiration for not only Crosthwaite's tale but also SF pioneer George Griffith's "A Photograph of the Invisible", published only a few months earlier in *Pearson's Magazine* (in this issue, readers could also find the essay "A Wizard of To-Day", featuring an interview with Röntgen himself), as well as H. G. Wells's far more famous *The Invisible Man*, serialised the following year. X-ray photography was also very quickly linked with the occult in the popular mind (though the above-mentioned stories carry no such overtones), while the idea of X-ray vision, a boon to pulp and comic heroes like Olga Mesmer and Superman, would also be exploited for horrific purposes, most famously in Roger Corman's 1963 film *X: The Man with the X-Ray Eyes* (the prolific pulpster Edmond Hamilton, of "Captain Future" fame, had used the same title, minus the initial "X", in the 1930s).

was educated at Cambridge, and after taking a respectable degree I adopted bacteriology and analytical chemistry as my profession. But after some years, part of which time was spent in the service of the Indian Government in the chase after the cholera microbe, I inherited some money, retired to England, and married. We had lived some years a country life, and had several children. I never altogether abandoned my favourite pursuit, and I had a laboratory built on to my house. My wife painted fairly for an amateur, and excelled in photography. The interest I took in her work led me to the study of light and all the phenomena connected with it, and this study became more and more absorbing. Nevertheless, a considerable portion of my time was given to outdoor pursuits and the society of my family and friends. No one could accuse me of overworking myself, or suspect me of yielding to the delusions of imagination. I trouble the reader with this preface lest in the statement I am about to make he should suspect he was reading the fictions of a diseased brain.

I was on the track of a great discovery. I was sure of it. A little more time, a little more toil, and the reward would be mine. I, Herbert Newton, should be hailed as the greatest benefactor of the human race in modern times. It was about the time that Röntgen published the wonderful results of his experiments with what he called the X-rays, and the whole world of scientific men felt that they were on the verge of a great event. Every magazine had an article on the so-called photography of the invisible, and every lecture-hall resounded with explanations of these extraordinary phenomena. To me, a student in this same field, the possibilities which underlay this discovery seemed immeasurable. My excitement became intense, and I threw all my powers of mind and body into the work of following the path of research indicated by Röntgen. To my eager brain there appeared no limit to the power which might be acquired by one who could make the X-rays his servants, and compel them to obey him. In one science alone—that of medicine—what a revolution might be effected, what progress made, if the physician could see the working of the vital organs and their condition! He could then no longer be accused of pouring, he knows not what into he knows not what, to cure he knows not what. It was possible even now, as Röntgen had proved, to examine the skeleton. But so long as a tedious process was necessary there would be many cases to which the new discovery could not be applied, while as yet only the skeleton, and not the interior organs, could be portrayed. I was determined to go far beyond the goal reached by Röntgen. I would not rest until the physician should be able to see and examine any part of the human organism as the patient lay on his bed, and to study the anatomy of the body in health or in disease as if he had the eye of the Creator. Other and wider fields of ambition opened to me, and I pictured myself able to see into the bowels of the earth or the depths of the sea. The discovery of minerals and precious stones, the finding of lost treasures, the laying bare of the secrets of ancient cities—these were but a few of the vulgar applications of the power which I sought to possess. Far above and beyond these rose the hope of snatching from Nature the secret of life itself, and of making biology the supreme science. Animated by these thoughts, I redoubled my exertions. Hardly giving myself time to eat or sleep, I would not spare a moment for the ordinary duties of life, and to my wife and children I became like one in a trance.

Not without a hard struggle did my wife let me fall into these ways. She exhorted and implored me by my love for her and the children. She urged me to remember my duty to God and man. But I would hear nothing. I was like the opium-eater or the drunkard. I could not now resist the impulse that was hurrying me on. So the days went by. Nearer and nearer I seemed to the desired end, and yet more and more there was to do. More laborious became the search, more close and fatiguing the observation necessary, for I had brought my experiments now to such a point that they were microscopic in their minuteness. As I staggered to bed, generally at an hour long past midnight, I felt my head swim and reel with the weariness of my brain. Excitement and determination roused me early in the morning to fresh efforts. Nature, however, did not leave me without warning that I was transgressing her laws. I began to dread that my strength would fail me, and that I should break down before my task was accomplished. Sometimes in the midst of my studies a veil, as it were, would come over my thoughts. All of a sudden, just as if some fairy had touched me with an enchanted wand, my thoughts would cease, my mind become like an empty page, and the brain, which a moment before had been full of active movements, keen reasonings, and vivid perceptions of the conclusions, would be dull and inert. It was just as if a damp sponge had been passed over a slate. These were warnings. What were warnings to me? If I must die for my work, I would die. But I would die working.

At last it came. Not the ruin of my mind, but the glory and pride of my life. I had gone far beyond and away from Röntgen's experiments. His discoveries had sufficed to show that no objects were in themselves opaque or impervious. There were rays of light or waves of ether that could—and no doubt did—pass through every and any substance. But the retina of the human eye did not respond to them.

If the invisible ultraviolet rays can be made perceptible to the eye by means of the fluorescence they excite in certain substances, then why should not other rays, such as Röntgen's X-rays, be made visible to the eye by some chemical means? As no bodies are really opaque, some rays must pass through matter of every kind, and some means can probably be found of making these rays visible to the eye. A power of sight able to see with the Röntgen rays was the first object to be attained, and my researches were directed towards finding the means of gaining that power. My belief in the possibilities of achieving this result was confirmed by the evident and great differences in the sight of animals—differences which seemed to me due less to variations in the mechanism of the eye than to the capacity of the retina to respond to rays other than those which go to form what to the human eye is light.

I am not going, however, to weary the reader with the details of my discovery. What I wish to tell is the effect and consequences of it.

It was past midnight, and I had been absorbed in work for many hours. I was eager, and flushed with excitement. My experiments during the day had been unusually successful and fertile. I thought I had the object of my desire within my grasp; and my mind was full of visions of the field of knowledge about to be laid open to it.

There was one faithful friend who never left me all these weary days. My children, poor things! seldom came near me. My wife had wellnigh ceased to come into my laboratory except at stated hours to call me to meals. My dog never left me. He had true faith. He knew well that the time would come when, my work being done, I should seize my gun and we should both go forth again into the sweet-smelling fields and the pleasant woods, full of scent and adventure to him. He seemed to know that I was not working for pleasure or caprice, and that I had no choice but to be about my business. At first, when the usual hour for going out arrived, he would bark and jump on me, and urge me to come as only a dog can urge; but after a few days he understood and accepted the reasons which bound me to my chair, and never again, irksome though the confinement was to him, did he importune me to leave my work. This faithful friend was lying at my feet now. He was sleeping, half on his back, with limbs extended and head thrown a little back. It was; as I have said, past midnight. The house was still as a tomb. All were asleep. My laboratory was at the end of a passage, away from the bedrooms of the family. I thought I had found at last how to make a liquid which, applied to the eyes, might make them sensitive to the X-rays, and perhaps to other waves of ether yet unknown. Taking a camel's-hair brush, I inserted a little of this preparation under the half-open eyelids of the sleeping dog. I knew it would give him no pain, and the longer it remained undisturbed upon the eyes the more likely its action to be effectual. Scarcely moving under my touch, which he knew and loved, the dog slept on. I sat down again to wait the result. I was excited and impatient: my nerves, suffering from overwork, were as tense as those of a condemned man listening in his cell for the footsteps of the executioner. I heard every little weird and awesome sound that breaks the silence of a sleeping house to a nervous watcher—the creaking of the stairs under stealthy footsteps; the sigh of suppressed breathings; the fearful whisper of voices that must speak, yet dread to be heard. Hark! What is that at my door? I must have been half asleep. I jumped up from my chair with a start, trembling with fear, yet ashamed of my fears and my childish lack of nerve. Ah! there it is again! I was stepping forward to open my door, when just at that moment the dog awoke. He rose lazily, stretched himself, yawned, and then came up slowly and stiffly, stretching his hind legs, and wagging his tail to greet me after his sleep, and suggest that it was time to move. He rubbed his nose against my knee, and then looked up in my face. Ah! What is it? The brute's eyes dilated with terror, his hair bristled on his back, he shrank back from me slowly, paralysed by deadly fear. And then there went forth from him a cry of horror too awful for words to tell. It was unearthly, unfleshly—such a cry as a damned soul may give forth on hearing its condemnation. I have read of the shrieks of wounded horses on the field of battle; I have heard the groans of man in mortal agony; in the depths of the jungle I have heard the piteous cry of the deer seized by a beast of prey,—all sounds eloquent of pain and fear. But these were as voices of joy compared to that cry of terror and despair that froze the blood in my veins and bade my pulse cease to beat. When that awful cry pierced the stillness of the night, the knocking at the door became loud and impatient. I heard my wife's voice imploring me to let her in. I opened the door and she rushed in, her face white and distorted with terror.

"Oh, my God," she cried, "protect me! What terrible cry was that? Herbert, what was it? It has nearly killed me with fear; and if the children had heard it? Oh, my children, my children! Speak, Herbert! Would you drive me mad?"

The dog was lying moaning under the table against the wall. Hearing my wife's voice, he came out trembling, and crouching as a hound that dreads the lash.

"Poor fellow," she said, "poor old fellow. What's the matter, Dash? What is it?"

Hearing the kind and well-known voice, the poor beast crawled to her feet and looked up. Instantly the same look of horror came into his eyes, the same awful cry issued from his mouth, and he slunk back into his place of retreat under the table.

"What have you done to the poor beast?" cried my wife, indignation now taking the place of fear. "Surely you have not used him for some wicked experiment?"

Her anger was noble, and became her well. I could not tell her what I had done. Resorting to a subterfuge, I assured her that I had done nothing to hurt or injure the animal, who, as she knew, was my constant and loved companion. I began to realise that the dog's fear was caused by what he saw, and triumph in the success of my experiments was driving every other consideration and feeling out of my mind.

"Come, dear," I said to my wife, "I am wearied out. Let us to bed. The dog was asleep, and must have dreamt of something that terrified him. Let us leave him alone. He will soon recover himself."

Fearing lest he should see either of us again and a fresh fit of horror should seize him, I switched off the electric light, and taking up a candle, which I lighted hastily, I led the way out of the room, and shut the doors on Dash.

Before we slept my wife once more attempted by her entreaties to induce me to forsake this, as she called it, mad pursuit. She pointed out the change which the last few weeks had wrought in my appearance, how I had aged, and how my strength and health were failing. She prayed me, if I did not care for myself, to have some thoughts for our children and for her, from whose life I was taking away all joy and happiness. She knew I was not thirsting for gain, and she acknowledged the loftiness of my motives. Nevertheless, ambition was the spirit that moved me, and I had, she urged, no right to sacrifice to it my wife and children. It was hard indeed for me to resist her. But how could I have the heart to turn back when I was, as I conceived, within sight of the goal. I tried to explain to her the enormous importance to mankind of the great discovery I was on the point of making. Only a few more days, it might be only a few more hours, were necessary to complete my work. Would she not have a little more patience? When I had accomplished my task I would shut up my laboratory and resume straightway my usual healthy way of life. This I solemnly promised her, and she had perforce to be content with it. But I could see that she whom I loved above everything, so far as my accursed ambition left me free to love, had lost faith in my assurances and was sorely grieved. It was long before I could find rest in sleep.

Early in the morning I rose, eager to verify the success I anticipated, and went down again to my laboratory to work. My dog lay fast asleep on the hearthrug. Hearing me enter, he got up, shook and stretched himself, and came across the room to greet his master. But when he saw me, again that fearful look came into his eyes, and once again that cry of terror, seeming to gather into one all the pain and agony of the brute creation, swept through the house. Knowing as I did the cause of his fear, and hailing it as a sure token of my success, yet that terrible sound unnerved me. I opened the door of my room with an unsteady hand, and the poor brute rushed, or rather tumbled, past me, and I saw him no more. I heard afterwards that he found his way into the garden, and into a thicket, whence no persuasion of voice or offer of food could tempt him, and where he perished miserably from fear and famine.

I pass over the confusion and panic which were caused in the house by the dog's cry of agony. Once more I had shut myself in my laboratory, and was preparing to try the experiment on my own eyes. Arrogant fool that I was, the dog's terror had no warning for me. It was true that I noticed with surprise that the effect had been more lasting than knowledge of the ingredients used had led me to anticipate. I had looked for a merely transient influence on the sight. The animal's eyes had retained the effects of the application for a considerable number of hours. It occurred to me as possible that the last attack of panic was only the result of the remembrance of what he had seen the night before. However this might be, no thought of applying the lesson to my own case and of holding my hand came into my mind. I was satisfied that I had made one of the most wonderful discoveries of modern times, and that by its publication my name would be made famous. By means practically as simple as that by which the surgeon dilates the pupil of his patient, I could now make the eye susceptible to those subtle rays or emanations to which few, perhaps none, of the objects surrounding us are dense or opaque. I was determined without delay to make the experiment on my own sight. Nor would anything have availed then to deter me, not even if I could have foreseen the suffering I was condemning myself to endure. I had in my grasp a talisman that would unlock for me the secrets of the universe. The fruit of the tree of knowledge hung within my reach. Ambition, desire, curiosity, tempted me. I must eat of it, even if the penalty were death, or worse.

As I have said, I had shut the door of my laboratory and was alone. I took the phial which contained the liquid I had applied to the dog's eyes, and carefully painted with it the insides of my eyelids. Then I sat down in my easy chair, with closed eyes, to give the drug a fair chance of showing its power.

I had sat thus for a considerable time, my mind full of the great discovery I had made, and dwelling on all its possible consequences, immense in their results, endless in their variations, when it occurred to me to write at once to Professor ——, with whom I was in correspondence on the subject of my researches, to tell him how far they had gone, and the extraordinary phenomena in the case of the dog. I turned to my writing-table for this purpose. For a moment I thought my brain must have given way and that my imagination was playing me a trick.

I could see nothing like a table. The whole room had taken a fantastic and ghostly appearance. Instead of the mahogany bureau which held my writing-materials, there was a misty and barely visible outline, which I can only compare to that of a ship looming through a dense fog. Upon the surface of this mist, floating, or rather upheld in their places by some magical and invisible support, were the brass handles, ornaments, locks, and keyholes of the drawers. There was nothing else to be seen with a distinct and defined outline, except here and there a screw or an angle-iron which had been used in the joining, and a bunch of keys and some gold seals which I kept in one of the drawers.

Pens or paper, although I knew there was plenty of them about, I could see none. I put out my hand to feel for them, and a shudder passed through me when I saw it was a skeleton hand. However, by the sense of touch I found some paper and a pen; but I could see neither, and after attempting to write a letter in ink which I could not see, on paper I could not see, on an invisible table, and with an invisible pen in a skeleton hand, I gave it up in despair, and threw myself back in my chair. I began now to realise what I had done, and to feel that knowledge might be too perfect. Up to this time I had not paid much attention to anything beyond my table and my own hands and arms. Rising now from my chair, I saw that to my eyes I was a skeleton, with metal buttons and a watch and chain belonging to it in some mysterious way without touching it. I could see that my legs were nothing but bones without either clothes or flesh, although I was strangely conscious of the presence of both. It was a ghastly and sickening sight to look down at my legs and body and see the bare bones of my own skeleton, and watch the motions of the uncovered, or apparently uncovered, joints. Between excitement and over-worry and the neglect to take proper food, rest, and exercise, my nerves were no better than those of a drunkard. I could hardly endure the sights which I had imposed upon myself. It seemed to me that it was near our breakfast-hour, and I took out my watch to see the time. I could see the hands, but the dial was invisible, while the works below it were clearly seen. The feeling of existence and reality conveyed by the sense of touch and the perception of warmth seemed the one barrier left between me and death.

My wife's voice at the door recalled me to myself. It was her practice, if I had not left the laboratory, to fetch me to breakfast, and usually our youngest child, a fine, stout little boy, came with her. Prepared as I was to some extent for what I was to see, the reality—if anything can be called real in this wonderful world—came upon me with a shock I could hardly bear. I tottered back, and clutched for support at the misty and uncanny object which I knew to be my table. I dared for one moment to look again, and in that one moment I suffered enough to make me regret for ever the ambition to see with the Divine eye. Two living skeletons walked in, the larger leading the little one by the hand; two chattering, gibbering skeletons, the smaller dancing and hopping along, and waving his little bony hands. Nearer they came, and although I heard the loved and familiar voices of the mother and child, and knew that they were living creatures of flesh as well as bone, I could not master the terrors and the dreadful feeling of disgust and repulsion that came over me. I could not endure to meet their embrace. Closing my eyes, I would have fallen if I had not supported myself against the table.

During the moment I looked at her my glance must have betrayed me, for my wife exclaimed—

"Herbert, what is the matter? Why do you look at me in such a way? You have overworked yourself. I was afraid it would all come to this."

It was some comfort to feel the warm, living touch of her hand and her breath on my face as she guided me to a chair. I sat down, resting my head on her shoulder, but not daring to look up. A little warm hand was laid upon mine, and a little voice lisped—

"Farder dear, dear farder, look at baby!"

Unable to withstand the entreating little voice, I opened my eyes. Oh God! how terrible! There at my knee was a little skeleton, mouthing at me and aping the motions of life. I closed my eyes again, and my tongue refused to speak.

"Herbert," said my wife, "speak to us. You are ill, dear. Speak, I entreat you; tell me what is the matter."

With all the force of my will I commanded myself, and looked at her.

"I am not feeling quite right, dear," I answered. "I have been overworking myself, as you say, and I want my breakfast. I must take things more easy for a time."

I tried to regard her with my usual look. I could not. It was not in my power. No one can imagine the grotesque horror of what I saw. Remember it was my wife, the woman I loved above everyone else, in whose beauty I rejoiced, the light of whose eyes was the sunshine of my life. I looked, and what did I see? Instead of the comely face with its loving smile, a grinning skull, all the more dreadful because it was alive. Instead of the shapely figure, a ghastly skeleton, whose bony hands were outstretched to touch me. In the most tragic events there is sometimes an element of the ludicrous, so there was something of the ridiculous in this horrible travesty of life. There were hairpins hovering, as it were, over the skull, and a necklace of gold floating round the bones of the neck, moved by the breathing, yet appearing to touch nothing; the steel stiffenings of the corset showed like bars placed unmeaningly in front of the ribs, while a shoe-buckle sat lightly and uncannily above the bony instep of each foot. The rings she wore encircled without touching the bones of her fingers. It was a skeleton masquerading in the skeleton of a dress.

To turn to the child was only to see still uglier horrors—the gaping suture in the baby skull, gaps where the joints should be, hands and feet connected by a hardly visible film with the limbs. For some reason the outlines of the flesh and the larger organs were more distinct than in the woman. David might have had some such vision when he truly said we are fearfully and wonderfully made.

"Come, Herbert," said my wife, in an anxious tone of voice, "I cannot see you like this. Your nerves are suffering from overwork, and you will be seriously ill if you do not rest. Come, now, and have something to eat, and then we will go out together. It is a lovely, bright morning, and when we come in you will lie down and take a sleep."

I suffered her to lead me out of the room, turning my eyes away from her. It was difficult for me to see my way in any case, as I saw little but a kind of mist, and I remember wondering how Dash had found his way out of my room. She led me into the breakfast-room, and I forced myself to look about me. I was not ill, I was not mad. It was childish and foolish to be thus upset by the sight of the human frame. I reasoned with myself, and tried to conquer and overcome my disgust, but it was impossible. It was not merely that I saw my family in the form of skeletons sitting round me. The horror lay in the life of the skeletons. They were not like the dry bones in a museum of anatomy or in the valley of death. They looked fresh and clammy, and the skulls wagged and mouthed at me in a manner that made my skin creep with disgust to see them eating or pretending to eat, lifting the bony fingers to the gumless jaws, which they moved in the act of chewing. The Egyptians may have been able to feast with a quiet, unobtrusive skeleton at the board—one amongst many living. The most callous cynic could not have enjoyed his dinner with such company as I had. Besides, I could not see to eat or drink. Nothing was visible to me except the metal of the plate and knives. I could not help myself, and I could not or would not explain to my wife what had happened. I was afraid she would think me labouring under a delusion, and I was more afraid that, if she believed me, she would feel outraged and offended that I should see her thus, and a barrier would be raised between us. I made an effort to look natural and unconcerned and find something to eat and drink. I succeeded only in upsetting a cup of tea that had been handed to me, and sweeping the crockery off the table. My wife gave a cry of distress and came over to me. She evidently thought, as she had good cause for thinking, that my intellect was failing.

As the only means of escape I said I was not feeling very well and must lie down. I was giddy and could hardly see. If she would take me upstairs and help me to lie down, I thought I should be better, and some food on a tray might be sent up to me.

Accordingly, with my wife's aid, I went upstairs and lay down. Some breakfast was brought up on a tray, which happened to be of silver or plated metal. As this was visible to me, and I knew the limits within which I had to search, I was able without much difficulty to find what I wanted and to take the food of which I was in sore need. This done, I lay still and tried to sleep. My care now was how to get rid of the power which I had striven so hard to gain, to the possession of which I had looked forward as the main object of living. It was mine, and what was the result? Everything in the outer world which had given me pleasure and happiness had gone from me. All beauty of shape and colour had for me vanished away. So far as I was concerned, this ancient world, with all the lovely forms of life it contains, had disappeared, and I lived in the older time of chaos, when the earth was without form and void.

I must have fallen asleep and slept for some time. I was awakened by the door opening and some one entering with a soft and cautious step. I heard my wife speaking in a whisper. I called her to me without opening my eyes, lest the pleasure of her presence and of her soft, warm touch should be destroyed by the sight of the bones, living indeed, but without sinews or flesh. It was something to know that I could close my eyes to what I did not wish to see, and that the pleasure of feeling her touch and hearing her voice remained to me and was enhanced. The cheerfulness of the blind became intelligible to me.

"How are you now, dear," she said; "you have been a long time asleep. I have brought Dr. B—— to see you," she went on, naming a well-known London physician whom I knew well. "He came down an hour ago, but I did not let him come up as you were asleep, and he arrived tired and hungry."

"I am glad to see you, B——," said I, holding out my hand to him. "But I do not think I need your professional help."

I turned to look at him as I spoke, and felt that my eyes must have belied my lips.

"What is the matter, Newton?" said he; "are you in pain? You seemed to start when you looked at me."

It was very difficult to tell him. I could not tell him that he seemed to me a grinning skeleton with a complete set of false teeth and a pince-nez. Yet that would have been the simple truth. He seemed to me a framework of living bones with a few metal buttons, like the satellites of a planet, unconnected and yet attached.

He was a somewhat corpulent man, and the way in which his handsome watch and chain hovered, as it were, several inches in front of his ribs was peculiarly ludicrous. It was a horrible and ghastly sight. But the absurdity of this grotesque collection of bones being an eminent London physician so tickled my fancy that I broke into a loud laugh, which even to my own ears sounded like the laugh of a maniac. When I looked at B—— I was not overcome by the horror which I felt at seeing my wife and children in this manner. In the case of my friend it was the ridiculous side of the picture which affected me most. He did not understand the cause of my merriment. I could see by his attitude that he was beginning to take my case seriously.

"Newton," he said, in a grave voice, "you are not well, and I must insist on your being calm and quiet. Let me feel your pulse."

I put out my hand, and when I saw the skeleton with its false teeth and gold pince-nez holding my skeleton wrist with one bony hand, while in the other it held a watch at which it appeared to gaze attentively, I threw myself back on the pillow and fairly screamed with laughter. He was a handsome, well-mannered man, and had a large practice amongst the fashionable ladies of London. How many of these fair patients would consult him, thought I, if he appeared to them in this guise? Not many of those, at least, who suffered from nerves. To him my laugh must have sounded absolutely inept. What on earth was there to laugh at? From the tone of his voice I gathered that he was alarmed for me. We had known each other long, and were close friends.

"Newton," he said gravely, "you must compose yourself. Your wife has told me how you have been working for months, and how this attack came on. I must order you to keep perfectly quiet, and to remain in bed until I give you leave to get up. You will have an attack of brain fever and lose your life, perhaps worse, unless you obey me. Dear Mrs. Newton," he said, turning to my wife, "leave us for a few minutes. I should like to have some conversation with your husband."

When she had gone, B—— came and sat down in a chair beside me. I was compelled to shut my eyes, as the appearance of this solemn spectacled skeleton bending over me with that professional bedside manner which the physician has, or acquires, was more than my sense of humour could stand. About the man, as he was in the flesh, there was nothing absurd, but the skeleton, and especially the skull, had an air of priggish conceit that moved me to assault him. He felt my pulse again and examined me carefully with a stethoscope, took my temperature, looked at my tongue, and questioned me closely as to the state of my health. Then he began, evidently of a purpose, to discuss current events and everyday topics. It required all the self-control of which I was capable to look at him and keep my countenance while this was going on. The solemn movements of the physician-skeleton were sublimely burlesque. I could see that he was fairly puzzled. At last, after all the tappings and touchings and auscultations were over—

"Well, Newton," he said, "I cannot see that there is anything bodily wrong with you, except that you are rather run down from too much work and too little air and exercise. But from the account your wife has given me, and from what I have seen of you, I am not at all satisfied about you. You appear to be in a very excitable state, liable to fits of horror when those you love come near you, and at other times to attacks of causeless laughter. What do you find so ludicrous in me, or so horrible in your wife and children? I cannot understand your case, unless you are either feigning madness—a supposition which, as regards you, is impossible—or suffering from one of those hallucinations or delusions with which Nature punishes us for overtaxing our brain power. Now that your wife has left the room, tell me why her appearance causes you to shrink from her. You can rely on my discretion."

"My dear fellow," said I, "there is no mystery about it, except Nature, the mystery of all mysteries. I have made a wonderful discovery."

And I told him the history of the matter, from the experiment on the dog up to his arrival. I could see that he thought my mind had gone astray, and did not believe a word I was saying.

"My dear B——," I said, "I see you think I have lost my senses and that I am talking nonsense. I admit that I have been working too much, and became very excited by my experiments. My nerves are no doubt overstrung, otherwise I should not have been so much disturbed by what I have seen. But as to the facts, what I have told you is the simple truth. Indeed, in some respects it is less than the truth, as words cannot convey to you more than a very imperfect idea of the kind of world into which I have plunged. I have torn away the veil mercifully spread over our eyes. Blindness itself were preferable to the perfect vision I have sought and acquired."

I was going to offer to prove by experiment that my assertions were true when, more convinced than ever that I was raving, he cut me short—

"Come now, Newton, I must forbid you to talk any more at present. I will come to see you again shortly, and we can discuss this matter. Meanwhile remain in bed. Keep absolutely quiet, and sleep as much as you can. I will order you a sleeping draught. Good-bye until the day after tomorrow."

"Stop, B——!" I cried. "I can prove to you easily that you are mistaken and that I am telling the truth."

But before I had finished the sentence he was away and the door shut. Like many of his kind, he had no scientific imagination, and took little interest in anything that did not in his view lead to some practical end in his profession. I determined to obey him all the same, because his advice, although founded on a very mistaken view of my case, coincided with my own opinion. It was very probable that absolute rest and sleep were the best means of allowing the effects of the drug to wear off, and of restoring my eyes to their ordinary state. Accordingly I remained in bed, kept my eyes closed, and got my wife to read an amusing book to me.

It is needless to write down all the incidents of the day. Let me hasten to the end. I occasionally looked round, but found that my sight was still in the same state. I took the sleeping draught at night, and slept soundly without even a dream. How refreshed I felt when I awoke in the early morning! I was lying on my side, with my face towards a window which looked out on part of the garden. There was an old oak tree not far off, and it was my fancy to leave the curtains undrawn so that I might see the tree with the background of the morning sky when I awoke. No beautiful picture awaited me this morning. My eyes were still, to my dismay, under the influence of the drug and sensitive to the X-rays. I turned hastily away from the window to my other side. An indescribable horror seized me. There in her accustomed place beside me lay my wife's skeleton, as it were the skeleton of one who had died in her sleep long years ago and had been left to lie undisturbed. There it lay beside me, and I nearly touched the skull as I turned. I put out my hands to save my face from the hateful contact, when the arms began to move as if they would enfold me in their embrace. I could control my terror no longer. With the shriek of a madman I leapt from the bed. The skeleton rose with a start and tried to grasp me. I heard my wife's voice uttering a cry of fear. I tried to escape; my foot caught in something, I fell heavily, and I remember no more.

It was a lovely summer morning when I came to myself. I felt weak, and did not desire to move. I was lying in bed, turned towards the window I have mentioned before. I could tell that it was early morning. The sun was not high. The pale greenish-blue of the sky was mottled with delicate rosy clouds. Birds were singing, and a soft flower-scented breath was coming in through the open window. It was some time before full consciousness returned and I could recall to mind what had happened to me. Then the dreadful recollection came upon me, and, forgetting the present evidence of my senses, I turned with an awful dread that the same sight might await me again.

It may be a confession of weakness, but never before or since, though I may have had much greater cause, have I been so really and earnestly thankful. It may seem but a small thing comparatively to be saved from a disagreeable sight, especially when it is the consequence of a power that may be turned to great purposes. I had my wife and children with me still. I could still hear their voices and feel their touch unchanged, even though I could see only the most unlovely portion of their bodies. Yet I believe, although it is a terrible thing to say, that I would have chosen rather to part with them forever than to see them as I saw them during those terrible days. I was indeed glad and thankful in the inmost depths of my being when, turning myself slowly and feebly on that lovely morning, full of fear of what I might see, I saw lying there, close beside me, the gracious form of my wife, her comely head with its soft brown hair almost touching mine.

It was not long before I had quite regained my strength and spirits. I recognised that I was not of the stuff of which the pioneers and heroes of science are made. I had been ill and unconscious for many days. My wife had taken the reins for the time into her own hands, and I found she had effected a complete clearance of my laboratory and its contents. She believed that I had worked myself into a state of madness, and as I never explained the facts to her, and for the reasons already given did not wish to explain them, I took no pains to undeceive her. If it had not been for the fate of my poor dog, who had not shared in his master's scientific labours, I might have persuaded myself that I had been the sport of a diseased imagination.

My note-books, I found, had escaped the ruthless hand which had turned my laboratory into a billiard-room. In them was a record of my researches and their results, more or less complete. This I sent to my friend Professor Gleichen, to use the results as he thought fit, provided he did not connect the discovery with my name. The Herr Professor worked them out, and verified them at once by experiment on his own sight. I received a letter from him, written by an amanuensis in the first flush of his pleasure, full of what he hoped to achieve by this new faculty. He was an old man, he said, and even if he found that his sight was permanently altered, and that he could not recover his normal vision, he did not object to unpleasantness and inconvenience suffered in the cause of knowledge.

Some weeks afterwards he wrote in a less cheerful and hopeful strain, notwithstanding some remarkable discoveries he had been able to make. When some months had passed, I heard of his sudden death. Whether he died from natural causes, or whether he found life under such conditions a burden not to be endured even by a German savant, who can tell?

THE DEVIL'S FANTASIA

Bernard Capes

An extremely prolific writer of popular fiction, Bernard Edward Joseph Capes (1854–1918) is little remembered today. That he has not been forgotten altogether is due in large part to his resurrection by anthologist Hugh Lamb, who placed Capes with Robert Louis Stevenson, Arthur Conan Doyle, and H. Rider Haggard among "the leading talents of Victorian fantasy", calling him one of "the most imaginative writers of his day". "The Devil's Fantasia", from Capes's collection *Plots* (1902), is a story E. T. A. Hoffmann might have written had he lived in the age of sound recording. Though it had precursors, notably Édouard-Léon Scott's phonautograph (this graphically captured voices in 1860 which were finally able to be digitised and replayed in 2008), Thomas Edison's phonograph (1877) was the first working device for the reproduction of sound. Edison used cylinders (first foil-covered, then wax-coated), while Emile Berliner's Gramophone, patented a decade later, used disc records. Both were still widely used at the turn of the century; Capes does not explicitly say which kind of device features in his story, but the fact that this "toy" has apparently been bought for home recording use, and that it is not referred to as a "Gramophone", suggests a cylinder phonograph, perhaps something similar to the Edison "Standard" or "Gem" models popular at the time.

(Note that the story opens with a discussion of "Signor Marconi" and his new invention, which threatens to make "the old cables" of the electric telegraph redundant—the subject of the next story in this collection.)

"ignor Marconi," said I, "is confident that in a little while New York and Land's End will be able to talk together without the need of wires."

"The whole world will be one whispering-gallery," said George. "If you sit here, Johnny, and turn a deaf ear to me—as you very often do—I shall only have to show you my back, and speak a matter of twenty-three thousand miles into your other ear."

"Crikey!" said young Bob, in great admiration; "wouldn't Mr. Markham have fits just!"

Nevertheless, Bob was pleased with the fancy; for, though not yet out of Eton jackets—a tailless cub, *qui ne respirait que plaies et bosses*—he had a turn for practical science, and was permeated at that very moment with a wriggling and itching consciousness of proprietorship in one of its most characteristic toys—a phonograph, to wit—which his guardian brother George had presented to him that morning for a New Year's gift, and which was even then gloating sleekly on the sideboard, in anticipation of its opening, and so far unresolved-upon, charge.

"What a wheeze!" said Bobby; "and the old cables'll be pretty sick, I *don't* think. They'll have to reconcile 'emselves to slow freight, you know—sermons, and marriages, and poetry, and rot like that."

Crack! went a chestnut in the fire, round which we were all sitting.

"There goes another!" said George. "Take care, Lucy; there's a bit blown on to your dress."

Lucy flicked the fragment of shell away.

"I wish it was Signor what's-his-name's theory exploded," said she quite plaintively. "You didn't prick them, George. I must say I think this world is going to be made a detestable place for people who don't want to know everything."

"What don't you want to know, miss?" said Bobby brazenly. "Anything old Sneak's been tryin' to teach you?"

"You infernal young ——" began George, roaring; but Lucy hushed him immediately, and addressed the monkey in a quiet enough voice, though her face was white.

"Don't speak about Mr. Schneck again, Bobby. I'm afraid you're particularly inclined to tonight, because you see it annoys me."

George subsided; and both he and I showed, I am sure, some small embarrassment.

"Well, anyhow, you've got to have him, or he you, about that old Philippine nut," muttered the boy mutinously; and then, though I was a little sick in the heart, I came to the rescue of the situation.

Lucy was a china shepherdess and the proudest little virtuosa in one. She was a born musician—so much to her finger-tips, that out of those poured the love and melody that are wont to issue elsewhere from lips. She could teach the old piano a trick or two, Bobby said; and indeed he was right. In taking her hand, one felt that one was half-way to her heart.

But even native gifts must be disciplined; and in Mr. Schneck, a naturalised *musiklehrer*, Lucy had found a professional director and confessor. After her heart? Well, sometimes I was unhappily constrained to think so—and in the double sense.

But he was popular with none other of us—not with George, who felt him, I think, a rather ugly responsibility; not with Bob, who loathed him; not certainly with George's partner, Mr. Markham, because that gentleman, at least, did believe him to be altogether too much after Lucy's own heart.

And then, suddenly, Miss Virtuosa herself, who had for months sat at the man's great feet—Miss Lucy, who had been Spring, froze to him. Why? Had he presumed beyond his engagement? I knew nothing, except that Schneck was a dangerous beast to offend.

The last time I had seen him was when, some evenings before at these Hessels' dinner table, he had secured the half of a double-kernelled nut that Lucy had cracked. That was Bobby's allusion. Pupil and teacher might be estranged (and, indeed, it seemed that they were, as effectually as unaccountably); yet each, by an absurd superstition, held the means to a playful forfeit of the other.

"I quite agree with you, Miss Hessel," said I. "There's too much of this sifting of the grain. What are we going to do, I should like to know, when we've worked out the sum of our own little corner of creation?"

"Kill the scientists and be haunted by their ghosts," said George.

"Yes," said Lucy, "that would be capital. It would be hoisting the creatures with their own—"

She stopped with an uncomfortable look. It had suddenly occurred to her that, not knowing the meaning of the word, she might be committing herself to a quotation from an un-Bowdlerised Shakespeare.

I quoted, in my turn, with a nervous glance at Bobby—

> "'When Science from Creation's face
>   Enchantment's veil withdraws,
> What lovely visions yield their place
>   To cold material laws!'"

"Look here," said George hurriedly, for he saw Bobby prepared to explode, "I'll read the three of you a passage from a book I was looking into before dinner. It ought to reconcile you all—science and romance and the rest of it—because it makes poetry out of progress," and he collared the volume and went at it—

"'I never hold with those who cry that hollow are delights—that first is but the beginning of last. Life flies before, and the ecstasy is in the chase. Shall man's soul be a lesser thing than his imagination? Shall the hunt end with the running down of the quarry? Ah, the glimpses, the vistas, the wild voices, seen and heard in the racing! We have gained upon, we have outstripped them in the rush; but, when we stop, they overtake and pass us, and we must on once more. It is not given to us to rest for ever in quiet pastures. The spirits of those we have slain we must follow, for every sacrifice we make to death robs us of a part of our independence, and always we are ready to yield that part for a song. Forward! forward! with every pace the imagination extends its horizon. Forward! forward! and what if over the edge of the world? Does not the sound of horns blown from other stars echo down to us?

"'And, should we run the live game to earth? Earth is sweet and lovable—its fields, its flowers, its roads; the warm and hearty tenements compacted of its clay; the wine of its grapes, the fragrant smoke of its leaf, the bread and headstrong drink yielded of its grain. Give me life and a sunny road; good-humour and a cool tavern.'"

He came to a stop.

"And no phonographs," said Lucy defiantly.

Bobby scowled, and turned a superior shoulder on his sister.

"What bally rot, George!" said he. "That's the stuff to go by slow freight."

Lucy smiled, serene and aggravating.

"Well," said she, "I prefer fancy to its imitations; and I wish every phonograph was burnt; and I declare I'd rather be haunted by a voice from the grave, than by one from a walnut-wood box."

The room door had been opened very softly.

"*Bon jour, Philippine!*" said a voice there.

We all started, and Lucy gasped like a frightened bird. Then Bobby gave a great rude laugh.

"Miss Fancy, Miss Fancy," crowed he, clapping his hands; "Mr. Sneak's got you first, and you'll have to pay forfeit!"

George rose, his instinct of hospitality bettering in him some natural restraint. After all, he was without warrant for implying a closure of the intimacy that had often hitherto found this visitor a guest at his fireside. Schneck, being better acquainted with the facts, must be judge of the propriety of his own conduct.

I stole a look at the girl. She was frowning—biting her lip. It was ignoble in me, perhaps, but my heart gave a little skip of exultation to read—or to think that it read—some signs in her face of implacable offence.

Schneck came heavily to the fire, nodding and humming, and smiling a little to himself. He was an unwieldy man, with a face one mask of hair, and a great nose—disgustedly pinched and pommelled out of shape in the modelling—that drew in at the wings, when he filled his chest for laughter. His clothes were like evangelical misfits. His voice tore every decent sentiment to rags. Yet he carried force on his shoulders, and his eyes were burning-glasses. An Englishman and pretty obstinate, I had always felt, up to now, that I had had little chance against this man.

Suddenly he spoke, his bass finding out a wire in the piano, that jarred to it.

"Pravo, Miss Lucy! Boetry from a parrel-organ? Ach Himmel! One would find as soon consistency in a woman. To be py fear, or remorse, or a melody haunted—yes, that is understoot; but py a mechanical hopgoblin! Indeet the world is going to pe made a detestaple blace for beoples who don't want to know everything."

He had no shame, it will be observed, in making this implicit confession of eavesdropping. He intended that it should suggest his knowledge of some personalities, of which he had been the subject long before he revealed himself. There was an air of hardly repressed ferocity about him, under which we all, I am sure, though conscious enough of guilt, found it difficult to regard *les convenances*.

Lucy, leaning back in her chair, took no notice whatever of his address. Her face was set in a studied indifference—pink and hard as china; but it was not the hardness that waits to be courted from its mood.

Schneck put away roughly the cigarette box proffered by George.

"I do not stop here," he said, "not more than a few minutes. I com to my forfeit claim, dat is all."

He nodded and laughed, and pinching out from his bagging waistcoat pocket his bit of a nut, held it up for evidence.

"*Bon jour, Philippine*," says he, repeating himself. "It shall pe for you the task of all the easiest. Dat is jchost to blay me a little God-speed pefore I am on a long journey brojected."

George alone amongst us had the nerve, or the decency, to murmur something vaguely significative of a polite concern over this intimation of leave-taking. Schneck only growled in response, as if he were wishing to spit, the beast.

But Miss Hessel was on her feet immediately, her eyes expressing a relief that her lips would not acknowledge. It was evident that the question of the nut had been upon her mind (a mind—God bless her!—quite orthodox in its superstitions), and that the indifferent penalty exacted disburdened that of some apprehensions.

"I am ready, Herr Schneck," said she. "What shall it be?"

Perhaps he had hoped against hope for some expression of regret, of protest, at least of surprise over his departure. He looked into the fire a moment, biting at his underlip till the hair on it rose like the withers of a dog; and then he put a hand into his inner breast-pocket, reluctantly, as if he were robbing his heart, and brought out a single yellow sheet of music.

"It is this," he said, his eyes lowered, while he fidgeted the paper eternally in his hands. "Somthing that has a very strange recollegtion. It was giffen me wonce by a man—a musician—that picked it up corked into a pottle and vloating at sea. I haf it myself never blayed, and he only wonce. He was ill that same night. He was neffer petter. On his death-ped he for me sent, and boot this into my hands. Now, at last, I would hear it. It is to regord a long farewell."

We all, I think, longed to get this unprofitable sentimentality over; yet we couldn't in decency rally Lucy on the situation. She accepted the faded sheet from the hand that held it out to her, and looked at it with some instinctive curiosity.

"It is very old," she said; "a figured bass."

"It is old," said Schneck quietly.

"And incomplete," said the girl wonderingly; "a duet, it seems, with the treble left out."

Schneck did not answer.

"Am I to play it," she asked, "unscored, imperfect, just as it is?"

He bowed, as if he could not trust himself to speak, and withdrawing as she crossed to the piano, halted between her and the door, his arms folded over his chest. As he thus stood motionless, the shaded gaslight, streaming upon his head, seemed to melt his every knot and feature into rivulets of gall, that flowed down and were merged into his beard.

Lucy, as sweet and native a musician as ever perched on a stool, settled herself, and paid out the first notes of her forfeit.

"Good God!" cried George, getting hurriedly to his feet; "not again, Lucy. We've had enough."

I came out of a nightmare, and stared at him. His face was livid. Bobby, crouched down in the chimney-corner, was snivelling. And Schneck was gone—had vanished in the thick of that infernal cacophony as if blown to the winds.

Once, twice, thrice had Lucy gone through the devilish duet— duet! was the girl hideously exalted, inspired, reduplicated?—and now a fourth time she was restarting on it.

"Oh, do stop her!" whimpered Bob.

George, in a loud, shaky voice, asserted his authority.

"That's enough, Lucy. Mr. Schneck's gone, and we don't care about any more. Damn it!" he screamed, "*will* you stop!"

I saw the girl's face peering evilly at us over the top of the piano; but the rush and explosion of notes never ceased. Yet, physically, she did not seem agitated in any degree proportionate with the hell she was raising. Her face looked calm, and shockingly evil—just that.

I felt as sick as a rat in a trap; but in a moment I was across the room and by her side—had put down my hands upon hers as they danced upon the keyboard. As I did so, I heard an appalling little sound through the rest. It was her teeth grinding at me. Then, in pure, unadulterated horror, I snatched my arms away and stood glaring. Her hands were flashing and glancing in the bass. She was responsible for no more than her share of the *duo diabolique*. But, up in the treble, nevertheless, the keys were pitting and pattering in a furious gambade, *though there were no fingers there to work them.*

"Come away, *in God's name!*" I muttered.

A chord so dissonant answered me, that I felt as if a bullet had crashed through my jaws and teeth.

"I can't—I wont!" she whined, her voice hopping in time to her hands. "I've chosen to bind myself, and I must go on—for ever and ever. Please stand away. It's the most wicked and delightful thing—not heavenly, but delightful."

I heard George breathing at my ear.

"What's happened to her? Who is she?"

And in an instant he had thrust me aside, and was making as if to tear her from her seat.

"Ah!" she shrieked hoarsely, crouching aside from him with a hateful look (and it was horrible to see that in her facile memory the *thing* was now so scored that she had no longer need to consult the manuscript). "Ah!—if you dare—if you touch me, I will scream the house down!"

Her fingers never stopped while she spoke—hers, or those others. He staggered back as if she had flung her little fist into his face.

"What are we to do?" he said in a thick, sick voice.

Suddenly he was flinging about, stamping, beating his ears, swearing like a madman.

"That devil!" he screeched. "Someone must go after him, kill him, bring him back at once—you, Markham!"

I turned and seized and held him steady.

"Not I, George. You, you. Leave me alone with her. You know why. It may bring her to herself. Listen, man: it may bring her to herself, I say."

He stared a moment, reeled, and went floundering towards the door. There he stopped and twisted about, fumbling drunkenly behind him for the handle.

"Come, Bobby," he muttered.

The boy edged, sobbing and slinking, by the wall, made a little final rush, and hustled him from the room. The door closed upon them.

With an indescribable desperate feeling of exaltation in my heart, I turned and fell on my knees by the girl. The sweet young bedevilled face had a smile of triumph on it. She laughed softly, with an infamous happiness. In the midst of her ecstasy, her gloating eyes were moved to look into the pain of mine. Immediately something—it was like a breath coming and going very faintly on a mirror—pulsed in her cheek.

"I can't help it, you know," she said, in a bewildered, but much gentler voice; "and I don't think I want to. But I wish you wouldn't look so troubled. If you loved me really" (I had spoken no word to her), "you wouldn't wish to rob me of such a transport."

I put my arms about her waist, and my lips to the little shining band of satin that imprisoned it from me.

"I do love you!" I cried. "Oh, my little girl, with my whole soul of love and sorrow!"

I felt a tremor go through her, and I thought the music rose suddenly in gasps and bounds, as if she were urging herself, or were being urged reluctant, to a new intoxication. Then in an instant she was moaning—

"If I could get rid of it! If someone would take it from me, as I took it from him!"

I scrambled to my feet and snatched (it was inexplicable we had not thought of it sooner) the damned sheet from the stand, and hurrying with it to the fire, threw it and stamped it upon the burning coals.

It caught, blazed into a roar and hiss, and went wobbling piecemeal in ashes up the chimney... Still the accursed fantasia went on, and I was back at her side.

"Lucy!" I cried, heart-sick.

She laughed horribly.

"It's no good, unless someone can catch it—take my place—take it from me. And how can they do it, now you've burnt the score?"

Someone! It was all one to me. I knew no more, George knew no more, Bobby knew no more, about music than an organ-grinder. If she should die or go mad at her post! I was desperate now to keep her going till—till when? What would justify us in transmitting the scourge to another—an expert—even if we could find one demented enough to—

My brain crackled. In a frenzy of horror I ran round her, and flogged down with my hands at the hands I could not see.

"Take care!" said Lucy. "It's turning its nails up."

I fell back, and upon an inspiration. In a moment I was across the room, had seized Bobby's new year's gift from the sideboard, had turned the key in the lock. Here at least was such an instrument as I had experimented with and could manipulate. My nerves were strung to snapping. My hands were steady as a hangman's.

The duet leapt to its close. As the little ringing pause, that preluded a renewal of the horror, succeeded, I had all in readiness. Before Lucy's fingers rose for the opening swoop, I had dumped the naked machine down on the piano lid.

Now I set my teeth, and stood, and endured. I had something more than the others to uphold me; but the tension was terrible. As the riot swept on, I felt burning drops trickling down my forehead. The performance was more astounding, more delirious, more shattering than ever. It rose to a pitch, a fury that was scarce endurable.

I wanted to outscream it; I took a step forward, and it slammed to an end. Standing rigid, as I had moved, I waited—waited, thinking I should die on my feet. Would the terrible white fingers lift and poise again? A minute passed—crawled into another. Suddenly she was swaying—drooping a little forward. I tore her into my arms, looked into her face, dropped my lips to her shut eyes, to her open mouth, looked again in agony. I had healed that wound—at least, had closed it; and a little smile was come about its corners. For the rest, she did not seem swooning so much as fallen into a deep, exhausted sleep. Murmuring incoherently, I carried her to a sofa, and laid her gently to rest there.

I had but drawn back, panting, regarding her, when the door hurriedly opened, and George re-entered the room. His face was like ashes.

"Johnny! my God!" he said.

I signalled silence to him.

"Yes," I whispered, "she's asleep. It's all right; I've managed it," and I told him.

He stared, but was so far from being incredulous that he fell in at once with the practical solution of the problem. This was a demonology that one could understand—the psychical brought accountable to the physical; the supernatural brought up to date.

"That skunk—" he snarled.

"Did you find him—kill him?"

"He was gone—had packed up his luggage (a comb and a sausage, I suppose), and left his lodgings before he came here. He can keep now for a bit."

"And—and that there? what shall we do with it?"

"Why, the thing's got in; it's *taken* it, you know. There's no help for it. We must treat it as they treat infected bed-clothes."

"Burn it?"

He nodded.

"We'll not leave a rivet. We'll sweep the very ashes to the devil. I'll speak to Bobby; go and get rid of the servants. Two of them met me crying just now, and cook is leaving at a moment's notice. We score on that. I notice there's back in the stand a silver-knobbed umbrella that's been missing for months. She wouldn't embezzle goods with the devil's hall-mark on 'em. I expect this is going to be quite an event—a resurrection of unconsidered trifles. I'm looking forward quite touchingly to renewing my acquaintance with a dozen little matters of personal furniture, that from time to time have mysteriously vanished in the very face of large-eyed innocence, leaving not a rack behind. Stay here a moment."

His head was blown with relief, I think. He returned in a few minutes, carrying a lantern.

"Now, Johnny," said he, "you've done much, but, by your own account, you've been rather overpaid than under. I'm not going to be modest about it. Lucy's a plum for any man. You must win her up to the hilt. A deed half done is a deed undone. It's for you to finish—to take up that abomination and carry it downstairs."

I set my mouth. I would sooner have handled an adder. But I would not have had another complete my work. Gingerly I dismembered the mechanism, as I would have unscrewed the cap of a gorged shell; breathlessly I reconsigned all to the box, and, holding that at arm's length, followed George out into the hall and down to the basement. At the door of the kitchen I paused, while he lit the gas. Then, ghost-like, I stalked in. Black beetles—my detestation—exploded beneath my feet. I took no heed. Had I not fairly won my love at last?

Fortunately a great fire was burning. Deliberately, at scorching risk, I placed the box on the top of it, and then we seized upon pokers and fell back.

It was long in catching, but at length, with a jarring bang, it was riven and in full blast. As the case burst and fell asunder, the metal rose writhing from it like a Pharaoh's serpent. The black beetles, I could swear it, stood up on their hind legs and cheered. The chimney was become a hellish trumpet, roaring shrieks and laughter into the night. At last, chord by chord, the turmoil died away and the fire sank into an exhausted glimmer.

Lucy remembered nothing of it all, but that she had dreamed she was mated to the devil. It was for me to disabuse her mind of that extravagance, and I have no reason to suppose that I failed in doing so.

Once upon a time business carried George to Germany. He returned at the end of two or three weeks, sound enough in health, but with a long scar across his temple. He had got it in a fall, he said.

But in the evening he opened quietly upon me—

"I have come across him, Johnny; he is bandmaster in a Bavarian regiment. I had a little talk with him. He treated the whole thing as a joke. It was very true, he said, that the manuscript had come out of a bottle that had been picked up on the seashore by a professional friend of his; that this friend had carried the prize home and had, then and there, in Schneck's presence, played over the piece; that he had been very queerly seized, it appeared as a consequence; that he, Schneck, being a powerful man, had succeeded in dragging his friend away from the piano, but unavailingly, for that the victim had succumbed a few days later to something in the nature of brain fever. 'And how was I to know,' says he, 'that the resbonsibility was to anything bot the artistic *Empfindlichkeit* of my vrent?' But a little pressure brought something else from the brute—that there had been extracted from the flask a second paper, which, being presently examined, was found to relate how the composer of the score had, for some unnamable atrocity, been put overboard from a West-Indiaman (whether marooned or cast adrift, I don't know), and how this accursed conjuration of his, found after his departure, had been bottled and committed to the sea, none daring to destroy it. Schneck, I think, had not meant to tell me that, but his hate got the better of him. Anyhow, he did tell me, and—"

"What?"

"I laid my whip across his face."

I nodded.

"And you met the next morning?"

"His first bullet," said George, "took me here, where you see. I was stunned by the shock and the wind of it, and Schneck thought he had accounted for me. He was unhurt himself, and he cleared out. I was well in a week. I wish I had killed him."

He broke off as his brother entered the room.

"Hullo, Bobby!" said he. "Got tired of poetry and the imaginative arts yet?"

"Oh, rot!" said Bobby.

"WIRELESS"

Rudyard Kipling

As the unofficial "poet laureate" of the British Empire at its height, the India-born Rudyard Kipling (1865–1936) is best remembered today for *The Jungle Book* and *Kim*, though aficionados of the supernatural relish such grim classics as "The Phantom Rickshaw", "The Mark of the Beast", and "They". Kipling's fascination with technology, including information technology, left its mark on many of his stories, which explore the electric telegraph, photography, cinema, and the telephone, among other media. He was particularly struck by the parallels between communications technology and authorship: "We are only telephone wires", he once told Rider Haggard, adding, "You didn't write *She* you know... something wrote it through you!" In "The Finest Story in the World" (1891), Kipling likens an unimaginative city clerk channelling episodes from his past lives to a telephone. The eponymous technology in "'Wireless'" plays a less metaphorical, if highly mysterious, role in facilitating an uncanny transmission from the ether, albeit one which generates wonder rather than terror. Wireless telegraphy—"this Marconi business", as the technologically uninterested Shaynor calls it—was then in its infancy, and still associated with the point-to-point transmission of Morse signals rather than the "broadcasting" of voices and music; indeed, an electrical engineers' magazine of this period warned: "messages scattered broadcast only waste energy by travelling with futile persistence towards celestial space". (The end of "'Wireless'" strikes a similar note of "futility".) In 1899 Marconi had successfully signalled across the English Channel, spanning the Atlantic in 1901. Kipling's presentation here of Shaynor as a medium, albeit an unwitting one (he thinks they are all frauds), mirroring a media technology echoes pre-wireless associations of the electric telegraph with spiritualism and the occult (such associations were forged with other new media as well, as in the later nineteenth-century emergence of "ghost" or "spirit" photography).

The story is set in an unnamed resort town on the south coast of England, but there can be little doubt that it is Brighton. Kipling was himself living in the adjacent village of Rottingdean at the time (Marconi came to visit him there in 1899), and other details ring true as well, such as the Victorian "big hotels" (here is also a nod to Marconi's own experiments at the Haven Hotel in Poole, where Kipling places the story's other operator) and the prevalence of the co-op stores which Shaynor (a Cumbrian transplant) abominates. I would wager that Kipling based his chemist's shop on a real one then extant at 5 Lewes Road in Brighton, which appears to have been next to a grocery and "Italian warehouse". There was no St. Agnes Church in Brighton, but one (initially a Mission Hall) was about to be constructed in nearby Hove; possibly Kipling had read about the appeal for funds for its construction two years earlier and connected the name with the 1820 narrative poem by Keats, "The Eve of St. Agnes", which plays an important role in the story.

"'Wireless'" was first published in *Scribner's* in 1902.

"It's a funny thing, this Marconi business, isn't it?" said Mr. Shaynor, coughing heavily. "Nothing seems to make any difference, by what they tell me—storms, hills, or anything; but if that's true we shall know before morning."

"Of course it's true," I answered, stepping behind the counter. "Where's old Mr. Cashell?"

"He's had to go to bed on account of his influenza. He said you'd very likely drop in."

"Where's his nephew?"

"Inside, getting the things ready. He told me that the last time they experimented they put the pole on the roof of one of the big hotels here and the batteries electrified all the water-supply and"—he giggled—"the ladies got shocked when they took their baths."

"I never heard of that."

"The hotel wouldn't exactly advertise it, would it? Just now, by what young Mr. Cashell tells me, they're trying to signal from here to Poole, and they're using stronger batteries than ever. But, you see, he being the guvnor's nephew and all that (and it will be in the papers, too), it doesn't matter how they electrify things in this house. Are you going to watch?"

"Very much. I've never seen this game. Aren't you going to bed?"

"We don't close till ten on Saturdays. There's a good deal of influenza in town, too, and there'll be a dozen prescriptions coming in before morning. I generally sleep in the chair here. It's warmer than jumping out of bed every time. Bitter cold, isn't it?"

"Freezing hard. I'm sorry your cough's worse."

"Thank you. I don't mind cold so much. It's this wind that fair cuts me to pieces." He coughed again, hard and hackingly, as an old lady came in for ammoniated quinine. "We've just run out of it in bottles, madam," said Mr. Shaynor, returning to the professional tone, "but if you will wait two minutes, I'll make it up for you, madam."

I had used the shop for some time, and my acquaintance with the proprietor had ripened into friendship. It was Mr. Cashell who revealed to me the purpose and power of Apothecaries' Hall what time a fellow-chemist had made an error in a prescription of mine, had lied to cover his sloth, and when error and lie were brought home to him had written vain letters.

"A disgrace to our profession," said the thin mild-eyed man, hotly, after studying the evidence. "You couldn't do a better service to the profession than report him to Apothecaries' Hall."

I did so, not knowing what djinns I should evoke; and the result was such an apology as one might make who had spent a night on the rack. I conceived great respect for Apothecaries' Hall and esteem for Mr. Cashell, a zealous craftsman who magnified his calling. Until Mr. Shaynor came down from the North his assistants had by no means agreed with Mr. Cashell. "They forget," said he, "that first and foremost the compounder is a medicine-man. On him depends the physician's reputation. He holds it literally in the hollow of his hand, sir."

Mr. Shaynor's manners had not, perhaps, the polish of the grocery and Italian warehouse next door, but he knew and loved his dispensary work in every detail. For relaxation he seemed to go no farther afield than the romance of drugs—their discovery, preparation, packing, and export—but it led him to the ends of the earth, and on this subject, and the Pharmaceutical Formulary, and Nicholas Culpepper, most confident of physicians, we met.

Little by little I grew to know something of his beginnings and his hopes—of his mother, who had been a school-teacher in one of the northern counties, and of his red-headed father, a small jobbing master at Kirby Moors, who died when he was a child; of the examinations he had passed (Apothecaries' Hall is a hard master in this respect); of his dreams of a shop in London; of his hate for the price-cutting co-operative stores; and, most interesting, of his mental attitude toward customers.

"There's a way you get into," he told me, "of serving them quite carefully, and, I hope, politely, without stopping your own thinking. I've been reading Christie's 'New Commercial Plants' all this autumn, and that needs keeping your mind on it, I can tell you. So long as it isn't a prescription, of course, I can carry as much as half a page of Christie in my head, and at the same time I could sell out all that window twice over, and not a penny wrong at the end. As to prescriptions, I think I could make up the general run of 'em in my sleep, almost."

For reasons of my own, I was deeply interested in Marconi experiments at their outset in England; and it was of a piece with Mr. Cashell's unvarying thoughtfulness that, when his nephew the electrician appropriated the house for a long-range installation, he should, as I have said, invite me to see the result.

The old lady went away with her medicine, and Mr. Shaynor and I stamped on the tiled floor behind the counter to keep ourselves warm. The shop, by the light of the many electrics, looked like a Paris-diamond mine, for Mr. Cashell believed in all the ritual of his craft. Three superb glass jars—red, green, and blue—of the sort that led Rosamond to parting with her shoes, blazed in the broad plate-glass windows, and there was a confused smell of orris, Kodak films, vulcanite, tooth-powder, sachets, and almond-cream in the air. Mr.

Shaynor fed the dispensary stove, and we sucked cayenne-pepper jujubes for our stomach's sake. The brutal east wind had cleared the streets, and the few passers-by were muffled to their puckered eyes. In the Italian warehouse next door some gay feathered birds and game, hung upon hooks, sagged to the wind across the left edge of our window-frame.

"They ought to take these poultry in—all knocked about like that," said Mr. Shaynor. "Doesn't it make you feel perishing? See that old hare! The wind's nearly blowing the fur off him."

I saw the belly-fur of the dead beast blown apart in ridges and streaks as the wind caught it, showing bluish skin underneath. "Bitter cold," said Mr. Shaynor, shuddering. "Fancy going out on a night like this! Oh, here's young Mr. Cashell."

The door of the inner office behind the dispensary opened, and an energetic, spade-bearded man stepped forth, rubbing his hands.

"I want a bit of tin-foil, Shaynor," he said. "Good-evening. My uncle told me you might be coming." This to me, as I began the first of a hundred questions.

"I've everything in order," he replied. "We're only waiting until Poole calls us up. Excuse me a minute. You can come in whenever you like—but I'd better be with the instruments. Give me that tin-foil. Thanks."

While we were talking, a girl—evidently no customer—had come into the shop, and the face and bearing of Mr. Shaynor changed. She leaned confidently across the counter.

"But I can't," I heard him whisper uneasily—the flush on his cheek was dull red, and his eyes shone like a drugged moth's. "I can't. I tell you I'm alone in the place."

"No, you aren't. Who's *that*? Let him look after it for half an hour. A brisk walk will do you good. Ah, come now, John."

"But he isn't—"

"I don't care. I want you to; we'll only go round by the church. If you don't—"

He crossed to where I stood in the shadow of the dispensary counter, and began some sort of broken apology about a lady-friend.

"Yes," she interrupted. "You take the shop for half an hour—to oblige *me*, won't you?"

She had a singularly rich and promising voice that well matched her outline.

"All right," I said. "I'll do it—but you'd better wrap yourself up, Mr. Shaynor."

"Oh, a brisk walk ought to help me. We're only going round by St. Agnes Church." I heard him cough grievously as they went out together.

I refilled the stove, and, after profligate expenditure of Mr. Cashell's coal, drove much warmth into the shop. I explored many of the glass-knobbed drawers that lined the walls, tasted some disconcerting drugs, and, by the aid of a few cardamoms, ground ginger, chloric-ether, and dilute alcohol, manufactured a new and wildish drink, of which I bore a glassful to young Mr. Cashell, busy in the back office. He laughed shortly when I told him that Mr. Shaynor had stepped out—but a frail coil of wire held all his attention, and he had no word for me bewildered among the batteries and rods. The noise of the sea on the beach began to make itself heard as the traffic in the street ceased. Then briefly, but very lucidly, he gave me the names and uses of the mechanism that crowded the tables and the floor.

"When do you expect to get the messages from Poole?" I demanded, sipping my liquor out of a graduated glass.

"About midnight, if everything is in order. We've got our installation-pole fixed to the roof of the house. I shouldn't advise you to turn on a tap or anything tonight. We've connected up with the plumbing, and all the water will be electrified." He repeated to me the history of the agitated ladies at the hotel at the time of the first installation.

"But what *is* it?" I asked. "Electricity is out of my beat altogether."

"Ah, if you knew *that* you'd know something nobody knows. It's just It—what we call Electricity, but the magic—the manifestations—the Hertzian waves—are all revealed by *this*. The coherer, we call it."

He picked up a glass tube not much thicker than a thermometer, in which, almost touching, were two tiny silver plugs and between them an infinitesimal pinch of metallic dust. "That's all," he said, proudly, as though himself responsible for the wonder. "That is the thing that will reveal to us the powers—whatever the powers may be—at work—through space—a long distance away."

Just then Mr. Shaynor returned alone and stood coughing his heart out on the mat.

"Serves you right for being such a fool," said young Mr. Cashell, as annoyed as myself at the interruption. "Never mind—we've all the night before us to see wonders."

Shaynor clutched the counter, his handkerchief to his lips. When he brought it away I saw two bright red stains.

"I—I've got a bit of a rasped throat from smoking cigarettes," he panted. "I think I'll try a cubeb."

"Better take some of this. I've been compounding while you've been away." I handed him the brew.

"'Twon't make me drunk, will it? I'm almost a teetotaller. My word! That's grateful and comforting."

He set down the empty glass to cough afresh.

"Brr! But it was cold out there! I shouldn't care to be lying in my grave a night like this. Don't *you* ever have a sore throat from smoking?" He pocketed his handkerchief after a furtive peep.

"Oh, yes, sometimes," I replied, wondering, while I spoke, into what agonies of terror I should fall if ever I saw those bright-red danger-signals under my nose. Young Mr. Cashell among the batteries coughed slightly to show that he was quite ready to continue his scientific explanations, but I was thinking still of the girl with the rich voice and the significantly cut mouth, at whose command I had taken charge of the shop. It flashed across me that she distantly resembled the seductive shape on a gold-framed toilet-water advertisement whose charms were unholily heightened by the glare from the red bottle in the window. Turning to make sure, I saw Mr. Shaynor's eyes bent in the same direction, and by instinct recognised that the flamboyant thing was to him a shrine. "What do you take for your—cough?" I asked.

"Well, I'm the wrong side of the counter to believe much in patent medicines. But there are asthma cigarettes and there are pastilles. To tell you the truth, if you don't object to the smell, which is very like incense, I believe, though I'm not a Roman Catholic, Blaudet's Cathedral Pastilles relieve me as much as anything."

"Let's try." My chances of raiding chemists' shops are few, and I make the most of them. We unearthed the pastilles—brown, gummy cones of benzoin—and set them alight under the toilet-water advertisement, where they fumed in thin blue spirals.

"Of course," said Mr. Shaynor, to my question, "what one uses in the shop for one's self comes out of one's own pocket. Why, stocktaking in our business is nearly the same as with jewellers—and I can't say more than that. But one gets them"—he pointed to the pastille-box—"at trade prices." Evidently this censing of the gay, seven-tinted wench was an established ritual which cost something.

"And when do we shut up shop?"

"We stay like this all night. The guv—old Mr. Cashell—doesn't believe in locks and shutters as compared with electric light. Besides it brings trade. I'll just sit here in the chair by the stove and doze off, if you don't mind. Electricity isn't my prescription."

The energetic young Mr. Cashell snorted within and Shaynor settled himself up in his chair over which he had thrown a staring red, black, and yellow Austrian jute blanket, rather like a table-cover. I cast about, amid patent-medicine pamphlets, for something to read, but finding little, returned to the manufacture of the new drink. The Italian warehouse took down its game and went to bed. Across the street blank shutters flung back the gaslight in cold smears; the dried pavement seemed to rough up in goose-flesh under the scouring of the savage wind, and we could hear, long ere he passed, the policeman flapping his arms to keep himself warm. Within, the flavours of cardamoms and chloric-ether disputed those of the pastilles and a score of drug and perfume and soap scents. Our electric lights, set low down in the windows before the tun-bellied Rosamond jars, flung inward three monstrous daubs of red, blue, and green, that broke into kaleidoscopic lights on the faceted knobs of the drug-drawers, the cut-glass scent flagons, and the bulbs of the sparklet bottles. They flushed the white tiled floor in gorgeous patches; splashed along the nickel-silver counter-rails and turned the polished mahogany counter-panels to the likeness of intricate grained marbles—slabs of porphyry and malachite. Mr. Shaynor unlocked a drawer and took out a meagre bundle of letters. From my place by the stove, I could see the scalloped edges of the paper with a flaring monogram in the corner and could even smell the reek of chypre. At each page he turned toward the toilet-water lady of the advertisement and devoured her with luminous eyes. He had drawn the Austrian blanket over his shoulders and among those warring lights he looked more than ever the incarnation of a drugged moth—a tiger moth as I thought.

He put his letter into an envelope, stamped it with stiff mechanical movements, and dropped it in the drawer. Then I became aware of the silence of a great city asleep—the silence that underlaid the even voice of the breakers along the sea-front—a thick, tingling quiet of warm life stilled down for its appointed time, and unconsciously I moved about the glittering shop as one moves in a sick-room. Young Mr. Cashell was adjusting some wire that crackled from time to time with the tense, knuckle-stretching sound of the electric spark. Upstairs, where a door shut and opened swiftly, I could hear his uncle coughing abed.

"Here," I said, when the drink was properly warmed, "take some of this, Mr. Shaynor."

He jerked in his chair with a start and a wrench, and held out his hand for the glass. The mixture, of a rich port-wine colour, frothed at the top.

"It looks," he said, suddenly, "it looks—those bubbles—like a string of pearls winking at you—rather like the pearls round that young lady's neck." He turned again to the advertisement where the female in the dove-coloured corset had seen fit to put on all her pearls before she cleaned her teeth.

"Not bad, is it?" I said.

"Eh?"

He rolled his eyes heavily full on me, and, as I stared, I beheld all meaning and consciousness die out of the swiftly dilating pupils. His figure lost its stark rigidity, softened into the chair, and, chin on chest, hands dropped before him, he rested open-eyed, absolutely still.

"I'm afraid I've rather cooked Shaynor's goose," I said, bearing the fresh drink to young Mr. Cashell. "Perhaps it was the chloric-ether."

"Oh, he's all right." The spade-bearded man glanced at him pityingly. "Consumptives go off in those sort of dozes very often. It's exhaustion...

I don't wonder. I daresay the liquor will do him good. It's grand stuff," he finished his share appreciatively. "Well, as I was saying—before he interrupted—about this little coherer. The pinch of dust, you see, is nickel-filings. The Hertzian waves, you see, come out of space from the station that despatches 'em and all these little particles are attracted together—cohere, we call it—for just so long as the current passes through them. Now, it's important to remember that the current is an induced current. There are a good many kinds of induction—"

"Yes, but what *is* induction?"

"That's rather hard to explain untechnically. But the long and the short of it is that when a current of electricity passes through a wire there's a lot of magnetism present round that wire; and if you put another wire parallel to, and within what we call its magnetic field— why then, the second wire will also become charged with electricity."

"On its own account?"

"On its own account."

"Then let's see if I've got it correctly. Miles off, at Poole, or wherever it is—"

"It will be anywhere in ten years."

"You've got a charged wire—"

"Charged with Hertzian waves which vibrate, say, two hundred and thirty million times a second." Mr. Cashell snaked his forefinger rapidly through the air.

"All right—a charged wire at Poole, giving out these waves into space. Then this wire of yours sticking out into space—on the roof of the house—in some mysterious way gets charged with those waves from Poole—"

"Or anywhere—it only happens to be Poole tonight."

"And those waves set the coherer at work, just like an ordinary telegraph-office ticker?"

"No! That's where so many people make the mistake. The Hertzian waves wouldn't be strong enough to work a great heavy Morse instrument like ours. They can only just make that dust cohere, and while it coheres (a little while for a dot and a longer time for a dash) the current from this battery—the home battery"—he laid his hand on the thing—"can get through to the Morse printing-machine to record the dot or dash. Let me make it clearer. Do you know anything about steam?"

"Very little. But go on."

"Well, the coherer's like a steam-valve. Any child can open a valve and start a steamer's engines, because a turn of the hand lets in the main steam, doesn't it? Now, this home battery here is the main steam, ready to print. The coherer is the valve, always ready to be turned on. The Hertzian wave is the child's hand that turns it."

"I see. That's marvellous."

"Marvellous, isn't it? And, remember, we're only at the beginning. There's nothing we sha'n't be able to do in ten years. I want to live—my God, how I want to live, and see things happen!" He looked through the door at Shaynor breathing lightly in his chair. "Poor beast! And he wants to keep company with Fanny Brand."

"Fanny *who*?" I said, for the name struck an obscurely familiar chord in my brain—something connected with a stained handkerchief, and the word "arterial."

"Fanny Brand—the girl you kept shop for!" He laughed. "That's all I know about her, and for the life of me I can't see what Shaynor sees in her, or she in him."

"*Can't* you see what he sees in her?" I insisted.

"Oh, yes, if *that's* what you mean. She's a great big fat lump of a girl and so on—I suppose that's why he's so crazy after her. She isn't his sort. Well, it doesn't matter. My uncle says he's bound to die before the year's out. Your drink's given him a good sleep, at any rate." Young Mr. Cashell could not catch Mr. Shaynor's face, which was half turned to the advertisement.

I stoked the stove anew, for the room was growing cold, and lighted another pastille. Mr. Shaynor in his chair, never moving, looked through and over me with eyes as wide and lustreless as those of a dead hare.

"Poole's late," said young Mr. Cashell, when I stepped back. "I'll just send them a call."

He pressed a key in the semi-darkness and with a rending crackle there leaped between two brass knobs a spark, streams of sparks, and sparks again.

"Grand, isn't it? *That's* the Power—our unknown Power—kicking and fighting to be let loose," said young Mr. Cashell. "There she goes—kick—kick—kick into space. I never get over the strangeness of it when I work a sending-machine—waves going into space, you know. T. R. is our call. Poole ought to answer with L. L. L."

We waited two, three, five minutes. In that silence, of which the boom of the tide was an orderly part, I caught the clear "*kiss— kiss—kiss*" of the halliards on the roof, as they were blown against the installation-pole.

"Poole is not ready. I'll stay here and call you when he is."

I returned to the shop, and set down my glass on a marble slab with a careless clink. As I did so, Shaynor rose to his feet, his eyes fixed once more on the advertisement, where the young woman bathed in the light from the red jar simpered pinkly over her pearls. His lips moved without cessation. I stepped nearer to listen. "And threw—and threw—and threw," he repeated, his face all sharp with some inexplicable agony.

I moved forward astonished. But it was then he found words— delivered roundly and clearly. These:

And threw warm gules on Madeleine's young breast.

The trouble passed off his countenance, and he returned lightly to his place, rubbing his hands.

It had never occurred to me, though we had many times discussed reading and prize-competitions as a diversion, that Mr. Shaynor ever read Keats, or could quote him at all appositely. There was, after all, a certain stained-glass effect of light on the high bosom of the highly polished picture which might, by stretch of fancy, suggest, as a vile chromo recalls some incomparable canvas, the line he had spoken. Night, my drink, and solitude were evidently turning Mr. Shaynor into a poet. He sat down again and wrote swiftly on his villainous notepaper, his lips quivering.

I shut the door into the inner office and moved up behind him. He made no sign that he saw or heard; I looked over his shoulder and read, amid half-formed words, sentences, and wild scratches:

—very cold it was. Very cold
The hare—the hare—the hare—
The birds—

He raised his head sharply, and frowned toward the blank shutters of the poulterer's shop where they jutted out against our window. Then one clear line came:

The hare, in spite of fur, was very cold—.

The head, moving machine-like, turned right to the advertisement where the Blaudet's Cathedral pastille reeked abominably. He grunted and went on:

Incense in a censer—
Before her darling picture framed in gold—
Maiden's picture—angel's portrait—

"Hsh," said Mr. Cashell, guardedly, from the inner office as though in the presence of spirits. "There's something coming through from somewhere; but it isn't Poole." I heard the crackle of sparks as he depressed the keys of the transmitter. In my own brain, too, something crackled, or it might have been the hair on my head. Then I heard my own voice in a harsh whisper: "Mr. Cashell, there is something coming through here, too. Leave me alone till I tell you."

"But I thought you'd come to see this wonderful thing—sir," indignantly at the end.

"Leave me alone till I tell you. Be quiet."

I watched—I waited. Under the blue-veined hand—the dry hand of the consumptive—came away clear, without erasure:

And my weak spirit fails
To think how the dead must freeze [he shivered as he
wrote]
Beneath the churchyard mould.

Then he stopped, laid the pen down, and leaned back.

For an instant, that was half an eternity, the shop spun before me in a rainbow-tinted whirl, in and through which my own soul most dispassionately considered my own soul as that fought with an overmastering fear. Then I smelt the strong smell of cigarettes from Mr. Shaynor's clothing and heard, as though it had been the rending of trumpets, the rattle of his breathing. I was still in my place of observation, much as one would watch a rifle-shot at the butts, half bent, hands on my knees and head within a few inches of the black, red, and yellow blanket of his shoulder. I was whispering encouragingly, evidently to my other self, sounding sentences, such as men pronounce in dreams.

"If he has read Keats, it proves nothing. If he hasn't—like causes *must* beget like effects. There is no escape from this law. *You* ought to be grateful that you know 'St. Agnes' Eve' without the book; because, given the circumstances, such as Fanny Brand, who is the key of the enigma and approximately represents the latitude and longitude of Fanny Brawne; allowing also for the bright red colour of the arterial blood upon the handkerchief, which was what you were puzzling over in the shop just now; and counting the effect of the professional environment, here almost perfectly duplicated—the result is logical and inevitable. As inevitable as induction."

Still the other half of my soul refused to be comforted. It was cowering in some minute and inadequate corner—at an immense distance.

Hereafter, I found myself one person again, my hands still gripping my knees and my eyes glued on the page before Mr. Shaynor. As dreamers accept and explain the upheaval of landscapes and the resurrection of the dead with excerpts from the evening hymn or the multiplication-table, so I had accepted the facts, whatever they might be, that I should witness, and had devised a theory, sane and plausible to my mind, that explained them all. Nay, I was even in advance of my facts, walking hurriedly before them, assured that they would fit my theory. And all that I now recall of that epoch-making theory are the lofty words: "If he has read Keats it's the chloric-ether. If he hasn't, it's the identical bacillus, or Hertzian wave of tuberculosis, *plus* Fanny Brand and the professional status which in conjunction with the main stream of subconscious thought, common to all mankind, has produced, temporarily, the induced Keats."

Mr. Shaynor returned to his work, erasing and rewriting as before, with incredible swiftness. Two or three blank pages he tossed aside. Then wrote, muttering:

"The little smoke of a candle that goes out."

"No," he muttered. "Little smoke—little smoke—little smoke. What else?" He thrust his chin forward toward the advertisement, whereunder the last of the Blaudet's Cathedral pastilles fumed in its holder. "Ah!" Then with relief:

The little smoke that dies in moonlight cold.

Evidently he was snared by the rhymes of his first verse, for he wrote and rewrote "gold—cold—mould" many times. Again he sought inspiration from the advertisement and set down, without erasure, the line I had overheard:

And threw warm gules on Madeleine's young breast.

As I remembered the original it is "fair"—a trite word—instead of "young," and I found myself nodding approval, though I admitted spaciously that the attempt to reproduce "its little smoke in pallid moonlight died" was a failure.

Followed without a break, ten or fifteen lines of bald prose—the naked soul's confession of its physical yearning for its beloved—unclean as we count uncleanliness; unwholesome, but human exceedingly—the raw material, so it seemed to me in that hour and in that place, whence Keats wove the twenty-sixth, seventh, and eighth stanzas of his poem. Shame I had none in overseeing this revelation; and my fear had gone like the smoke of the pastille.

"That's it," I murmured. "That's how it's blocked out. Go on! Ink it in, man. Ink it in."

Mr. Shaynor returned to broken verse wherein "loveliness" was made to rhyme with a desire to look upon "her empty dress." He picked up a fold of the gay, soft blanket, spread it over one hand, caressed it with infinite tenderness, thought, muttered, traced some snatches which I could not decipher, shut his eyes drowsily, shook his head, and dropped the stuff. Here I found myself at fault, for I could not then see (as I do now) in what manner a red, black, and yellow Austrian blanket bore upon his dreams.

In a few minutes he laid aside his pen, and, chin on hand, considered the shop with intelligent and thoughtful eyes. He threw down the blanket, rose, passed along a line of drug-drawers, and read the names on the labels aloud. Returning, he took from his desk Christie's "New Commercial Plants" and the old Culpepper that I had given him; opened and laid them side by side with a clerkly air, all trace of passion gone from his face; read first in one and then in the other and paused with the pen behind his ear.

"What wonder of Heaven's coming now?" I thought.

"Manna—manna—manna," he said at last, under wrinkled brows. "That's what I wanted. Good! Now then! Now then! Good! Good! Oh, by God, that's good!" His voice rose and he spoke richly and fully without a falter:

> Candied apple, quince and plum and gourd,
> And jellies smoother than the creamy curd,
> And lucent sirups tinct with cinnamon,
> Manna and dates in Argosy transferred

From Fez; and spiced dainties everyone
From silken Samarcand to cedared Lebanon.

He repeated it once more, using "blander" for "smoother" in the second line: then wrote it down without erasure, but this time (my set eyes missed no hairstroke of any word) he substituted "soother" for his atrocious second-thought, so that it came away under his hand as it is written in the book—as it is written in the book.

A wind went shouting down the street, and on the heels of the wind followed a spurt and rattle of rain.

After a smiling pause—and good right had he to smile—he began anew, always tossing the last sheet over his shoulder:

The sharp rain falling on the window-pane,
Rattling sleet—the windblown sleet.

Then prose: "It is very cold of mornings when the wind brings rain and sleet with it. I heard the sleet on the window-pane outside and thought of you, my darling. I am always thinking of you. I wish we could both run away like two lovers into the storm and get that little cottage by the sea which we were always thinking about, my own dear darling. We could sit and watch the sea beneath our windows. It would be a fairyland all of our own—a fairy sea—a fairy sea..."

He stopped, raised his head and listened. The steady drone of the Channel along the sea-front that had borne us company so long, leaped up a note to the sudden fuller surge that signals the change from ebb to flood. It beat in like the change of step throughout an army—this renewed pulse of the sea—and filled our ears till they, accepting it, marked it no longer.

> A fairyland for you and me
> Across the foam—beyond...
> A magic foam, a perilous sea.

He grunted again with effort and bit his underlip. My throat dried, but I dared not gulp to moisten it lest I should break the spell that was drawing him nearer and nearer to the high-water mark but two of the sons of Adam have reached. Remember that in all the millions permitted there are no more than five—five little lines—of which one can say: "These are the Magic. These are the Vision. The rest is only poetry." And Mr. Shaynor was playing hot and cold with two of them!

I vowed no unconscious thought of mine should influence the blindfold soul and pinned myself desperately to the other three, repeating and re-repeating:

> A savage spot as holy and enchanted
> As e'er beneath a waning moon was haunted
> By woman wailing for her demon lover.

But though I believed my brain thus occupied, my every sense hung upon the writing under the dry, bony hand, all brown-fingered with chemicals and cigarette smoke.

> Our windows fronting on the dangerous foam,

(he wrote, after long, irresolute snatches); and then

> Our open casements facing desolate seas
> Forlorn—forlorn—

Here again his face grew peaked and anxious with that sense of loss I had first seen when the power snatched him. But this time the agony was tenfold keener. As I watched, it mounted like mercury in the tube. It lighted his face from within till I thought the visibly scourged soul must leap forth naked between his jaws, unable to endure. A drop of sweat trickled from my forehead down my nose and splashed on the back of my hand.

> Our windows facing on the desolate seas
> And perilous foam of magic fairyland—

"Not yet—not yet," he muttered, "wait a minute. *Please*, wait a minute. I shall get it then.

> Our magic windows fronting on the sea,
> The dangerous foam of desolate seas... for aye.

Ouh, my God!"

From head to heel he shook—shook from the marrow of his bones outward—then leaped to his feet with raised arms, and slid the chair screeching across the tiled floor where it struck the drawers behind and fell with a jar. Mechanically, I stooped to recover it.

As I rose, Mr. Shaynor was stretching and yawning at leisure.

"I've had a bit of a doze," he said. "How did I come to knock the chair over? You look rather—"

"The chair startled me," I answered. "It was so sudden in this quiet."

Young Mr. Cashell behind his shut door was offendedly silent.

"I suppose I must have been dreaming," said Mr. Shaynor.

"I suppose you must," I said. "Talking of dreams—I—I noticed you writing—before—"

He flushed consciously.

"I meant to ask you if you've ever read anything written by a man called Keats."

"Oh! I haven't much time to read poetry and I can't say that I remember the name exactly. Is he a popular writer?"

"Middling. I thought you might know him because he's the only poet who ever was a druggist. And he's rather what's called the lover's poet."

"Indeed? I must look into him. What did he write about?"

"A lot of things. Here's a sample that may interest you."

Then and there, carefully, I repeated the verse he had twice spoken and once written not ten minutes ago.

"Ah. Anybody could see he was a druggist from that line about the tinctures and sirups. It's a fine tribute to our profession."

"I don't know," said young Mr. Cashell, with icy politeness, opening the door one-half inch, "if you still happen to be interested in our trifling experiments. But, should such be the case—"

I drew him aside, whispering, "Shaynor seemed going off into some sort of fit when I spoke to you just now. I thought, even at the risk of being rude, it wouldn't do to take you off your instruments just as the call was coming through. Don't you see?"

"Granted—granted as soon as asked," he said, unbending. "I *did* think it a shade odd at the time. So that was why he knocked the chair down?"

"I hope I haven't missed anything," I said.

"I'm afraid I can't say that but you're just in time for a rather curious performance. You can come in, too, Mr. Shaynor. Listen, while I read it off."

The Morse instrument was ticking furiously. Mr. Cashell interpreted: "'K.K.V. *Can make nothing of your signals.*'" A pause. "'*M. M.*

V. M. M. V. Signals unintelligible. Purpose anchor Sandown Bay. Examine instruments tomorrow.' Do you know what that means? It's a couple of men-o'-war working Marconi signals off the Isle of Wight. They are trying to talk to each other. Neither can read the other's messages, but all their messages are being taken in by our receiver here. They've been going on for ever so long, I wish you could have heard it."

"Good heavens!" I said. "Do you mean we're overhearing Portsmouth ships trying to talk to each other—that we're eavesdropping across half South England?"

"Just that. Their transmitters are all right, but their receivers are out of order, so they only get a dot here and a dash there. Nothing clear."

"Why is that?"

"God knows—and Science will know tomorrow. Perhaps the induction is faulty; perhaps the receivers aren't tuned to receive just the number of vibrations per second that the transmitter sends. Only a word here and there. Just enough to tantalise."

Again the Morse sprang to life.

"That's one of 'em complaining now. Listen: '*Disheartening—most disheartening.*' It's quite pathetic. Have you ever seen a spiritualistic seance? It reminds me of that sometimes—odds and ends of messages coming out of nowhere—a word here and there. No good at all."

"But mediums are all impostors," said Mr. Shaynor, in the doorway, lighting an asthma-cigarette. "They only do it for the money they can make. I've seen 'em."

"Here's Poole, at last—clear as a bell. L. L. L. *Now* we sha'n't be long." Mr. Cashell rattled the keys merrily. "Anything you'd like to tell 'em?"

"No, I don't think so," I said. "I'll go home and get to bed. I'm feeling a little tired."

POOR LUCY RIVERS

Bernard Capes

In 1714 one Henry Mill, an English engineer, obtained a patent for a machine for "the impressing or transcribing of letters singly or progressively one after another, as in writing, whereby all writings whatsoever may be engrossed in paper or parchment so neat and exact as not to be distinguished from print". Over the next century and a half, numerous inventors tried their hand at building writing machines of various kinds. But the typewriter as we know it (or used to know it, before the ubiquity of the personal computer) was the brainchild of the American inventor and printer Christopher Sholes, who worked with the Remington company, manufacturers of guns and sewing machines, to make his dream a reality. Like many another invention, the "typewriter", first marketed in 1874, did not take off until its makers discovered its real customer base—not private individuals but businesses. For some time, the word "typewriter" could refer either to the machine or its operator, and as Capes's story (taken from the 1906 collection *Loaves and Fishes*) shows, many "typewriters" were women: indeed, Sholes's invention played a major role in bringing middle-class women into the workforce. Media scholar Chris Keep notes that "[d]espite its poor pay and limited opportunities for advancement, work as a typist proved to be an attractive option for many women in the latter decades of the nineteenth century... it was one of the few occupations that allowed them to earn an independent income without significant loss of class standing, and which lower-middle-class women might use as a means of social advancement". He might be describing either of the precariously employed women in Capes's story.

T he following story was told to a friend—with leave, conditionally, to make it public—by a well-known physician who died last year.

I was in Paul's typewriting exchange (says the professional narrator), seeing about some circulars I required, when a young lady came in bearing a box, the weight of which seemed to tax her strength severely. She was a very personable young woman, though looking ill, I fancied—in short, with those diathetic symptoms which point to a condition of hysteria. The manager, who had been engaged elsewhere, making towards me at the moment, I intimated to him that he should attend to the new-comer first. He turned to her.

"Now, madam?" said he.

"I bought this machine second-hand off you last week," she began, after a little hesitation. He admitted his memory of the fact. "I want to know," she said, "if you'll change it for another."

"Is there anything wrong with it, then?" he asked.

"Yes," she said; "No!" she said; "Everything!" she said, in a crescendo of spasms, looking as if she were about to cry. The manager shrugged his shoulders.

"Very reprehensible of us," said he; "and hardly our way. It is not customary; but, of course—if it doesn't suit—to give satisfaction—" he cleared his throat.

"I don't want to be unfair," said the young woman. "It doesn't suit *me*. It might another person."

He had lifted, while speaking, its case off the typewriter, and now, placing the machine on a desk, inserted a sheet or two of paper, and ran his fingers deftly over the keys.

"Really, madam," said he, removing and examining the slip, "I can detect nothing wrong."

"I said—perhaps—only as regards myself."

She was hanging her head, and spoke very low.

"But!" said he, and stopped—and could only add the emphasis of another deprecatory shrug.

"Will you do me the favour, madam, to try it in my presence?"

"No," she murmured; "please don't ask me. I'd really rather not." Again the suggestion of strain—of suffering.

"At least," said he, "oblige me by looking at this."

He held before her the few lines he had typed. She had averted her head during the minute he had been at work; and it was now with evident reluctance, and some force put upon herself, that she acquiesced. But the moment she raised her eyes, her face brightened with a distinct expression of relief.

"Yes," she said; "I know there's nothing wrong with it. I'm sure it's all my fault. But—but, if you don't mind. So much depends on it."

Well, the girl was pretty; the manager was human. There were a dozen young women, of a more or less pert type, at work in the front office. I dare say he had qualified in the illogic of feminine moods. At any rate, the visitor walked off in a little with a machine presumably another than that she had brought.

"Professional?" I asked, to the manager's resigned smile addressed to me.

"So to speak," said he. "She's one of the 'augment her income' class. I fancy it's little enough without. She's done an occasional job for us. We've got her card somewhere."

"Can you find it?"

He could find it, though he was evidently surprised at the request—scarce reasonably, I think, seeing how he himself had just given me an instance of that male inclination to the attractive, which is so calculated to impress woman in general with the injustice of our claims to impartiality.

With the piece of pasteboard in my hand, I walked off then and there to commission "Miss Phillida Gray" with the job I had intended for Paul's. Psychologically, I suppose, the case interested me. Here was a young person who seemed, for no *practical* reason, to have quarrelled with her unexceptionable means to a livelihood.

It raised more than one question; the incompleteness of woman as a wage earner, so long as she was emancipated from all but her fancifulness; the possibility of the spontaneous generation of soul—the *divina particula auræ*—in man-made mechanisms, in the construction of which their makers had invested their whole of mental capital. Frankenstein loathed the abortion of his genius. Who shall say that the soul of the inventor may not speak antipathetically, through the instrument which records it, to that soul's natural antagonist? Locomotives have moods, as any engine-driver will tell you; and any shaver, that his razor, after maltreating in some fit of perversity one side of his face, will repent, and caress the other as gently as any sucking-dove.

I laughed at this point of my reflections. Had Miss Gray's typewriter, embodying the soul of a blasphemer, taken to swearing at her?

It was a bitterly cold day. Snow, which had fallen heavily in November, was yet lying compact and unthawed in January. One had the novel experience in London of passing between piled ramparts of it. Traffic for some two months had been at a discount; and walking, for one of my years, was still so perilous a business that I was long in getting to Miss Gray's door.

She lived West Kensington way, in a "converted flat," whose title, like that of a familiar type of Christian exhibited on platforms, did not convince of anything but a sort of paying opportunism. That is to say, at the cost of some internal match-boarding, roughly fitted and stained, an unlettable private residence, of the estimated yearly rental of forty pounds, had been divided into two "sets" at thirty-five apiece—whereby fashion, let us hope, profited as greatly as the landlord.

Miss Gray inhabited the upper section, the door to which was opened by a little Cockney drab, very smutty, and smelling of gas stoves.

"Yes, she was in." (For all her burden, "Phillida," with her young limbs, had outstripped me.) "Would I please to walk up?"

It was the dismallest room I was shown into—really the most unattractive setting for the personable little body I had seen. She was not there at the moment, so that I could take stock without rudeness. The one curtainless window stared, under a lid of fog, at the factory-like rear of houses in the next street. Within was scarce an evidence of dainty feminine occupation. It was all an illustration of the empty larder and the wolf at the door. How long would the bolt withstand him? The very walls, it seemed, had been stripped for sops to his ravening—stripped so nervously, so hurriedly, that ribbons of paper had been flayed here and there from the plaster. The ceiling was falling; the common grate cold; there was a rag of old carpet on the floor—a dreary, deadly place! The typewriter—the new one—laid upon a little table placed ready for its use, was, in its varnished case, the one prominent object, quite healthy by contrast. How would the wolf moan and scratch to hear it desperately busy, with click and clang, building up its paper rampart against his besieging!

I had fallen of a sudden so depressed, into a spirit of such premonitory haunting, that for a moment I almost thought I could hear the brute of my own fancy snuffling outside. Surely there was something breathing, rustling near me—something—

I grunted, shook myself, and walked to the mantelpiece. There was nothing to remark on it but a copy of some verses on a sheet of notepaper; but the printed address at the top, and the signature at the foot of this, immediately caught my attention. I trust, under the circumstances (there was a coincidence here), that it was not dishonest, but I took out my glasses, and read those verses—or, to be strictly accurate, the gallant opening quatrain—with a laudable coolness. But inasmuch as the matter of the second and third stanzas, which I had an opportunity of perusing later, bears upon one aspect of my story, I may as well quote the whole poem here for what it is worth.

> Phyllis, I cannot woo in rhyme,
>   As courtlier gallants woo,
> With utterances sweet as thyme
>   And melting as the dew.
>
> An arm to serve; true eyes to see;
>   Honour surpassing love;
> These, for all song, my vouchers be,
>   Dear love, so thou'lt them prove.
>
> Bid me—and though the rhyming art
>   I may not thee contrive—
> I'll print upon thy lips, sweetheart,
>   A poem that shall live.

It may have been derivative; it seemed to me, when I came to read the complete copy, passable. At the first, even, I was certainly conscious of a thrill of secret gratification. But, as I said, I had mastered no more than the first four lines, when a rustle at the door informed me that I was detected.

She started, I could see, as I turned round. I was not at the trouble of apologising for my inquisitiveness.

"Yes," I said; "I saw you at Paul's Exchange, got your address, and came on here. I want some circulars typed. No doubt you will undertake the job?"

I was conning her narrowly while I spoke. It was obviously a case of neurasthenia—the tendril shooting in the sunless vault. But she had more spirit than I calculated on. She just walked across to the empty fireplace, collared those verses, and put them into her pocket. I rather admired her for it.

"Yes, with pleasure," she said, sweetening the rebuke with a blush, and stultifying it by affecting to look on the mantelpiece for a card, which eventually she produced from another place. "These are my terms."

"Thank you," I replied. "What do you say to a contra account— you to do my work, and I to set my professional attendance against it? I am a doctor."

She looked at me mute and amazed.

"But there is nothing the matter with me," she murmured, and broke into a nervous smile.

"O, I beg your pardon!" I said. "Then it was only your instrument which was out of sorts?"

Her face fell at once.

"You heard me—of course," she said. "Yes, I—it was out of sorts, as you say. One gets fancies, perhaps, living alone, and typing—typing."

I thought of the discordant clack going on hour by hour—the dead words of others made brassily vociferous, until one's own individuality would become merged in the infernal harmonics.

"And so," I said, "like the dog's master in the fable, you quarrelled with an old servant."

"O, no!" she answered. "I had only had it for a week—since I came here."

"You have only been here a week?"

"Little more," she replied. "I had to move from my old rooms. It is very kind of you to take such an interest in me. Will you tell me what I can do for you?"

My instructions were soon given. The morrow would see them attended to. No, she need not send the copies on. I would myself call for them in the afternoon.

"I hope *this* machine will be more to the purpose," I said.

"*I* hope so, too," she answered.

"Well, she seems a lady," I thought, as I walked home; "a little anæmic flower of gentility." But sentiment was not to the point.

That evening, "over the walnuts and the wine," I tackled Master Jack, my second son. He was a promising youth; was reading for the Bar, and, for all I knew, might have contributed to the "Gownsman."

"Jack," I said, when we were alone, "I never knew till today that you considered yourself a poet."

He looked at me coolly and inquiringly, but said nothing.

"Do you consider yourself a marrying man, too?" I asked.

He shook his head, with a little amazed smile.

"Then what the devil do you mean by addressing a copy of love verses to Miss Phillida Gray?"

He was on his feet in a moment, as pale as death.

"If you were not my father"—he began.

"But I am, my boy," I answered, "and an indulgent one, I think you'll grant."

He turned, and stalked out of the room; returned in a minute, and flung down a duplicate draft of *the* poem on the table before me. I put down the crackers, took up the paper, and finished my reading of it.

"Jack," I said, "I beg your pardon. It does credit to your heart—you understand the emphasis? You are a young gentleman of some prospects. Miss Gray is a young lady of none."

He hesitated a moment; then flung himself on his knees before me. He was only a great boy.

"Dad," he said; "dear old Dad; you've seen them—you've seen her?"

I admitted the facts. "But that is not at all an answer to me," I said.

"Where is she?" he entreated, pawing me.

"You don't know?"

"Not from Adam. I drove her hard, and she ran away from me. She said she would, if I insisted—not to kill those same prospects of mine. My prospects! Good God! What are they without her? She left her old rooms, and no address. How did you get to see her—and my stuff?"

I could satisfy him on these points.

"But it's true," he said; "and—and I'm in love, Dad—Dad, I'm in love."

He leaned his arms on the table, and his head on his arms.

"Well," I said, "how did *you* get to know her?"

"Business," he muttered, "pure business. I just answered her advertisement—took her some of my twaddle. She's an orphan—daughter of a Captain Gray, navy man; and—and she's an angel."

"I hope he is," I answered. "But anyhow, that settles it. There's no marrying and giving in marriage in heaven."

He looked up.

"You don't mean it? No! you dearest and most indulgent of old Dads! Tell me where she is."

I rose.

"I may be all that; but I'm not such a fool. I shall see her tomorrow. Give me till after then."

"O, you perfect saint!"

"I promise absolutely nothing."

"I don't want you to. I leave you to her. She could beguile a Saint Anthony."

"Hey!"

"I mean as a Christian woman should."

"O! that explains it."

The following afternoon I went to West Kensington. The little drab was snuffling when she opened the door. She had a little hat on her head.

"Missus wasn't well," she said; "and she hadn't liked to leave her, though by rights she was only engaged for an hour or two in the day."

"Well," I said, "I'm a doctor, and will attend to her. You can go."

She gladly shut me in and herself out. The clang of the door echoed up the narrow staircase, and was succeeded, as if it had started it, by the quick toing and froing of a footfall in the room above. There was something inexpressibly ghostly in the sound, in the reeling dusk which transmitted it.

I perceived, the moment I set eyes on the girl, that there was something seriously wrong with her. Her face was white as wax, and quivered with an incessant horror of laughter. She tried to rally, to greet me, but broke down at the first attempt, and stood as mute as stone.

I thank my God I can be a sympathetic without being a fanciful man. I went to her at once, and imprisoned her icy hands in the human strength of my own.

"What is it? Have you the papers ready for me?"

She shook her head, and spoke only after a second effort.

"I am very sorry."

"You haven't done them, then? Never mind. But why not? Didn't the new machine suit either?"

I felt her hands twitch in mine. She made another movement of dissent.

"That's odd," I said. "It looks as if it wasn't the fault of the tools, but of the workwoman."

All in a moment she was clinging to me convulsively, and crying—

"You are a doctor—you'll understand—don't leave me alone—don't let me stop here!"

"Now listen," I said; "listen, and control yourself. Do you hear? I have come *prepared* to take you away. I'll explain why presently."

"I thought at first it was my fault," she wept distressfully, "working, perhaps, until I grew light-headed" (Ah, hunger and loneliness and that grinding labour!); "but when I was sure of myself, still it went on, and I could not do my tasks to earn money. Then I thought—how can God let such things be!—that the instrument itself must be haunted. It took to going at night; and in the morning"—she gripped my hands—"I burnt them. I tried to think I had done it myself in my sleep, and I always burnt them. But it didn't stop, and at last I made up my mind to take it back and ask for another—another—you remember?"

She pressed closer to me, and looked fearfully over her shoulder.

"It does the same," she whispered, gulping. "It wasn't the machine at all. It's the place—itself—that's haunted."

I confess a tremor ran through me. The room was dusking—hugging itself into secrecy over its own sordid details. Out near the window, the typewriter, like a watchful sentient thing, seemed grinning at us with all its ivory teeth. She had carried it there, that it might be as far from herself as possible.

"First let me light the gas," I said, gently but resolutely detaching her hands.

"There is none," she murmured.

None. It was beyond her means. This poor creature kept her deadly vigils with a couple of candles. I lit them—they served but to make the gloom more visible—and went to pull down the blind.

"O, take care of it!" she whispered fearfully, meaning the typewriter. "It is awful to shut out the daylight so soon."

God in heaven, what she must have suffered! But I admitted nothing, and took her determinedly in hand.

"Now," I said, returning to her, "tell me plainly and distinctly what it is that the machine does."

She did not answer. I repeated my question.

"It writes things," she muttered—"things that don't come from me. Day and night it's the same. The words on the paper aren't the words that come from my fingers."

"But that is impossible, you know."

"So I should have thought once. Perhaps—what is it to be possessed? There was another typewriter—another girl—lived in these rooms before me."

"Indeed! And what became of her?"

"She disappeared mysteriously—no one knows why or where. Maria, my little maid, told me about her. Her name was Lucy Rivers, and—she just disappeared. The landlord advertised her effects, to be claimed, or sold to pay the rent; and that was done, and she made no sign. It was about two months ago."

"Well, will you now practically demonstrate to me this reprehensible eccentricity on the part of your instrument?"

"Don't ask me. I don't dare."

"I would do it myself; but of course you will understand that a more satisfactory conclusion would be come to by my watching your fingers. Make an effort—you needn't even look at the result—and I will take you away immediately after."

"You are very good," she answered pathetically; "but I don't know that I ought to accept. Where to, please? And—and I don't even know your name."

"Well, I have my own reasons for withholding it."

"It is all so horrible," she said; "and I am in your hands."

"They are waiting to transfer you to mamma's," said I.

The name seemed an instant inspiration and solace to her. She looked at me, without a word, full of wonder and gratitude; then asked me to bring the candles, and she would acquit herself of her task. She showed the best pluck over it, though her face was ashy, and her mouth a line, and her little nostrils pulsing the whole time she was at work.

I had got her down to one of my circulars, and, watching her fingers intently, was as sure as observer could be that she had followed the text verbatim.

"Now," I said, when she came to a pause, "give me a hint how to remove this paper, and go you to the other end of the room."

She flicked up a catch. "You have only to pull it off the roller," she said; and rose and obeyed. The moment she was away I followed my instructions, and drew forth the printed sheet and looked at it.

It may have occupied me longer than I intended. But I was folding it very deliberately, and putting it away in my pocket when I walked across to her with a smile. She gazed at me one intent moment, and dropped her eyes.

"Yes," she said; and I knew that she had satisfied herself. "Will you take me away now, at once, please?"

The idea of escape, of liberty once realised, it would have been dangerous to baulk her by a moment. I had acquainted mamma that I might possibly bring her a visitor. Well, it simply meant that the suggested visit must be indefinitely prolonged.

Miss Gray accompanied me home, where certain surprises, in addition to the tenderest of ministrations, were awaiting her. All that becomes private history, and outside my story. I am not a man of sentiment; and if people choose to write poems and make general asses of themselves, why—God bless them!

The problem I had set *my*self to unravel was what looked deucedly like a tough psychologic poser. But I was resolute to face it, and had formed my plan. It was no unusual thing for me to be out all night. That night, after dining, I spent in the "converted" flat in West Kensington.

I had brought with me—I confess to so much weakness—one of your portable electric lamps. The moment I was shut in and established, I pulled out the paper Miss Gray had typed for me, spread it under the glow and stared at it. Was it a copy of my circular? Would a sober "First Aid Society" Secretary be likely, do you think, to require circulars containing such expressions as *"William! William! Come back to me! O, William, in God's name! William! William! William!"*—in monstrous iteration—the one cry, or the gist of it, for lines and lines in succession?

I am at the other end from humour in saying this. It is heaven's truth. Line after line, half down the page, went that monotonous, heart-breaking appeal. It was so piercingly moving, my human terror of its unearthliness was all drowned, absorbed in an overflowing pity.

I am not going to record the experiences of that night. That unchanging mood of mine upheld me through consciousnesses and sub-consciousnesses which shall be sacred. Sometimes, submerged in these, I seemed to hear the clack of the instrument in the window, but at a vast distance. I may have seen—I may have dreamt—I accepted it all. Awaking in the chill grey of morning, I felt no surprise at seeing some loose sheets of paper lying on the floor. *"William! William!"* their text ran down, *"Come back to me!"* It was all that same wail of a broken heart. I followed Miss Gray's example. I took out my match-box, and reverently, reverently burned them.

An hour or two later I was at Paul's Exchange, privately interviewing my manager.

"Did you ever employ a Miss Lucy Rivers?"

"Certainly we did. Poor Lucy Rivers! She rented a machine of us. In fact—"

He paused.

"Well?"

"Well—it is a mere matter of business—she 'flitted,' and we had to reclaim our instrument. As it happens, it was the very one purchased by the young lady who so interested you here two days ago."

"The first machine, you mean?"

"The first—*and* the second." He smiled. "As a matter of fact, she took away again what she brought."

"Miss Rivers's?"

He nodded.

"There was absolutely nothing wrong with it—mere fad. Women start these fancies. The click of the thing gets on their nerves, I suppose. We must protect ourselves, you see; and I'll warrant she finds it perfection now."

"Perhaps she does. What was Miss Rivers's address?"

He gave me, with a positive grin this time, the "converted" flat.

"But that was only latterly," he said. "She had moved from—"

He directed me elsewhere.

"Why," said I, taking up my hat, "did you call her 'poor Lucy Rivers'?"

"O, I don't know!" he said. "She was rather an attractive young lady. But we had to discontinue our patronage. She developed the most extraordinary—but it's no business of mine. She was one of the submerged tenth; and she's gone under for good, I suppose."

I made my way to the *other* address—a little lodging in a shabby-genteel street. A bitter-faced landlady, one of the "preordained" sort, greeted me with resignation when she thought I came for rooms, and with acerbity when she heard that my sole mission was to inquire about a Miss Lucy Rivers.

"I won't deceive you, sir," she said. "When it come to receiving gentlemen privately, I told her she must go."

"Gentlemen!"

"I won't do Miss Rivers an injustice," she said. "It was *ha* gentleman."

"Was that latterly?"

"It was not latterly, sir. But it was the effects of its not being latterly which made her take to things."

"What things?"

"Well, sir, she grew strange company, and took to the roof."

"What on earth do you mean?"

"Just precisely what I say, sir; through the trap-door by the steps, and up among the chimney-pots. *He'd* been there with her before, and perhaps she thought she'd find him hiding among the stacks. He called himself an astronomer; but it's my belief it was another sort of star-gazing. I couldn't stand it at last, and I had to give her notice."

It was falling near a gloomy midday when I again entered the flat, and shut myself in with its ghosts and echoes. I had a set conviction, a set purpose in my mind. There was that which seemed to scuttle, like a little demon of laughter, in my wake, now urging me on, now slipping round and above to trip me as I mounted. I went steadily on and up, past the sitting-room door, to the floor above. And here, for the first time, a thrill in my blood seemed to shock and hold me for a moment. Before my eyes, rising to a skylight, now dark and choked with snow, went a flight of steps. Pulling myself together, I mounted these, and with a huge effort (*the bolt was not shot*) shouldered the trap open. There were a fall and rustle without; daylight entered; and, levering the door over, I emerged upon the roof.

Snow, grim and grimy and knee-deep, was over everything, muffling the contours of the chimneys, the parapets, the irregularities of the leads. The dull thunder of the streets came up to me; a fog of thaw was in the air; a thin drizzle was already falling. I drove my foot forward into a mound, and hitched it on something. In an instant I was down on my knees, scattering the sodden raff right and left, and—my God!—a face!

She lay there as she had been overwhelmed, and frozen, and preserved these two months. She had closed the trap behind her, and nobody had known. Pure as wax—pitiful as hunger—dead! Poor Lucy Rivers!

Who was she, and who the man? We could never learn. She had woven his name, his desertion, her own ruin and despair into the texture of her broken life. Only on the great day of retribution shall he answer to that agonised cry.

BENLIAN

Oliver Onions

To fans of horror fiction, the name Oliver Onions (1873–1961) sparks an immediate synaptic connection to the much-anthologised novella "The Beckoning Fair One" and not, in all likelihood, much else. This is a shame, because such finely crafted stories as "Rooum", "The Painted Face", and the present story, "Benlian", show him to be one of the masters of the psychological ghost story in the early twentieth century. (His Sheridan Le Fanu-like Gothic novel *The Hand of Kornelius Voyt* is also well worth reading.) Onions's early training as an artist (he was also a magazine illustrator and book designer) is evident in "Benlian", whose eponymous character is a sculptor and whose narrator is a painter of portrait miniatures, an especially English artistic tradition dating back to the days of the Tudors. But when the French artist Louis Daguerre, following in the footsteps of his partner Nicéphore Niépce, succeeded in perfecting a process for photographically capturing images, the days of the miniature were numbered. Or at least its heyday: there was a revival of sorts at the end of the Victorian era, with the founding of the Royal Society of Miniature Painters in 1896 (still in existence today), whose "Aims are to Esteem, Protect, and Practise the traditional 16th Century art of miniature work". One suspects that the story's narrator is not a member—he sees himself as a down-to-earth tradesman, and since he primarily copies from photographs, he is a photographer himself as well. By this time, portable cameras were in widespread use—a craze for "snapshots" had begun soon after the introduction of the first Kodak camera in 1888—but "Pudgie" has a real professional's set-up: we should picture a heavy box camera mounted on a tripod, using glass negatives which are then contact-printed in the printing-frames he sets "out on the window-sash". Night photography, as we see here, requires the flash of ignited magnesium. Late in the story we also encounter an X-ray machine, which is now, a decade and a half after George Griffith and Charles Crosthwaite's tales, in widespread use in hospitals, complete with the generator it needs to provide the thousands of volts necessary for their conversion into X-rays in the vacuum tube.

"Benlian" appeared in 1911 in both *The Fortnightly Review* and Onions's landmark collection *Widdershins*.

t would be different if you had known Benlian. It would be different if you had had even that glimpse of him that I had the very first time I saw him, standing on the little wooden landing at the top of the flight of steps outside my studio door. I say "studio"; but really it was just a sort of loft looking out over the timber-yard, and I used it as a studio. The real studio, the big one, was at the other end of the yard, and that was Benlian's.

Scarcely anybody ever came there. I wondered many a time if the timber-merchant was dead or had lost his memory and forgotten all about his business; for his stacks of floorboards, set criss-crosswise to season (you know how they pile them up) were grimy with soot, and nobody ever disturbed the rows of scaffold-poles that stood like palisades along the walls. The entrance was from the street, through a door in a billposter's hoarding; and on the river not far away the steamboats hooted, and, in windy weather, the floorboards hummed to keep them company.

I suppose some of these real, regular artists wouldn't have called me an artist at all; for I only painted miniatures, and it was trade-work at that, copied from photographs and so on. Not that I wasn't jolly good at it, and punctual too (lots of these high-flown artists have simply no idea of punctuality); and the loft was cheap, and suited me very well. But, of course, a sculptor wants a big place on the ground floor; it's slow work, that with blocks of stone and marble that cost you twenty pounds every time you lift them; so Benlian had the studio.

His name was on a plate on the door, but I'd never seen him till this time I'm telling you of.

I was working that evening at one of the prettiest little things I'd ever done: a girl's head on ivory, that I'd stippled up just like... oh, you'd never have thought it was done by hand at all. The daylight had gone, but I knew that "Prussian" would be about the colour for the eyes and the bunch of flowers at her breast, and I wanted to finish.

I was working at my little table, with a shade over my eyes; and I jumped a bit when somebody knocked at the door—not having heard anybody come up the steps, and not having many visitors anyway. (Letters were always put into the box in the yard door.)

When I opened the door, there he stood on the platform; and I gave a bit of a start, having come straight from my ivory, you see. He was one of these very tall, gaunt chaps, that make us little fellows feel even smaller than we are; and I wondered at first where his eyes were, they were set so deep in the dark caves on either side of his nose. Like a skull, his head was; I could fancy his teeth curving round inside his cheeks; and his zygomatics stuck up under his skin like razorbacks (but if you're not one of us artists you'll not understand that). A bit of smoky, greenish sky showed behind him; and then, as his eyes moved in their big pits, one of them caught the light of my lamp and flashed like a well of lustre.

He spoke abruptly, in a deep, shaky sort of voice.

"I want you to photograph me in the morning," he said. I supposed he'd seen my printing-frames out on the window-sash some time or other.

"Come in," I said. "But I'm afraid, if it's a miniature you want, that I'm retained—my firm retains me—you'd have to do it through them. But come in, and I'll show you the kind of thing I do—though you ought to have come in the daylight..."

He came in. He was wearing a long, grey dressing-gown that came right down to his heels and made him look something like a Noah's-ark figure. Seen in the light, his face seemed more ghastly bony still; and as he glanced for a moment at my little ivory he made a sound of contempt—I know it was contempt. I thought it rather cheek, coming into my place and—

He turned his cavernous eyeholes on me.

"I don't want anything of that sort. I want you to photograph me. I'll be here at ten in the morning."

So, just to show him that I wasn't to be treated that way, I said, quite shortly, "I can't. I've an appointment at ten o'clock."

"What's that?" he said—he'd one of these rich deep voices that always sound consumptive. "Take that thing off your eyes, and look at me," he ordered.

Well, I was awfully indignant.

"If you think I'm going to be told to do things like this—" I began.

"Take that thing off," he just ordered again.

I've got to remember, of course, that you didn't know Benlian. *I* didn't then. And for a chap just to stalk into a fellow's place, and tell him to photograph him, and order him about... but you'll see in a minute. I took the shade off my eyes, just to show him that *I* could browbeat a bit too.

I used to have a tall strip of looking-glass leaning against my wall; for though I didn't use models much, it's awfully useful to go to Nature for odd bits now and then, and I've sketched myself in that glass, oh, hundreds of times! We must have been standing in front of it, for all at once I saw the eyes at the bottom of his pits looking rigidly over my shoulder. Without moving his eyes from the glass, and scarcely moving his lips, he muttered:

"Get me a pair of gloves, get me a pair of gloves."

It was a funny thing to ask for; but I got him a pair of my gloves from a drawer. His hands were shaking so that he could hardly get them on, and there was a little glistening of sweat on his face, that looked like the salt that dries on you when you've been bathing in the sea. Then I turned, to see what it was that he was looking so earnestly and profoundly at in the mirror. I saw nothing except just the pair of us, he with my gloves on.

He stepped aside, and slowly drew the gloves off. I think *I* could have bullied *him* just then. He turned to me.

"Did that look all right to you?" he asked.

"Why, my dear chap, whatever ails you?" I cried.

"I suppose," he went on, "you couldn't photograph me tonight—now?"

I could have done, with magnesium, but I hadn't a scrap in the place. I told him so. He was looking round my studio. He saw my camera standing in a corner.

"Ah!" he said.

He made a stride towards it. He unscrewed the lens, brought it to the lamp, and peered attentively through it, now into the air, now at his sleeve and hand, as if looking for a flaw in it. Then he replaced it, and pulled up the collar of his dressing-gown as if he was cold.

"Well, another night of it," he muttered; "but," he added, facing suddenly round on me, "if your appointment was to meet your God Himself, you must photograph me at ten tomorrow morning!"

"All right," I said, giving in (for he seemed horribly ill). "Draw up to the stove and have a drink of something and a smoke."

"I neither drink nor smoke," he replied, moving towards the door.

"Sit down and have a chat, then," I urged; for I always like to be decent with fellows, and it was a lonely sort of place, that yard.

He shook his head.

"Be ready by ten o'clock in the morning," he said; and he passed down my stairs and crossed the yard to his studio without even having said "Good night."

Well, he was at my door again at ten o'clock in the morning, and I photographed him. I made three exposures; but the plates were some that I'd had in the place for some time, and they'd gone off and fogged in the developing.

"I'm awfully sorry," I said; "but I'm going out this afternoon, and will get some more, and we'll have another shot in the morning."

One after the other, he was holding the negatives up to the light and examining them. Presently he put them down quietly, leaning them methodically up against the edge of the developing-bath.

"Never mind. It doesn't matter. Thank you," he said; and left me.

After that, I didn't see him for weeks; but at nights I could see the light of his roof-window, shining through the wreathing river-mists, and sometimes I heard him moving about, and the muffled knock-knocking of his hammer on marble.

II

Of course I did see him again, or I shouldn't be telling you all this. He came to my door, just as he had done before, and at about the same time in the evening. He hadn't come to be photographed this time, but for all that it was something about a camera—something he wanted to know. He'd brought two books with him, big books, printed in German. They were on Light, he said, and Physics (or else it was Psychics—I always get those two words wrong). They were full of diagrams and equations and figures; and, of course, it was all miles above my head.

He talked a lot about "hyper-space," whatever that is; and at first

I nodded, as if I knew all about it. But he very soon saw that I didn't, and he came down to my level again. What he'd come to ask me was this: Did I know anything, of my own experience, about things "photographing through"? (You know the kind of thing: a name that's been painted out on a board, say, comes up in the plate.)

Well, as it happened, I *had* once photographed a drawing for a fellow, and the easel I had stood it on had come up through the picture; and I knew by the way Benlian nodded that that was the kind of thing he meant.

"More," he said.

I told him I'd once seen a photograph of a man with a bowler hat on, and the shape of his crown had showed through the hat.

"Yes, yes," he said, musing; and then he asked: "Have you ever heard of things not photographing at all?"

But I couldn't tell him anything about that; and off he started again, about Light and Physics and so on. Then, as soon as I could get a word in, I said, "But, of course, the camera isn't Art." (Some of my miniatures, you understand, were jolly nice little things.)

"No—no," he murmured absently; and then abruptly he said: "Eh? What's that? And what the devil do *you* know about it?"

"Well," said I, in a dignified sort of way, "considering that for ten years I've been—"

"Chut!... Hold your tongue," he said, turning away.

There he was, talking to me again, just as if I'd asked him in to bully me. But you've got to be decent to a fellow when he's in your own place; and by-and-by I asked him, but in a cold, off-hand sort of way, how his own work was going on. He turned to me again.

"Would you like to see it?" he asked.

"*Aha!*" thought I, "he's got to a sticking-point with his work! It's all very well," I thought, "for you to sniff at my miniatures, my friend, but we all get stale on our work sometimes, and the fresh eye, even of a miniature-painter..."

"I shall be glad if I can be of any help to you," I answered, still a bit huffish, but bearing no malice.

"Then come," he said.

We descended and crossed the timber-yard, and he held his door open for me to pass in.

It was an enormous great place, his studio, and all full of mist; and the gallery that was his bedroom was up a little staircase at the farther end. In the middle of the floor was a tall structure of scaffolding, with a stage or two to stand on; and I could see the dim ghostly marble figure in the gloom. It had been jacked up on a heavy base; and as it would have taken three or four men to put it into position, and scarcely a stranger had entered the yard since I had been there, I knew that the figure must have stood for a long time. Sculpture's weary, slow work.

Benlian was pottering about with a taper at the end of a long rod; and suddenly the overhead gas-ring burst into light. I placed myself before the statue—to criticise, you know.

Well, it didn't seem to me that he needed to have turned up his nose at my ivories, for I didn't think much of his statue—except that it was a great, lumping, extraordinary piece of work. It had an outstretched arm that, I remember thinking, was absolutely misshapen—disproportioned, big enough for a giant, ridiculously out of drawing. And as I looked at the thing this way and that, I knew that his eyes in their deep cellars never left my face for a moment.

"It's a god," he said by-and-by.

Then I began to tell him about that monstrous arm; but he cut me very short.

"I say it's a god," he interrupted, looking at me as if he would have eaten me. "Even you, child as you are, have seen the gods men have made for themselves before this. Half-gods they've made, all good or all evil (and then they've called them the Devil). This is *my* god—the god of good and of evil also."

"Er—I see," I said, rather taken aback (but quite sure he was off his head for all that). Then I looked at the arm again; a child could have seen how wrong it was...

But suddenly, to my amazement, he took me by the shoulders and turned me away.

"That'll do," he said curtly. "I didn't ask you to come in here with a view to learning anything from you. I wanted to see how it struck you. I shall send for you again—and again—"

Then he began to jabber, half to himself.

"Bah!" he muttered. "'Is that all?' they ask before a stupendous thing. Show them the ocean, the heavens, infinity, and they ask, 'Is that all?' If they saw their God face to face they'd ask it!... There's only one Cause, that works now in good and now in evil, but show It to them and they put their heads on one side and begin to appraise and patronise It!... I tell you, what's seen at a glance flies away at a glance. Gods come slowly over you, but presently, ah! they begin to grip you, and at the end there's no fleeing from them! You'll tell me more about my statue by-and-by!... What was that you said?" he demanded, facing swiftly round on me. "That arm? Ah, yes; but we'll see what you say about that arm six months from now! Yes, the arm... Now be off!" he ordered me. "I'll send for you again when I want you!"

He thrust me out.

"An asylum, Mr. Benlian," I thought as I crossed the yard, "is the place for you!" You see, I didn't know him then, and that he wasn't to be judged as an ordinary man is. Just you wait till you see...

And straight away, I found myself vowing that I'd have nothing more to do with him. I found myself resolving that, as if I were making up my mind not to smoke or drink—and (I don't know why) with a similar sense that I was depriving myself of something. But, somehow, I forgot, and within a month he'd been in several times to see me, and once or twice had fetched me in to see his statue.

In two months I was in an extraordinary state of mind about him. I was familiar with him in a way, but at the same time I didn't know one scrap more about him. Because I'm a fool (oh, yes, I know quite well, now, what I am) you'll think I'm talking folly if I even begin to tell you what sort of a man he was. I don't mean just his knowledge (though I think he knew everything—sciences, languages, and all that) for it was far more than that. Somehow, when he was there, he had me all restless and uneasy; and when he wasn't there I was (there's only the one word for it) jealous—as jealous as if he'd been a girl! Even yet I can't make it out...

And he knew how unsettled he'd got me; and I'll tell you how I found that out.

Straight out one night, when he was sitting up in my place, he asked me: "Do you like me, Pudgie?" (I forgot to say that I'd told him they used to call me Pudgie at home, because I was little and fat; it was odd, the number of things I told him that I wouldn't have told anybody else.)

"Do you like me, Pudgie?" he said.

As for my answer, I don't know how it spurted out. I was much more surprised than he was, for I really didn't intend it. It was for all the world as if somebody else was talking with my mouth.

"*I loathe and adore you!*" it came; and then I looked round, awfully startled to hear myself saying that.

But he didn't look at me. He only nodded.

"Yes. Of good and evil too—" he muttered to himself. And then all of a sudden he got up and went out.

I didn't sleep for ever so long after that, thinking how odd it was I should have said that.

Well (to get on), after that something I couldn't account for began to come over me sometimes as I worked. It began to come over me, without any warning, that he was thinking of me down there across the yard. I used to *know* (this must sound awfully silly to you) that he was down yonder, thinking of me and doing something to me. And one night I was so sure that it wasn't fancy that I jumped straight up from my work, and I'm not quite sure what happened then, until I found myself in his studio, just as if I'd walked there in my sleep.

And he seemed to be waiting for me, for there was a chair by his own, in front of the statue.

"What is it, Benlian?" I burst out.

"Ah!" he said... "Well, it's about that arm, Pudgie; I want you to tell me about the arm. Does it look so strange as it did?"

"No," I said.

"I thought it wouldn't," he observed. "But I haven't touched it, Pudgie—"

So I stayed the evening there.

But you must not think he was always doing that thing—whatever it was—to me. On the other hand, I sometimes felt the oddest sort of release (I don't know how else to put it)... like when, on one of these muggy, earthy-smelling days, when everything's melancholy, the wind freshens up suddenly and you breathe again. And that (I'm trying to take it in order, you see, so that it will be plain to you) brings me to the time I found out that *he* did that too, and knew when he was doing it.

I'd gone into his place one night to have a look at his statue. It was surprising what a lot I was finding out about that statue. It was still all out of proportion (that is to say, I knew it must be—remembered

I'd thought so—though it didn't annoy me now quite so much. I suppose I'd lost *my* fresh eye by that time). Somehow, too, my own miniatures had begun to look a bit kiddish; they made me impatient; and that's horrible, to be discontented with things that once seemed jolly good to you.

Well, he'd been looking at me in the hungriest sort of way, and I looking at the statue, when all at once that feeling of release and lightness came over me. The first I knew of it was that I found myself thinking of some rather important letters my firm had written to me, wanting to know when a job I was doing was going to be finished. I thought myself it was time I got it finished; I thought I'd better set about it at once; and I sat suddenly up in my chair, as if I'd just come out of a sleep. And, looking at the statue, I saw it as it had seemed at first—all misshapen and out of drawing.

The very next moment, as I was rising, I sat down again as suddenly as if somebody had pulled me back.

Now a chap doesn't like to be changed about like that; so, without looking at Benlian, I muttered a bit testily, "Don't, Benlian!"

Then I heard him get up and knock his chair away. He was standing behind me.

"Pudgie," he said, in a moved sort of voice, "I'm no good to you. Get out of this. Get out—"

"No, no, Benlian!" I pleaded.

"Get out, do you hear, and don't come again! Go and live somewhere else—go away from London—don't let me know where you go—"

"Oh, what have I done?" I asked unhappily; and he was muttering again.

"Perhaps it would be better for me too," he muttered; and then he added, "Come, bundle out!"

So in home I went, and finished my ivory for the firm; but I can't tell you how friendless and unhappy I felt.

Now I used to know in those days a little girl—a nice, warm-hearted little thing, just friendly you know, who used to come to me sometimes in another place I lived at and mend for me and so on. It was an awful long time since I'd seen her; but she found me out one night—came to that yard, walked straight in, went straight to my linen-bag, and began to look over my things to see what wanted mending, just as she used to. I don't mind confessing that I was a bit sweet on her at one time; and it made me feel awfully mean, the way she came in, without asking any questions, and took up my mending.

So she sat doing my things, and I sat at my work, glad of a bit of company; and she chatted as she worked, just jolly and gentle and not at all reproaching me.

But as suddenly as a shot, right in the middle of it all, I found myself wondering about Benlian again. And I wasn't only wondering; somehow I was horribly uneasy about him. It came to me that he might be ill or something. And all the fun of her having come to see me was gone. I found myself doing all sorts of stupid things to my work, and glancing at my watch that was lying on the table before me.

At last I couldn't stand it any longer. I got up.

"Daisy," I said, "I've got to go out now."

She seemed surprised.

"Oh, why didn't you tell me I'd been keeping you!" she said, getting up at once.

I muttered that I was awfully sorry...

I packed her off. I closed the door in the hoarding behind her. Then I walked straight across the yard to Benlian's.

He was lying on a couch, not doing anything.

"I know I ought to have come sooner, Benlian," I said, "but I had somebody with me."

"Yes," he said, looking hard at me; and I got a bit red.

"She's awfully nice," I stammered; "but you never bother with girls, and you don't drink or smoke—"

"No," he said.

"Well," I continued, "you ought to have a little relaxation; you're knocking yourself up." And, indeed, he looked awfully ill.

But he shook his head.

"A man's only a definite amount of force in him, Pudgie," he said, "and if he spends it in one way he goes short in another. Mine goes—there." He glanced at the statue. "I rarely sleep now," he added.

"Then you ought to see a doctor," I said, a bit alarmed. (I'd felt sure he was ill.)

"No, no, Pudgie. My force is all going there—all but the minimum that can't be helped, you know... You've heard artists talk about 'putting their soul into their work,' Pudgie?"

"Don't rub it in about my rotten miniatures, Benlian," I asked him.

"You've heard them say that; but they're charlatans, professional artists, all, Pudgie. They haven't got any souls bigger than a sixpence to put into it... You know, Pudgie, that Force and Matter are the same thing—that it's decided nowadays that you can't define matter otherwise than as 'a point of Force'?"

"Yes," I found myself saying eagerly, as if I'd heard it dozens of times before.

"So that if they could put their souls into it, it would be just as easy for them to put their *bodies* into it?..."

I had drawn very close to him, and again—it was not fancy—I felt as if somebody, not me, was using my mouth. A flash of comprehension seemed to come into my brain.

"*Not that, Benlian?*" I cried breathlessly.

He nodded three or four times, and whispered. I really don't know why we both whispered.

"*Really that, Benlian?*" I whispered again.

"Shall I show you?... I tried my hardest not to, you know,..." he still whispered.

"Yes, show me!" I replied in a suppressed voice.

"Don't breathe a sound then! I keep them up there..."

He put his finger to his lips as if we had been two conspirators; then he tiptoed across the studio and went up to his bedroom in the gallery. Presently he tiptoed down again, with some rolled-up papers in his hand. They were photographs, and we stooped together over a little table. His hand shook with excitement.

"You remember this?" he whispered, showing me a rough print.

It was one of the prints from the fogged plates that I'd taken after that first night.

"Come closer to me if you feel frightened, Pudgie," he said. "You said they were old plates, Pudgie. No no; the plates were all right; it's *I* who am wrong!"

"Of course," I said. It seemed so natural.

"This one," he said, taking up one that was numbered "1," "is a plain photograph, in the flesh, before it started; *you* know! Now look at this, and this—"

He spread them before me, all in order.

"2" was a little fogged, as if a novice had taken it; on "3" a sort of cloudy veil partly obliterated the face; "4" was still further smudged and lost; and "5" was a figure with gloved hands held up, as a man holds his hands up when he is covered by a gun. The face of this one was completely blotted out.

And it didn't seem in the least horrible to me, for I kept on murmuring, "Of course, of course."

Then Benlian rubbed his hands and smiled at me.

"I'm making good progress, am I not?" he said.

"Splendid!" I breathed.

"Better than you know, too," he chuckled, "for you're not properly under yet. But you will be, Pudgie, you will be—"

"Yes, yes!... Will it be long, Benlian?"

"No," he replied, "not if I can keep from eating and sleeping and thinking of other things than the statue—and if you don't disturb me by having girls about the place, Pudgie."

"I'm awfully sorry," I said contritely.

"All right, all right; ssh!... This, you know, Pudgie, is my own studio; I bought it; I bought it purposely to make my statue, my god. I'm passing nicely into it; and when I'm quite passed—*quite* passed, Pudgie—you can have the key and come in when you like."

"Oh, thanks awfully," I murmured gratefully.

He nudged me.

"What would they think of it, Pudgie—those of the exhibitions and academies, who say 'their souls are in their work'? What would the cacklers think of it, Pudgie?"

"Aren't they fools!" I chuckled.

"And I shall have *one* worshipper, shan't I, Pudgie?"

"Rather!" I replied. "Isn't it splendid!... Oh, need I go back just yet?"

"Yes, you must go now; but I'll send for you again very soon... You know I tried to do without you, Pudge; I tried for thirteen days, and it nearly killed me! That's past. I shan't try again. Now off you trot, my Pudgie—"

I winked at him knowingly, and came skipping and dancing across the yard.

III

It's just silly—that's what it is—to say that something of a man doesn't go into his work.

Why, even those wretched little ivories of mine, the thick-headed fellows who paid for them knew my touch in them, and once spotted it instantly when I tried to slip in another chap's who was hard up. Benlian used to say that a man went about spreading himself over everything he came in contact with—diffusing some sort of influence (as far as I could make it out); and the mistake was, he said, that we went through the world just wasting it instead of directing it. And if Benlian didn't understand all about those things, I should jolly well like to know who does! A chap with a great abounding will and brain like him, it's only natural he should be able to pass himself on, to a statue or anything else, when he really tried—did without food and talk and sleep in order to save himself up for it!

"A man can't both *do* and *be*," I remember he said to me once. "He's so much force, no more, and he can either make himself with it or something else. If he tries to do both, he does both imperfectly. I'm going to do *one* perfect thing." Oh, he was a queer chap! Fancy, a fellow making a thing like that statue, out of himself, and then wanting somebody to adore him!

And I hadn't the faintest conception of how much I did adore him till yet again, as he had done before, he seemed to—you know— to take himself away from me again, leaving me all alone, and so wretched!... And I was angry at the same time, for he'd promised me he wouldn't do it again... (This was one night, I don't remember when.)

I ran to my landing and shouted down into the yard.

"Benlian! Benlian!"

There was a light in his studio, and I heard a muffled shout come back.

"Keep away—keep away—keep away!"

He was struggling—I knew he was struggling as I stood there on my landing—struggling to let me go. And I could only run and throw myself on my bed and sob, while he tried to set me free, who didn't want to be set free... he was having a terrific struggle, all alone there...

(He told me afterwards that he *had* to eat something now and then and to sleep a little, and that weakened him—strengthened him—strengthened his body and weakened the passing, you know.)

But the next day it was all right again. I was Benlian's again. And I wondered, when I remembered his struggle, whether a dying man had ever fought for life as hard as Benlian was fighting to get away from it and pass himself.

The next time after that that he fetched me—called me—whatever you like to name it—I burst into his studio like a bullet. He was sunk in a big chair, gaunt as a mummy now, and all the life in him seemed to burn in the bottom of his deep eye-sockets. At the sight of him I fiddled with my knuckles and giggled.

"You *are* going it, Benlian!" I said.

"Am I not?" he replied, in a voice that was scarcely a breath.

"You *meant* me to bring the camera and magnesium, didn't you?" (I had snatched them up when I felt his call, and had brought them.)

"Yes. Go ahead."

So I placed the camera before him, made all ready, and took the magnesium ribbon in a pair of pincers.

"Are you ready?" I said; and lighted the ribbon.

The studio seemed to leap with the blinding glare. The ribbon spat and spluttered. I snapped the shutter, and the fumes drifted away and hung in clouds in the roof.

"You'll have to walk me about soon, Pudgie, and bang me with bladders, as they do the opium-patients," he said sleepily.

"Let me take one of the statue now," I said eagerly.

But he put up his hand.

"No no. *That's* too much like testing our god. Faith's the food they feed gods on, Pudgie. We'll let the S.P.R. people photograph it when it's all over," he said. "Now get it developed."

I developed the plate. The obliteration now seemed complete.

But Benlian seemed dissatisfied.

"There's something wrong somewhere," he said. "It isn't so perfect as that yet—I can feel within me it isn't. It's merely that your camera isn't strong enough to find me, Pudgie."

"I'll get another in the morning," I cried.

"No," he answered. "I know something better than that. Have a cab here by ten o'clock in the morning, and we'll go somewhere."

By half-past ten the next morning we had driven to a large hospital, and had gone down a lot of steps and along corridors to a basement room. There was a stretcher couch in the middle of the room, and all manner of queer appliances, frames of ground glass, tubes of glass blown into extraordinary shapes, a dynamo, and a lot of other things all about. A couple of doctors were there too, and Benlian was talking to them.

"We'll try my hand first," Benlian said by-and-by.

He advanced to the couch, and put his hand under one of the frames of ground glass. One of the doctors did something in a corner. A harsh crackling filled the room, and an unearthly, fluorescent light shot and flooded across the frame where Benlian's hand was. The two doctors looked, and then started back. One of them gave a cry. He was sickly white.

"Put me on the couch," said Benlian.

I and the doctor who was not ill lifted him on the canvas stretcher. The green-gleaming frame of fluctuating light was passed over the whole of his body. Then the doctor ran to a telephone and called a colleague...

We spent the morning there, with dozens of doctors coming and going. Then we left. All the way home in the cab Benlian chuckled to himself.

"That scared 'em, Pudgie!" he chuckled. "A man they can't X-ray—that scared 'em! We must put that down in the diary—"

"Wasn't it ripping!" I chuckled back.

He kept a sort of diary or record. He gave it to me afterwards, but they've borrowed it. It was as big as a ledger, and immensely valuable, I'm sure; they oughtn't to borrow valuable things like that and not return them. The laughing that Benlian and I have had over that diary! It fooled them all—the clever X-ray men, the artists of the academies, everybody! Written on the fly-leaf was *"To My Pudgie."* I shall publish it when I get it back again.

Benlian had now got frightfully weak; it's awfully hard work, passing yourself. And he had to take a little milk now and then or he'd have died before he had quite finished. I didn't bother with miniatures any longer, and when angry letters came from my employers we just put them into the fire, Benlian and I, and we laughed—that is to say, I laughed, but Benlian only smiled, being too weak to laugh really. He'd lots of money, so that was all right; and I slept in his studio, to be there for the passing.

And that wouldn't be very long now, I thought; and I was always looking at the statue. Things like that (in case you don't know) have to be done gradually, and I supposed he was busy filling up the inside of it and hadn't got to the outside yet—for the statue was much the same to look at. But, reckoning off his sips of milk and snatches of sleep, he was making splendid progress, and the figure must be getting very full now. I was awfully excited, it was getting so near...

And then somebody came bothering and nearly spoiling all. It's odd, but I really forget exactly what it was. I only know there was a funeral, and people were sobbing and looking at me, and somebody said I was callous, but somebody else said, "No, look at him," and that it was just the other way about. And I think I remember, now, that it wasn't in London, for I was in a train; but after the funeral I dodged them, and found myself back at Euston again. They followed me, but I shook them off. I locked my own studio up, and lay as quiet as a mouse in Benlian's place when they came hammering at the door...

And now I must come to what you'll call the finish—though it's awfully stupid to call things like that "finishes."

I'd slipped into my own studio one night—I forget what for; and I'd gone quietly, for I knew they were following me, those people, and would catch me if they could. It was a thick, misty night, and the light came streaming up through Benlian's roof window, with the shadows of the window-divisions losing themselves like dark rays in the fog. A lot of hooting was going on down the river, steamers and barges... Oh, I know what I'd come into my studio for! It was for those negatives. Benlian wanted them for the diary, so that it could be seen there wasn't any fake about the prints. For he'd said he would make a final spurt that evening and get the job finished. It had taken a long time, but I'll bet *you* couldn't have passed *your*self any quicker.

When I got back he was sitting in the chair he'd hardly left for weeks, and the diary was on the table by his side. I'd taken all the scaffolding down from the statue, and he was ready to begin. He had to waste one last bit of strength to explain to me, but I drew as close as I could, so that he wouldn't lose much.

"Now, Pudgie," I just heard him say, "you've behaved splendidly, and you'll be quite still up to the finish, won't you?"

I nodded.

"And you mustn't expect the statue to come down and walk about, or anything like that," he continued. "*Those* aren't the really wonderful things. And no doubt people will tell you it hasn't changed; but you'll know better! It's much more wonderful that I should be there than that they should be able to prove it, isn't it?... And, of course, I don't know exactly how it will happen, for I've never done this before... You have the letter for the S.P.R.? They can photograph it if they want... By the way, you don't think the same of my statue as you did at first, do you?"

"Oh, it's wonderful!" I breathed.

"And even if, like the God of the others, it doesn't vouchsafe a special sign and wonder, it's Benlian, for all that?"

"Oh, do be quick, Benlian! I can't bear another minute!"

Then, for the last time, he turned his great eaten-out eyes on me.

"*I seal you mine, Pudgie!*" he said.

Then his eyes fastened themselves on the statue.

I waited for a quarter of an hour, scarcely breathing. Benlian's breath came in little flutters, many seconds apart. He had a little clock on the table. Twenty minutes passed, and half an hour. I was a little disappointed, really, that the statue wasn't going to move; but Benlian knew best, and it was filling quietly up with him instead. Then I thought of those zigzag bunches of lightning they draw on the electric-belt advertisements, and I was rather glad after all that the statue *wasn't* going to move. It would have been a little cheap, that... vulgar, in a sense... He was breathing a little more sharply now, as if in pain, but his eyes never moved. A dog was howling somewhere, and I hoped that the hooting of the tugs wouldn't disturb Benlian...

Nearly an hour had passed when, all of a sudden, I pushed my chair farther away and cowered back, gnawing my fingers, very frightened. Benlian had suddenly moved. He'd set himself forward in his chair, and he seemed to be strangling. His mouth was wide open, and he began to make long harsh "*Aaaaah-aaaah's!*" I shouldn't have thought passing yourself was such agony...

And then I gave a scream—for he seemed to be thrusting himself back in his chair again, as if he'd changed his mind and didn't want to pass himself at all. But just you ask anybody: When you get yourself just over half-way passed, the other's dragged out of you, and you can't help yourself. His "*Aaaaah's!*" became so loud and horrid that I shut my eyes and stopped my ears... Minutes that lasted; and then there came a high dinning that I couldn't shut out, and all at once the floor shook with a heavy thump. When all was still again I opened my eyes.

His chair had overturned, and he lay in a heap beside it.

I called "Benlian!" but he didn't answer...

He'd passed beautifully; quite dead. I looked up at the statue. It was just as Benlian had said—it didn't open its eyes, nor speak, nor anything like that. Don't you believe chaps who tell you that statues that have been passed into do that; they don't.

But instead, in a blaze and flash and shock, I knew now for the first time what a glorious thing that statue was! Have you ever seen anything for the first time like that? If you have, you never see very much afterwards, you know. The rest's all piffle after that. It was like coming out of fog and darkness into a split in the open heavens, my statue was so transfigured; and I'll bet if you'd been there you'd have clapped your hands, as I did, and chucked the tablecloth over the Benlian on the floor till they should come to cart that empty shell away, and patted the statue's foot and cried: "*Is it all right, Benlian?*"

I did this; and then I rushed excitedly out into the street, to call somebody to see how glorious it was...

They've brought me here for a holiday, and I'm to go back to the studio in two or three days. But they've said that before, and I think it's caddish of fellows not to keep their word—and not to return a valuable diary too! But there isn't a peephole in my room, as there is in some of them (the Emperor of Brazil told me that); and Benlian knows I haven't forsaken him, for they take me a message every day to the studio, and Benlian always answers that it's "*all right*, and I'm to stay where I am for a bit." So as long as he knows, I don't mind so much. But it is a bit rotten hanging on here, especially when the doctors themselves admit how reasonable it all is... Still, if Benlian says it's "*All right...*"

UNSEEN—UNFEARED

Francis Stevens

"The woman who invented dark fantasy", as she has been called, Francis Stevens (1883–1945) was really Gertrude Barrows, whose pulp stories and serialised novels—including *The Citadel of Fear* (1918), *The Heads of Cerberus* (1919), and *Claimed* (1920)—blended horror with science fiction and fantasy in innovative and disconcerting ways. Like the previous tale by Onions, "Unseen—Unfeared", originally published in *People's Favorite Magazine* in 1919, also centres upon photography and its power to see what the naked eye cannot—in this case the "unseen world" of microorganisms (and... other things). Stevens's mad scientist-showman describes his technical struggles in trying to combine colour photography with "microphotography"—properly photomicroscopy, the taking of pictures using a microscope. Both of these date to the mid-Victorian period: in 1861 the great Scottish scientist James Clerk Maxwell, working with English photographer Thomas Sutton, presented a colour photograph—of sorts—of a tartan ribbon, while in 1876, the pioneering German microbiologist Robert Koch not only discovered the bacterium which causes anthrax; he photographed it. The other optical medium in evidence here is the stereopticon (not the 3D-image-generating stereoscope, with which it is easily confused), a slide-projecting magic lantern used for both entertainment and educational purposes. In Stevens's story, "settlement workers"—something like volunteer social workers—have hired a man to project colour images of "various deadly bacilli" to teach the benighted immigrants living in this part of Lower Manhattan the virtues of cleanliness—a kind of hygienic "Scared Straight", for which there is a historical basis: in 1910 a US government agency announced a campaign to "stamp out typhoid fever" through sanitation and education efforts, noting that one "can usually get a good audience to attend popular lectures, with exhibits or stereopticon demonstrations". The visceral disgust Stevens's protagonist experiences upon encountering these slum dwellers may be partly explained by one of the twists in the plot (Stevens takes care to let us know that Blaisdell is himself startled by his own reaction), though the modern reader may find troubling echoes here of H. P. Lovecraft's description of "the polyglot abyss of New York's underworld" in "The Horror at Red Hook".

I

 had been dining with my ever interesting friend, Mark Jenkins, at a little Italian restaurant near South Street. It was a chance meeting. Jenkins is too busy, usually, to make dinner engagements. Over our highly seasoned food and sour, thin, red wine, he spoke of little odd incidents and adventures of his profession. Nothing very vital or important, of course. Jenkins is not the sort of detective who first detects and then pours the egotistical and revealing details of achievement in the ears of every acquaintance, however appreciative.

But when I spoke of something I had seen in the morning papers, he laughed. "Poor old 'Doc' Holt! Fascinating old codger, to any one who really knows him. I've had his friendship for years—since I was first on the city force and saved a young assistant of his from jail on a false charge. And they had to drag him into the poisoning of this young sport, Ralph Peeler!"

"Why are you so sure he couldn't have been implicated?" I asked.

But Jenkins only shook his head, with a quiet smile. "I have reasons for believing otherwise," was all I could get out of him on that score. "But," he added, "the only reason he was suspected at all is the superstitious dread of these ignorant people around him. Can't see why he lives in such a place. I know for a fact he doesn't have to. Doc's got money of his own. He's an amateur chemist and dabbler in different sorts of research work, and I suspect he's been guilty of

155

'showing off.' Result, they all swear he has the evil eye and holds forbidden communion with invisible powers. Smoke?"

Jenkins offered me one of his invariably good cigars, which I accepted, saying thoughtfully: "A man has no right to trifle with the superstitions of ignorant people. Sooner or later, it spells trouble."

"Did in his case. They swore up and down that he sold love charms openly and poisons secretly, and that, together with his living so near to—somebody else—got him temporarily suspected. But my tongue's running away with me, as usual!"

"As usual," I retorted impatiently, "you open up with all the frankness of a Chinese diplomat."

He beamed upon me engagingly and rose from the table, with a glance at his watch. "Sorry to leave you, Blaisdell, but I have to meet Jimmy Brennan in ten minutes."

He so clearly did not invite my further company that I remained seated for a little while after his departure; then took my own way homeward. Those streets always held for me a certain fascination, particularly at night. They are so unlike the rest of the city, so foreign in appearance, with their little shabby stores, always open until late evening, their unbelievably cheap goods, displayed as much outside the shops as in them, hung on the fronts and laid out on tables by the curb and in the street itself. Tonight, however, neither people nor stores in any sense appealed to me. The mixture of Italians, Jews and a few n—oes, mostly bareheaded, unkempt and generally unhygienic in appearance, struck me as merely revolting. They were all humans, and I, too, was human. Some way I did not like the idea.

Puzzled a trifle, for I am more inclined to sympathise with poverty than accuse it, I watched the faces that I passed. Never before had I observed how stupid, how bestial, how brutal were the countenances of the dwellers in this region. I actually shuddered when an old-clothes man, a grey-bearded Hebrew, brushed me as he toiled past with his barrow.

There was a sense of evil in the air, a warning of things which it is wise for a clean man to shun and keep clear of. The impression became so strong that before I had walked two squares I began to feel physically ill. Then it occurred to me that the one glass of cheap Chianti I had drunk might have something to do with the feeling. Who knew how that stuff had been manufactured, or whether the juice of the grape entered at all into its ill-flavoured composition? Yet I doubted if that were the real cause of my discomfort.

By nature I am rather a sensitive, impressionable sort of chap. In some way tonight this neighbourhood, with its sordid sights and smells, had struck me wrong.

My sense of impending evil was merging into actual fear. This would never do. There is only one way to deal with an imaginative temperament like mine—conquer its vagaries. If I left South Street with this nameless dread upon me, I could never pass down it again without a recurrence of the feeling. I should simply have to stay here until I got the better of it—that was all.

I paused on a corner before a shabby but brightly lighted little drug store. Its gleaming windows and the luminous green of its conventional glass show jars made the brightest spot on the block. I realised that I was tired, but hardly wanted to go in there and rest. I knew what the company would be like at its shabby, sticky soda fountain. As I stood there, my eyes fell on a long white canvas sign across from me, and its black-and-red lettering caught my attention.

SEE THE GREAT UNSEEN!
Come in! This Means You!
Free to All!

A museum of fakes, I thought, but also reflected that if it were a show of some kind I could sit down for a while, rest, and fight off this increasing obsession of nonexistent evil. That side of the street was almost deserted, and the place itself might well be nearly empty.

II

I walked over, but with every step my sense of dread increased. Dread of I knew not what. Bodiless, inexplicable horror had me as in a net, whose strands, being intangible, without reason for existence, I could by no means throw off. It was not the people now. None of them were about me. There, in the open, lighted street, with no sight nor sound of terror to assail me, I was the shivering victim of such fear as I had never known was possible. Yet still I would not yield.

Setting my teeth, and fighting with myself as with some pet animal gone mad, I forced my steps to slowness and walked along the sidewalk, seeking entrance. Just here there were no shops, but several doors reached in each case by means of a few iron-railed stone steps. I chose the one in the middle beneath the sign. In that neighbourhood there are museums, shops and other commercial enterprises conducted in many shabby old residences, such as were these. Behind the glazing of the door I had chosen I could see a dim, pinkish light, but on either side the windows were quite dark.

Trying the door, I found it unlocked. As I opened it a party of Italians passed on the pavement below and I looked back at them over my shoulder. They were gayly dressed, men, women and children, laughing and chattering to one another; probably on their way to some wedding or other festivity.

In passing, one of the men glanced up at me and involuntarily I shuddered back against the door. He was a young man, handsome after the swarthy manner of his race, but never in my life had I seen a face so expressive of pure, malicious cruelty, naked and unashamed. Our eyes met and his seemed to light up with a vile gleaming, as if all the wickedness of his nature had come to a focus in the look of concentrated hate he gave me.

They went by, but for some distance I could see him watching me, chin on shoulder, till he and his party were swallowed up in the crowd of marketers farther down the street.

Sick and trembling from that encounter, merely of eyes though it had been, I threw aside my partly smoked cigar and entered. Within there was a small vestibule, whose ancient tessellated floor was grimy with the passing of many feet. I could feel the grit of dirt under my shoes, and it rasped on my rawly quivering nerves. The inner door stood partly open, and going on I found myself in a bare, dirty hallway, and was greeted by the sour, musty, poverty-stricken smell common to dwellings of the very ill-to-do. Beyond there was a stairway, carpeted with ragged grass matting. A gas jet, turned low inside a very dusty pink globe, was the light I had seen from without.

Listening, the house seemed entirely silent. Surely, this was no place of public amusement of any kind whatever. More likely it was a rooming house, and I had, after all, mistaken the entrance.

To my intense relief, since coming inside, the worst agony of my unreasonable terror had passed away. If I could only get in some place where I could sit down and be quiet, probably I should be rid of it for good. Determining to try another entrance, I was about to leave the bare hallway when one of several doors along the side of it suddenly opened and a man stepped out into the hall.

"Well?" he said, looking at me keenly, but with not the least show of surprise at my presence.

"I beg your pardon," I replied. "The door was unlocked and I came in here, thinking it was the entrance to the exhibit—what do they call it?—the 'Great Unseen.' The one that is mentioned on that long white sign. Can you tell me which door is the right one?"

"I can."

With that brief answer he stopped and stared at me again. He was a tall, lean man, somewhat stooped, but possessing considerable dignity of bearing. For that neighbourhood, he appeared uncommonly well dressed, and his long, smooth-shaven face was noticeable because, while his complexion was dark and his eyes coal-black, above them the heavy brows and his hair were almost silvery-white. His age might have been anything over the threescore mark.

I grew tired of being stared at. "If you can and—won't, then never mind," I observed a trifle irritably, and turned to go. But his sharp exclamation halted me.

"No!" he said. "No—no! Forgive me for pausing—it was not hesitation, I assure you. To think that one—one, even, has come! All day they pass my sign up there—pass and fear to enter. But you are different. *You* are not of these timorous, ignorant foreign peasants. You ask me to tell you the right door? Here it is! Here!"

And he struck the panel of the door, which he had closed behind him, so that the sharp yet hollow sound of it echoed up through the silent house.

Now it may be thought that after all my senseless terror in the open street, so strange a welcome from so odd a showman would have brought the feeling back, full force. But there is an emotion stronger, to a certain point, than fear. This queer old fellow aroused my curiosity. What kind of museum could it be that he accused the passing public of fearing to enter? Nothing really terrible, surely, or it would have been closed by the police. And normally I am not an unduly timorous person. "So, it's in there, is it?" I asked, coming toward him. "And I'm to be sole audience? Come, that will be an interesting experience." I was half laughing now.

"The most interesting in the world," said the old man, with a solemnity which rebuked my lightness.

With that he opened the door, passed inward and closed it again—in my very face. I stood staring at it blankly. The panels, I remember, had been originally painted white, but now the paint was flaked and blistered, grey with dirt and dirty finger marks. Suddenly it occurred to me that I had no wish to enter there. Whatever was behind it could be scarcely worth seeing, or he would not choose such a place for its exhibition. With the old man's vanishing my curiosity had cooled, but just as I again turned to leave, the door opened and this singular showman stuck his white-eyebrowed face through the aperture. He was frowning impatiently. "Come in—come in!" he snapped, and promptly withdrawing his head, once more closed the door.

"He has something in there he doesn't want should get out," was the very natural conclusion which I drew. "Well, since it can hardly be anything dangerous, and he's so anxious I should see it—here goes!"

With that I turned the soiled white porcelain handle, and entered.

The room I came into was neither very large nor very brightly lighted. In no way did it resemble a museum or lecture room. On the contrary, it seemed to have been fitted up as a quite well-appointed laboratory. The floor was linoleum-covered, there were glass cases along the walls whose shelves were filled with bottles, specimen jars, graduates, and the like. A large table in one corner bore what looked like some odd sort of camera, and a larger one in the middle of the room was fitted with a long rack filled with bottles and test tubes, and was besides littered with papers, glass slides, and various paraphernalia which my ignorance failed to identify. There were several cases of books, a few plain wooden chairs, and in the corner a large iron sink with running water.

My host of the white hair and black eyes was awaiting me, standing near the larger table. He indicated one of the wooden chairs with a thin forefinger that shook a little, either from age or eagerness. "Sit down—sit down! Have no fear but that you will be interested, my friend. Have no fear at all—of anything!"

As he said it he fixed his dark eyes upon me and stared harder than ever. But the effect of his words was the opposite of their meaning. I did sit down, because my knees gave under me, but if in the outer hall I had lost my terror, it now returned twofold upon me. Out there the light had been faint, dingily roseate, indefinite. By it I had not perceived how this old man's face was a mask of living malice—of cruelty, hate and a certain masterful contempt. Now I knew the meaning of my fear, whose warning I would not heed. Now I knew that I had walked into the very trap from which my abnormal sensitiveness had striven in vain to save me.

III

Again I struggled within me, bit at my lip till I tasted blood, and presently the blind paroxysm passed. It must have been longer in going than I thought, and the old man must have all that time been speaking, for when I could once more control my attention, hear and see him, he had taken up a position near the sink, about ten feet away, and was addressing me with a sort of "platform" manner, as if I had been the large audience whose absence he had deplored.

"And so," he was saying, "I was forced to make these plates very carefully, to truly represent the characteristic hues of each separate organism. Now, in colour work of every kind the film is necessarily extremely sensitive. Doubtless you are familiar in a general way with the exquisite transparencies produced by colour photography of the single-plate type."

He paused, and, trying to act like a normal human being, I observed: "I saw some nice landscapes done in that way—last week at an illustrated lecture in Franklin Hall."

He scowled, and made an impatient gesture at me with his hand. "I can proceed better without interruptions," he said. "My pause was purely oratorical."

I meekly subsided, and he went on in his original loud, clear voice. He would have made an excellent lecturer before a much larger audience—if only his voice could have lost that eerie, ringing note. Thinking of that I must have missed some more, and when I caught it again he was saying:

"As I have indicated, the original plate is the final picture. Now, many of these organisms are extremely hard to photograph, and microphotography in colour is particularly difficult. In consequence, to spoil a plate tries the patience of the photographer. They are so sensitive that the ordinary dark-room ruby lamp would instantly ruin them, and they must therefore be developed either in darkness or by a special light produced by interposing thin sheets of tissue of a particular shade of green and of yellow between lamp and plate, and even that will often cause ruinous fog. Now I, finding it hard to handle them so, made numerous experiments with a view to discovering some glass or fabric of a colour which should add to the safety of the green, without robbing it of all efficiency. All proved equally useless, but intermittently I persevered—until last week."

His voice dropped to an almost confidential tone, and he leaned slightly toward me. I was cold from my neck to my feet, though my head was burning, but I tried to force an appreciative smile.

"Last week," he continued impressively, "I had a prescription filled at the corner drug store. The bottle was sent home to me wrapped in a piece of what I at first took to be whitish, slightly opalescent paper. Later I decided that it was some kind of membrane. When I questioned the druggist, seeking its source, he said it was a sheet of 'paper' that was around a bundle of herbs from South America. That he had no more, and doubted if I could trace it. He had wrapped my bottle so, because he was in haste and the sheet was handy.

"I can hardly tell you what first inspired me to try that membrane in my photographic work. It was merely dull white with a faint hint of opalescence, except when held against the light. Then it became quite translucent and quite brightly prismatic. For some reason it occurred to me that this refractive effect might help in breaking up the actinic rays—the rays which affect the sensitive emulsion. So that night I inserted it behind the sheets of green and yellow tissue, next the lamp, prepared my trays and chemicals, laid my plate holders to hand, turned off the white light and—turned on the green!"

There was nothing in his words to inspire fear. It was a wearisomely detailed account of his struggles with photography. Yet, as he again paused impressively, I wished that he might never speak again. I was desperately, contemptibly in dread of the thing he might say next.

Suddenly he drew himself erect, the stoop went out of his shoulders, he threw back his head and laughed. It was a hollow sound, as if he laughed into a trumpet. "I won't tell you what I saw! Why should I? Your own eyes shall bear witness. But this much I'll say, so that you may better understand—later. When our poor, faultily sensitive vision can perceive a thing, we say that it is visible. When the nerves of touch can feel it, we say that it is tangible. Yet I tell you there are beings intangible to our physical sense, yet whose presence is felt by the spirit, and invisible to our eyes merely because those organs are not attuned to the light as reflected from their bodies. But light passed through the screen which we are about to use has a wave length novel to the scientific world, and by it you shall see with the eyes of the flesh that which has been invisible since life began. Have no fear!"

He stopped to laugh again, and his mirth was yellow-toothed—menacing.

"*Have no fear!*" he reiterated, and with that stretched his hand toward the wall, there came a click and we were in black, impenetrable darkness. I wanted to spring up, to seek the door by which I had entered and rush out of it, but the paralysis of unreasoning terror held me fast.

I could hear him moving about in the darkness, and a moment later a faint green glimmer sprang up in the room. Its source was over the large sink, where I suppose he developed his precious "colour plates."

Every instant, as my eyes became accustomed to the dimness, I could see more clearly. Green light is peculiar. It may be far fainter than red, and at the same time far more illuminating. The old man was standing beneath it, and his face by that ghastly radiance had the exact look of a dead man's. Beside this, however, I could observe nothing appalling.

"That," continued the man, "is the simple developing light of which I have spoken—now watch, for what you are about to behold no mortal man but myself has ever seen before."

For a moment he fussed with the green lamp over the sink. It was so constructed that all the direct rays struck downward. He opened a flap at the side, for a moment there was a streak of comforting white luminance from within, then he inserted something, slid it slowly in—and closed the flap.

The thing he put in—that South American "membrane" it must have been—instead of decreasing the light increased it—amazingly.

The hue was changed from green to greenish-grey, and the whole room sprang into view, a livid, ghastly chamber, filled with—over-crawled by—what?

My eyes fixed themselves, fascinated, on something that moved by the old man's feet. It writhed there on the floor like a huge, repulsive starfish, an immense, armed, legged thing, that twisted convulsively. It was smooth, as if made of rubber, was whitish-green in colour; and presently raised its great round blob of a body on tottering tentacles, crept toward my host and writhed upward—yes, climbed up his legs, his body. And he stood there, erect, arms folded, and stared sternly down at the thing which climbed.

But the room—the whole room was alive with other creatures than that. Everywhere I looked they were—centipedish things, with yard-long bodies, detestable, furry spiders that lurked in shadows, and sausage-shaped translucent horrors that moved—and floated through the air. They dived here and there between me and the light, and I could see its brighter greenness through their greenish bodies.

Worse, though, far worse than these were the *things with human faces*. Masklike, monstrous, huge gaping mouths and slitlike eyes—I find I cannot write of them. There was that about them which makes their memory even now intolerable.

The old man was speaking again, and every word echoed in my brain like the ringing of a gong. "Fear nothing! Among such as these do you move every hour of the day and the night. Only you and I have seen, for God is merciful and has spared our race from sight. But I am not merciful! I loathe the race which gave these creatures birth—the race which might be so surrounded by invisible, unguessed but blessed beings—and chooses these for its companions! All the world shall see and know. One by one shall they come here, learn the truth, and perish. For who can survive the ultimate of terror? Then I, too, shall find peace, and leave the earth to its heritage of man-created horrors. Do you know what these are—whence they come?"

His voice boomed now like a cathedral bell. I could not answer him, but he waited for no reply. "Out of the ether—out of the omni-present ether from whose intangible substance the mind of God made the planets, all living things, and man—man has made these! By his evil thoughts, by his selfish panics, by his lusts and his interminable, never-ending hate he has made them, and they are everywhere! Fear nothing—they cannot harm your body—but let your spirit beware! Fear nothing—but see where there comes to you, its creator, the shape and the body of your FEAR!"

And as he said it I perceived a great Thing coming toward me—a Thing—but consciousness could endure no more. The ringing, threatening voice merged in a roar within my ears, there came a merciful dimming of the terrible, lurid vision, and blank nothingness succeeded upon horror too great for bearing.

IV

There was a dull, heavy pain above my eyes. I knew that they were closed, that I was dreaming, and that the rack full of coloured bot-tles which I seemed to see so clearly was no more than a part of the dream. There was some vague but imperative reason why I should rouse myself. I wanted to awaken, and thought that by staring very hard indeed I could dissolve this foolish vision of blue and yellow-brown bottles. But instead of dissolving they grew clearer, more solid and substantial of appearance, until suddenly the rest of my senses rushed to the support of sight, and I became aware that my eyes were open, the bottles were quite real, and that I was sitting in a chair, fallen sideways so that my cheek rested most uncomfortably on the table which held the rack.

I straightened up slowly and with difficulty, groping in my dulled brain for some clue to my presence in this unfamiliar place, this laboratory that was lighted only by the rays of an arc light in the street outside its three large windows. Here I sat, alone, and if the aching of cramped limbs meant anything, here I had sat for more than a little time.

Then, with the painful shock which accompanies awakening to the knowledge of some great catastrophe, came memory. It was this very room, shown by the street lamp's rays to be empty of life, which I had seen thronged with creatures too loathsome for description. I staggered to my feet, staring fearfully about. There were the glass-doored cases, the bookshelves, the two tables with their burdens, and the long iron sink above which, now only a dark blotch of shadow, hung the lamp from which had emanated that livid, terrifically revealing illumination. Then the experience had been no dream, but a frightful reality. I was alone here now. With callous indifference my strange host had allowed me to remain for hours unconscious, with not the least effort to aid or revive me. Perhaps, hating me so, he had hoped that I would die there.

At first I made no effort to leave the place. Its appearance filled me with reminiscent loathing. I longed to go, but as yet felt too weak and ill for the effort. Both mentally and physically my condition was deplorable, and for the first time I realised that a shock to the mind may react upon the body as vilely as any debauch of self-indulgence.

Quivering in every nerve and muscle, dizzy with headache and nausea, I dropped back into the chair, hoping that before the old man returned I might recover sufficient self-control to escape him. I knew that he hated me, and why. As I waited, sick, miserable, I understood the man. Shuddering, I recalled the loathsome horrors he had shown me. If the mere desires and emotions of mankind were daily carnified in such forms as those, no wonder that he viewed his fellow beings with detestation and longed only to destroy them.

I thought, too, of the cruel, sensuous faces I had seen in the streets outside—seen for the first time, as if a veil had been withdrawn from eyes hitherto blinded by self-delusion. Fatuously trustful as a month-old puppy, I had lived in a grim, evil world, where goodness is a word and crude selfishness the only actuality. Drearily my thoughts drifted back through my own life, its futile purposes, mistakes and activities. All of evil that I knew returned to overwhelm me. Our gropings toward divinity were a sham, a writhing sunward of slime-covered beasts who claimed sunlight as their heritage, but in their hearts preferred the foul and easy depths.

Even now, though I could neither see nor feel them, this room, the entire world, was acrawl with the beings created by our real natures. I recalled the cringing, contemptible fear to which my spirit had so readily yielded, and the faceless Thing to which the emotion had given birth.

Then abruptly, shockingly, I remembered that every moment I was adding to the horde. Since my mind could conceive only repulsive incubi, and since while I lived I must think, feel, and so continue to shape them, was there no way to check so abominable a succession? My eyes fell on the long shelves with their many-coloured bottles. In the chemistry of photography there are deadly poisons—I knew that. Now was the time to end it—now! Let him return and find his desire accomplished. One good thing I could do, if one only. I could abolish my monster-creating self.

V

My friend Mark Jenkins is an intelligent and usually a very careful man. When he took from "Smiler" Callahan a cigar which had every appearance of being excellent, innocent Havana, the act denoted both intelligence and caution. By very clever work he had traced the poisoning of young Ralph Peeler to Mr. Callahan's door, and he believed this particular cigar to be the mate of one smoked by Peeler just previous to his demise. And if, upon arresting Callahan, he had not confiscated this bit of evidence, it would have doubtless been destroyed by its regrettably unconscientious owner.

But when Jenkins shortly afterward gave me that cigar, as one of his own, he committed one of those almost inconceivable blunders which, I think, are occasionally forced upon clever men to keep them from overweening vanity. Discovering his slight mistake, my detective friend spent the night searching for his unintended victim, myself, and that his search was successful was due to Pietro Marini, a young Italian of Jenkins' acquaintance, whom he met about the hour of two a. m. returning from a dance.

Now, Marini had seen me standing on the steps of the house where Doctor Frederick Holt had his laboratory and living rooms, and he had stared at me, not with any ill intent, but because he thought I was the sickest-looking, most ghastly specimen of humanity that he had ever beheld. And, sharing the superstition of his South Street neighbours, he wondered if the worthy doctor had poisoned me as well as Peeler. This suspicion he imparted to Jenkins, who, however, had the best of reasons for believing otherwise. Moreover, as he informed Marini, Holt was dead, having drowned himself late the previous afternoon. An hour or so after our talk in the restaurant news of his suicide reached Jenkins.

It seemed wise to search any place where a very sick-looking young man had been seen to enter, so Jenkins came straight to the laboratory. Across the fronts of those houses was the long sign with its mysterious inscription, "See the Great Unseen," not at all mysterious to the detective. He knew that next door to Doctor Holt's the second floor had been thrown together into a lecture room, where at certain hours a young man employed by settlement workers displayed upon a screen stereopticon views of various deadly bacilli, the germs of diseases appropriate to dirt and indifference. He knew, too, that Doctor Holt himself had helped the educational effort along by providing some really wonderful lantern slides, done by microcolour photography.

On the pavement outside, Jenkins found the two-thirds remnant of a cigar, which he gathered in and came up the steps, a very miserable and self-reproachful detective. Neither outer nor inner door was locked, and in the laboratory he found me, alive, but on the verge of death by another means than he had feared.

In the extreme physical depression following my awakening from drugged sleep, and knowing nothing of its cause, I believed my adventure fact in its entirety. My mentality was at too low an ebb to resist its dreadful suggestion. I was searching among Holt's various bottles when Jenkins burst in. At first I was merely annoyed at the interruption of my purpose, but before the anticlimax of his explanation the mists of obsession drifted away and left me still sick in body, but in spirit happy as any man may well be who has suffered a delusion that the world is wholly bad—and learned that its badness springs from his own poisoned brain.

The malice which I had observed in every face, including young Marini's, existed only in my drug-affected vision. Last week's "popular science" lecture had been recalled to my subconscious mind—the mind that rules dreams and delirium—by the photographic apparatus in Holt's workroom. "See the Great Unseen" assisted materially, and even the corner drug store before which I had paused, with its green-lit show vases, had doubtless played a part. But presently, following something Jenkins told me, I was driven to one protest. "If Holt was not here," I demanded, "if Holt is dead, as you say, how do you account for the fact that I, who have never seen the man, was able to give you an accurate description which you admit to be that of Doctor Frederick Holt?"

He pointed across the room. "See that?" It was a life-size bust portrait, in crayons, the picture of a white-haired man with bushy eyebrows and the most piercing black eyes I had ever seen—until the previous evening. It hung facing the door and near the windows, and the features stood out with a strangely lifelike appearance in the white rays of the arc lamp just outside. "Upon entering," continued Jenkins, "the first thing you saw was that portrait, and from it your delirium built a living, speaking man. So, there are your white-haired showman, your unnatural fear, your colour photography and your pretty green golliwogs all nicely explained for you, Blaisdell, and thank God you're alive to hear the explanation. If you had smoked the whole of that cigar—well, never mind. You didn't. And now, my very dear friend, I think it's high time that you interviewed a real, flesh-and-blood doctor. I'll phone for a taxi."

"Don't," I said. "A walk in the fresh air will do me more good than fifty doctors."

"Fresh air! There's no fresh air on South Street in July," complained Jenkins, but reluctantly yielded.

I had a reason for my preference. I wished to see people, to meet face to face even such stray prowlers as might be about at this hour, nearer sunrise than midnight, and rejoice in the goodness and kindliness of the human countenance—particularly as found in the lower classes.

But even as we were leaving there occurred to me a curious inconsistency.

"Jenkins," I said, "you claim that the reason Holt, when I first met him in the hall, appeared to twice close the door in my face, was because the door never opened until I myself unlatched it."

"Yes," confirmed Jenkins, but he frowned, foreseeing my next question.

"Then why, if it was from that picture that I built so solid, so convincing a vision of the man, did I see Holt in the hall before the door was open?"

"You confuse your memories," retorted Jenkins rather shortly.

"Do I? Holt was dead at that hour, but—*I tell you I saw Holt outside the door!* And what was his reason for committing suicide?"

Before my friend could reply I was across the room, fumbling in the dusk there at the electric lamp above the sink. I got the tin flap open and pulled out the sliding screen, which consisted of two sheets of glass with fabric between, dark on one side, yellow on the other. With it came the very thing I dreaded—a sheet of whitish, parchmentlike, slightly opalescent stuff.

Jenkins was beside me as I held it at arm's length toward the windows. Through it the light of the arc lamp fell—divided into the most astonishingly brilliant rainbow hues. And instead of diminishing the light, it was perceptibly increased in the oddest way. Almost one thought that the sheet itself was luminous, and yet when held in shadow it gave off no light at all.

"Shall we—put it in the lamp again—and try it?" asked Jenkins slowly, and in his voice there was no hint of mockery.

I looked him straight in the eyes. "No," I said, "we won't. I was drugged. Perhaps in that condition I received a merciless revelation of the discovery that caused Holt's suicide, but I don't believe it. Ghost or no ghost, I refuse to ever again believe in the depravity of the human race. If the air and the earth are teeming with invisible horrors, they are *not* of our making, and—the study of demonology is better let alone. Shall we burn this thing, or tear it up?"

"We have no right to do either," returned Jenkins thoughtfully, "but you know, Blaisdell, there's a little too darn much realism about some parts of your 'dream.' I haven't been smoking any doped cigars, but when you held that up, to the light. I'll swear I saw—well, never mind. Burn it—send it back to the place it came from."

"South America?" said I.

"A hotter place than that. Burn it."

So he struck a match and we did. It was gone in one great white flash.

A large place was given by morning papers to the suicide of Doctor Frederick Holt, caused, it was surmised, by mental derangement brought about by his unjust implication in the Peeler murder. It seemed an inadequate reason, since he had never been arrested, but no other was ever discovered.

Of course, our action in destroying that "membrane" was illegal and rather precipitate, but, though he won't talk about it, I know that Jenkins agrees with me—doubt is sometimes better than certainty, and there are marvels better left unproved. Those, for instance, which concern the Powers of Evil.

SIGNALS

Stefan Grabiński

"Wonder and fear", the Polish master of the fantastic, Stefan Grabiński (1887–1936), once wrote, "these are my guiding motives". If his powerfully atmospheric fiction remains, even now, little known to Anglophone readers, it is because so much of his work remains untranslated. (A promised collection from the independent publishers Centipede Press will hopefully fill some of this gap.) Grabiński has been called both "the Polish Poe" and "the Polish Lovecraft", but in this story he might be more aptly likened to a "Polish Dickens"—the Dickens, at any rate, of the classic ghost story "The Signal-Man" (1866). Since the first appearance of the steam locomotive in Britain in the early nineteenth century, a number of signalling methods had been used for safety purposes, including semaphore-based systems, but soon after the invention of the electric telegraph in the 1830s, railway signalling took a giant step forward. The system described in Grabiński's tale does not differ much from the mid-Victorian one depicted in Dickens's: a code-based telegraphic bell signal comprises part of a "block" scheme designed to ensure that no more than one train is travelling along a particular length of track at the same time. In addition to the signalling telegraphs, located in stations and signal cabins, separate lines were maintained by the railway companies for internal communication (as we also see in Grabiński's story). "Signals" is taken from Grabiński's 1919 volume *The Motion Demon*, a collection of weird tales of the railway.

t the depot station, in an old postal car taken out of service long ago, several off-duty railwaymen were gathered for their usual chat: three train conductors, the old ticket collector, Trzpien, and the assistant stationmaster, Haszczyc.

Because the October night was rather chilly, they had lit a fire in a little iron stove whose pipe exited out of an opening in the roof. The group was indebted for this happy idea to the inventiveness of the conductor, Swita, who had personally brought over the rust-corroded heater, discarded from some waiting room, to adapt it so splendidly to the changed circumstances. Four wooden benches, their oilcloth covering torn, and a three-legged garden table, wide like a record turntable, completed the interior furnishings. A lantern, hanging on a hook above the heads of those who sat below, spread out along their faces a hazy, semi-obscure light.

So looked the "train casino" of the Przelecz station officials, an improvised refuge for homeless bachelors, a quiet, secluded stop for off-duty conductors. Here, in their spare moments, zapped of energy by their riding patrons, the old, grey "train wolves" converged to relax after the executed tour, and chat with professional comrades. Here, in the fumes of conductors' pipes, the tobacco smoke, the cigarettes, and cuds of chewing tobacco, wandered the echoes of tales, thousands of adventures and anecdotes: here spun out the yarn of a railwayman's fate.

And today the noisy meeting was also animated, the group exceptionally well-suited, just the cream of the station. A moment ago Trzpien had related an interesting episode from his own life and had managed to rivet the attention of his audience to such a degree that they forgot to feed their dying-out pipes, and they now held them in their teeth already cold and extinguished like cooled-down volcano craters.

Silence filled the car. Through the window, damp from the drizzle outside, one could see the wet roofs of train cars, shiny like steel armour under the light of reflectors. From time to time the lantern of a trackwalker flashed by, or the blue signal of a switching engine; from time to time the green reflection of the switch signal ploughed through the darkness, or the penetrating call of a trolley was heard. From afar, beyond the black entrenchment of slumbering cars, came the muffled buzz of the main station.

Through the gap between the cars, a portion of track was visible: several parallel strips of rail. On one of them an empty train slowly pulled in; its pistons, tired by a full day's race, operated sluggishly, transforming their motion to the rotations of the wheels.

At a certain moment the locomotive stopped. Under the chest of the machine whirls of vapours emerged, enfolding the rotund framework. The lantern lights at the front of the colossus began to bend in rainbow-coloured aureoles and golden rings, and became enveloped with a cloud of steam. Then came an optical illusion: the locomotive and, with it, the cars, rose above the layers of steam and remained suspended in the air. After several seconds the train returned to the rails, emitting from its organism the last puffs, to plunge itself into the reverie of a nightly repose.

"A beautiful illusion," remarked Swita, who had been looking for a long time through the window pane. "Did all of you see that apparent levitation?"

"Certainly," confirmed several voices.

"It reminded me of a rail legend I heard years ago."

"Tell us about it, Swita!" exhorted Haszczyc.

"Yes, go on!"

"Of course—the story isn't long; one can sum it up in a couple of words. There circulates among railwaymen a tale of a train that disappeared."

"What do you mean 'disappeared'? Did it evaporate or what?"

"Well, no. It disappeared—that doesn't mean that it stopped existing! It disappeared—that means its outward appearance is not to be seen by the human eye. In reality, it exists somewhere. Somewhere it dwells, though it's not known where. This phenomenon was supposed to have been created by a certain stationmaster, some real character and maybe even a sorcerer. This trick was performed by a series of specially arranged signals that followed each other. The occurrence caught him off guard, as he later maintained. He had been playing around with the signals, which he had arranged in the most varied ways, changing their progression and quality; until one time, after letting out seven of such signs, the train driving up to his station suddenly, at full speed, rose parallel to the track, wavered a few times in the air, and then, tipping at an angle, vanished. Since that time no one has seen either the train or the people who were riding in it. They say that the train will appear again when someone gives the same signals but in the reverse order. Unfortunately the stationmaster went insane shortly thereafter, and all attempts to extract the truth from him proved abortive. The madman took the key to the secret with him when he died. Most probably someone will hit upon the right signs by accident and draw out the train from the fourth dimension to the earth."

"A real fuss," remarked Zdanski, a train conductor. "And when did this wonderful event occur? Does the legend fix a date for it?"

"Some hundred years ago."

"Well, well. A pretty long time! In that case the passengers inside the train would be, at the present moment, older by an entire century. Please try and imagine what a spectacle it would be if today or tomorrow some lucky person were able to uncover the apocalyptic signals and remove the seven magical charms. From neither here nor there the missing train suddenly falls from the sky, suitably rested after a hundred-year hoisting, and throngs pour out stooping under the burden of a century of existence!"

"You forget that in the fourth dimension people apparently do not need to eat or drink, and they don't age."

"That's right," declared Haszczyc, "that's absolutely right. A beautiful legend, my friend, very beautiful."

Remembering something, he became silent. After a moment, referring to what Swita had related, he said thoughtfully:

"Signals, signals... I've something to say about them—only it's not a legend, but a true story."

"We're listening! Please, go ahead!" echoed back a chorus of railwaymen.

Haszczyc rested an elbow against the table top, filled his pipe, and, expelling a couple of milky spirals, began his story:

One evening, around seven o'clock, an alarm went out to the Dabrowa station with the signal "cars unattached." The hammer of the bell gave off four strokes by four strokes spaced apart by three seconds. Before Stationmaster Pomian could figure out from where the signal originated, a new signal flowed from the region. Three strikes alternating with two, repeated four times, could be heard. The official understood: they meant "stop all trains." Apparently the danger had increased.

Moving along the track slope and in the direction of a strong westerly wind, the detached cars were running towards the passenger train leaving the station at that moment.

It was necessary to stop the passenger train and back it up several kilometres and somehow cover the suspected part of the region.

The energetic young official gave the suitable orders. The passenger train was successfully turned back from its course and at the same time an engine was sent out with people whose job was to stop the racing separated cars. The locomotive moved carefully in the direction of danger, lighting up the way with three huge reflectors. Before it, at a distance of 700 metres, went two trackwalkers with lighted torches, examining the line attentively.

But to the amazement of the entire group, the runaway cars were not met with along the way, and, after a two-hour inspection to the end of the ride, the engine turned back to the nearest station at Glaszow. There, the stationmaster received the expedition with great surprise. Nobody knew anything about any signals, the region was absolutely clear, and no danger threatened from this side. The officials, worn-out by tracking, got on the engine and returned to Dabrowa near eleven at night.

Here, meanwhile, the unease had increased. Ten minutes before the engine's return, the bell sounded again, this time demanding the sending of a rescue locomotive with workers. The stationmaster was in despair. Agitated by the signals continually flowing from the direction of Glaszow, he was pacing restlessly about the platform, going out to the line to return again to the station office baffled, terrified, frightened.

In reality, it was a sorry situation. His comrade from Glaszow, alarmed by him every dozen or so minutes, answered at first with calm that everything was in order; later, losing his patience, he started to scold fools and lunatics. To Dabrowa, meanwhile, came signal after signal, entreating ever more urgently the dispatching of workers' cars.

Clinging on to the last plank like a drowning man, Pomian phoned the Zbaszyn station, in the opposite direction, supposing, he didn't know why, that the alarm was coming from there. Naturally he was answered in the negative; everything was in perfect order in that area.

"Have I gone crazy or is everyone not in their right minds?" he finally asked a passing blockman. "Mr. Sroka, have you heard these damned bell signals?"

"Yes, stationmaster, I heard them. There they go again! What the hell?"

Indeed, the relentless hammer struck the iron bell anew; it called for help from workers and doctors.

The clock already read past one.

Pomian flew into a rage.

"What business is this of mine? In this direction, everything's fine, in that direction, everything's in order—then what the hell do they want? Some joker is playing games with us, throwing the whole station upside-down! I'll make a report—and that's that!"

"I don't think so, stationmaster," his assistant calmly put in; "the affair is too serious to be grasped from this point of view. One rather has to accept a mistake."

"Some mistake! Haven't you heard, my friend, the answer from both of the stations nearest to us? It's not possible that these stations would not have heard any accidentally stray signals from stops beyond them. If these signals reached us, they would have to go through their regions first! Well?"

"So the simple conclusion is that these signals are coming from some trackwalker's booth between Dabrowa and Glaszow."

Pomian glanced at his subordinate attentively.

"From one of those booths, you say? Hmm... maybe. But why? For what purpose? Our people examined the entire line, step by step, and they didn't find anything suspicious."

The official spread out his arms.

"That I don't know. We can investigate this later in conjunction with Glaszow. In any case, I believe we can sleep peacefully tonight and ignore the signals. Everything that we had to do, we did—the region has been searched rigorously, on the line there isn't any trace of the danger we were warned about. I consider these signals as simply a so-called 'false alarm.'"

The assistant's calmness transferred itself soothingly to the stationmaster. He bid him leave and shut himself in his office for the rest of the night.

But the station personnel did not ignore this so easily. They gathered on the block around the switchman, whispering secretively among themselves. From time to time, when the quiet of the night was interrupted by a new ringing of the bell, the heads of the railway men, bent towards each other, turned in the direction of the signal post, and several pairs of eyes, wide with superstitious fear, observed the movements of the forged hammer.

"A bad sign," murmured Grzela, the watchman; "a bad sign!"

Thus the signals played on until the start of daybreak. But the closer morning came, the weaker and less distinct the sounds; then long gaps between each signal ensued, until the signals died down, leaving no trace at dawn. People sighed out, as if a nightmarish weight had been lifted from their chests.

That day Pomian turned to the authorities at Ostoi, giving a precise report of the occurrences of the preceding night. A telegraphed reply ordered him to await the arrival of a special commission that would examine the affair thoroughly.

During the day, the rail traffic proceeded normally and without a hitch. But when the clock struck seven in the evening, the alarm signals arrived once again, in the same succession as the night before. So, first came the "cars unattached" signal; then the order "stop all trains"; finally the command "send a locomotive with workers" and the distress call for help, "send an engine with workers and a doctor." The progressive excellence of the signals was characteristic; each new one presented an increase in the fictitious danger. The signals clearly complemented each other, forming, in distinctive punctuations, a chain that spun out an ominous story of some presumed accident.

And yet the affair seemed like a joke or a silly prank.

The stationmaster raged on, while the personnel behaved variously; some took the affair from a humorous point of view, laughing at the frantic signals, others crossed themselves superstitiously. Zdun, the blockman, maintained half-aloud that the devil was sitting inside the signal post and striking the bell out of contrariness.

In any event, no one took the signals seriously, and no suitable orders were given at the station. The alarm lasted, with breaks, until the morning, and only when a pale-yellow line cut through in the East did the bell quiet down.

Finally, after a sleepless night, the stationmaster saw the arrival of the commission around ten in the morning. From Ostoi came the most noble chief inspector, Turner—a tall, lean gentleman with maliciously blinking eyes—along with his entire staff of officials. The investigation began.

These gentlemen "from above" already had a preconceived view of the affair. In the opinion of the chief inspector the signals were originating from one of the trackwalker's booths along the Dabrowa-Glaszow line. It only needed to be ascertained which one. According to the official records, there were ten booths in this region; from this number, eight could be eliminated, as they did not possess the apparatus to give signals of this type. Consequently, the suspicion fell on the remaining two. The chief inspector decided to investigate both.

After a lavish dinner at the stationmaster's residence, the inquiry committee set out in a special train at noon. After a half-hour ride, the gentlemen got off before the booth of trackwalker Dziwota; he was one of the suspects.

The poor little fellow, terrified by the invasion of the unexpected visitors, forgot his tongue and answered questions as if awakened from a deep sleep. After an examination that lasted over an hour, the commission decided that Dziwota was as innocent as a lamb and ignorant about everything.

In order not to waste time, the chief inspector left him in peace, recommending to his people a further drive to the eighth trackwalker on the line, on whom his investigation was now focused.

Forty minutes later they stopped at the place. No one ran out to meet them. This made them wonder. The post looked deserted; no trace of life in the homestead, no sign of a living being about. No voice of the man of the house responded, no rooster crowed, no chicken grumbled.

Along steep, little stairs, framed by handrails, they went up the hill on which stood the house of trackwalker Jazwa. At the entrance they were met by countless swarms of flies—nasty, vicious, buzzing. As if angered at the intruders, the insects threw themselves on their hands, eyes, and faces.

The door was knocked on. No one answered from within. One of the railwaymen pressed down on the handle—the door was closed...

"Mr. Tuziak," beckoned Pomian to the station locksmith, "pick it."

"With pleasure, stationmaster."

Iron creaked, the lock crunched and yielded.

The inspector pried the door open with his leg and entered. But then he retreated to the open air, applying a handkerchief to his nose. A horrible foulness from inside hit those present. One of the officials ventured to cross the threshold and glanced into the interior.

By a table near the window sat the trackwalker with his head sunk on his chest, the fingers of his right hand resting on the knob of the signal apparatus.

The official advanced towards the table and, paling, turned back to the exit. A quick glance thrown at the trackwalker's hand had ascertained that it was not fingers that were enclosing the knob, but three naked bones, cleansed of meat.

At that moment the sitter by the table wavered and tumbled down like a log onto the ground. Jazwa's body was recognised in a state of complete decomposition. The doctor present ascertained that death came at least ten days earlier.

An official record was written down, and the corpse was buried on the spot, an autopsy being abandoned because of the greatly-advanced deterioration of the body.

The cause of death was not discovered. Peasants from the neighbouring village were queried, but could not shed any light on the matter other than that Jazwa had not been seen for a long time. Two hours later the commission returned to Ostoi.

Stationmaster Pomian slept calmly that night and the next, undisturbed by signals. But a week later a terrible collision occurred on the Dabrowa–Glaszow line. Cars that had come apart by an unfortunate accident ran into an express train bound for the opposite direction, shattering it completely. The entire train personnel perished, as well as eighty or so travellers.

THE STATEMENT OF RANDOLPH CARTER

H. P. Lovecraft

Howard Phillips Lovecraft (1890–1937), probably the most innovative and influential weird writer of the twentieth century, frequently included modern media technologies in his fiction: in
"The Whisperer in Darkness" we encounter buzzing alien voices
captured on the "blasphemous waxen cylinder" of a phonograph,
"Nyarlathotep" features a demonic cinema, and the sense-augmenting
machine in "From Beyond" (a tale which, I suspect, owes a very large
debt to the Francis Stevens story included in this collection), is a kind
of nightmarish ur-media device, monstrously expanding our powers
of perception by directly stimulating the pineal gland.

Much of the horror in "The Statement of Randolph Carter"—a
blend of old-fashioned Gothic and new-fangled technology—derives
from Lovecraft's treatment of the telephone, which is, along with the
radio, one of the most successful of the electric telegraph's offspring.
As everyone knows, the telephone was invented by Alexander Graham
Bell in 1876. Of course, it is not quite so simple as that: the Italian
inventor Antonio Meucci had made great strides in electromagnetic
telephony two decades earlier, while Bell's contemporary and rival
Elisha Gray has his champions even today (fans of *The Simpsons* will
remember Gray as a forlorn figure on a postage stamp accusing Bell
of stealing his idea). Among the technology's early adopters was
Mark Twain, who also explored its possibilities in his fiction. As with

the electric telegraph, it did not take long for writers to imagine the telephone wires "reaching out and touching someone" beyond the grave. In 1898, the German statesman Walter Rathenau playfully imagined a telephonic exchange in a cemetery in "Necropolis, Dakota, USA": intended as a safeguard against premature burial, it unexpectedly enables communication with the dead. (In James Joyce's *Ulysses* (1922), Leopold Bloom will muse about the possibility of installing "a telephone in the coffin", as well as "a gramophone in every grave".)

The "portable telephone outfit" which Harley Warren, one of Lovecraft's doomed "searchers after horror" (as he puts it in another tale), brings to the cemetery is apparently a field telephone, akin to those in widespread use during the recent Great War. The story appeared first in the magazine *The Vagrant* (1920) and later in *Weird Tales*.

repeat to you, gentlemen, that your inquisition is fruitless. Detain me here forever if you will; confine or execute me if you must have a victim to propitiate the illusion you call justice; but I can say no more than I have said already. Everything that I can remember, I have told with perfect candour. Nothing has been distorted or concealed, and if anything remains vague, it is only because of the dark cloud which has come over my mind—that cloud and the nebulous nature of the horrors which brought it upon me.

Again I say. I do not know what has become of Harley Warren, though I think—almost hope—that he is in peaceful oblivion, if there be anywhere so blessed a thing. It is true that I have for five years been his closest friend, and a partial sharer of his terrible researches into the unknown. I will not deny, though my memory is uncertain and indistinct, that this witness of yours may have seen us together as he says, on the Gainsville pike, walking toward Big Cypress Swamp, at half past 11 on that awful night. That we bore electric lanterns, spades, and a curious coil of wire with attached instruments, I will even affirm; for these things all played a part in the single hideous scene which remains burned into my shaken recollection. But of what followed, and of the reason I was found alone and dazed on the edge of the swamp next morning, I must insist that I know nothing save what I have told you over and over again. You say to me that there is nothing in the swamp or near it which could form the setting of that frightful episode. I reply that I knew nothing beyond what I saw. Vision or nightmare it may have been—vision or nightmare I fervently hope it was—yet it is all that my mind retains of what took place in those shocking hours after we left the sight of men. And why Harley Warren did not return, he or his shade—or some nameless *thing* I cannot describe—alone can tell.

As I have said before, the weird studies of Harley Warren were well known to me, and to some extent shared by me. Of his vast collection of strange, rare books on forbidden subjects I have read all that are written in the languages of which I am master; but these are few as compared with those in languages I cannot understand. Most, I believe, are in Arabic; and the fiend-inspired book which brought on the end—the book which he carried in his pocket out of the world—was written in characters whose like I never saw elsewhere. Warren would never tell me just what was in that book. As to the nature of our studies—must I say again that I no longer retain full comprehension? It seems to me rather merciful that I do not, for they were terrible studies, which I pursued more through reluctant fascination than through actual inclination. Warren always dominated me, and sometimes I feared him. I remember how I shuddered at his facial expression on the night before the awful happening, when he talked so incessantly of his theory, why certain corpses never decay, but rest firm and fat in their tombs for a thousand years. But I do not fear him now, for I suspect that he has known horrors beyond my ken. Now I fear *for* him.

Once more I say that I have no clear idea of our object on that night. Certainly, it had much to do with something in the book which Warren carried with him—that ancient book in undecipherable characters which had come to him from India a month before—but I swear I do not know what it was that we expected to find. Your witness says he saw us at half past 11 on the Gainsville pike, headed for Big Cypress Swamp. This is probably true, but I have no distinct memory of it. The picture seared into my soul is of one scene only, and the hour must have been long after midnight; for a waning crescent moon was high in the vaporous heavens.

The place was an ancient cemetery; so ancient that I trembled at the manifold signs of immemorial years. It was in a deep, damp hollow, overgrown with rank grass, moss, and curious creeping weeds, and filled with a vague stench which my idle fancy associated absurdly with rotting stone. On every hand were the signs of neglect and decrepitude, and I seemed haunted by the notion that Warren and I were the first living creatures to invade a lethal silence of centuries. Over the valley's rim a wan, waning crescent moon peered through the noisome vapours that seemed to emanate from unheard-of catacombs, and by its feeble, wavering beams I could distinguish a repellent array of antique slabs, urns, cenotaphs, and mausolean façades; all crumbling, moss-grown, and moisture-stained, and partly concealed by the gross luxuriance of the unhealthy vegetation.

My first vivid impression of my own presence in this terrible necropolis concerns the act of pausing with Warren before a certain half-obliterated sepulchre, and of throwing down some burdens which we seemed to have been carrying. I now observed that I had with me an electric lantern and two spades, whilst my companion was supplied with a similar lantern and a portable telephone outfit. No word was uttered, for the spot and the task seemed known to us; and without delay we seized our spades and commenced to clear away the grass, weeds, and drifted earth from the flat, archaic mortuary. After uncovering the entire surface, which consisted of three immense granite slabs, we stepped back some distance to survey the charnel scene; and Warren appeared to make some mental calculations. Then he returned to the sepulchre, and using his spade as a lever, sought to pry up the slab lying nearest to a stony ruin which may have been a monument in its day. He did not succeed, and motioned to me to come to his assistance. Finally our combined strength loosened the stone, which we raised and tipped to one side.

The removal of the slab revealed a black aperture, from which rushed an effluence of miasmal gases so nauseous that we started back in horror. After an interval, however, we approached the pit again, and found the exhalations less unbearable. Our lanterns disclosed the top of a flight of stone steps, dripping with some detestable ichor of the inner earth, and bordered by moist walls encrusted with nitre. And now for the first time my memory records verbal discourse, Warren addressing me at length in his mellow tenor voice; a voice singularly unperturbed by our awesome surroundings.

"I'm sorry to have to ask you to stay on the surface," he said, "but it would be a crime to let anyone with your frail nerves go down there. You can't imagine, even from what you have read and from what I've told you, the things I shall have to see and do. It's fiendish work, Carter, and I doubt if any man without ironclad sensibilities could ever see it through and come up alive and sane. I don't wish to offend you, and Heaven knows I'd be glad enough to have you with me; but the responsibility is in a certain sense mine, and I couldn't drag a bundle of nerves like you down to probable death or madness. I tell you, you can't imagine what the thing is really like! But I promise to keep you informed over the telephone of every move—you see I've enough wire here to reach to the centre of the earth and back!"

I can still hear, in memory, those coolly spoken words; and I can still remember my remonstrances. I seemed desperately anxious to accompany my friend into those sepulchral depths, yet he proved inflexibly obdurate. At one time he threatened to abandon the expedition if I remained insistent; a threat which proved effective, since he alone held the key to the *thing*. All this I can still remember, though I no longer know what manner of *thing* we sought. After he had obtained my reluctant acquiescence in his design, Warren picked up the reel of wire and adjusted the instruments. At his nod I took one of the latter and seated myself upon an aged, discoloured gravestone close by the newly uncovered aperture. Then he shook my hand, shouldered the coil of wire, and disappeared within that indescribable ossuary.

For a minute I kept sight of the glow of his lantern, and heard the rustle of the wire as he laid it down after him; but the glow soon disappeared abruptly, as if a turn in the stone staircase had been encountered, and the sound died away almost as quickly. I was alone, yet bound to the unknown depths by those magic strands whose insulated surface lay green beneath the struggling beams of that waning crescent moon.

In the lone silence of that hoary and deserted city of the dead, my mind conceived the most ghastly fantasies and illusions; and the grotesque shrines and monoliths seemed to assume a hideous personality—a half-sentience. Amorphous shadows seemed to lurk in the darker recesses of the weed-choked hollow and to flit as in some blasphemous ceremonial procession past the portals of the mouldering tombs in the hillside; shadows which could not have been cast by that pallid, peering crescent moon.

I constantly consulted my watch by the light of my electric lantern, and listened with feverish anxiety at the receiver of the telephone; but for more than a quarter of an hour heard nothing. Then a faint clicking came from the instrument, and I called down to my friend in a tense voice. Apprehensive as I was, I was nevertheless unprepared for the words which came up from that uncanny vault in accents more alarmed and quivering than any I had heard before from Harley

Warren. He who had so calmly left me a little while previously, now called from below in a shaky whisper more portentous than the loudest shriek:

"God! If you could see what I am seeing!"

I could not answer. Speechless, I could only wait. Then came the frenzied tones again:

"Carter, it's terrible—monstrous—unbelievable!"

This time my voice did not fail me, and I poured into the transmitter a flood of excited questions. Terrified, I continued to repeat, "Warren, what is it! What is it!"

Once more came the voice of my friend, still hoarse with fear, and now apparently tinged with despair:

"I can't tell you, Carter! It's too utterly beyond thought—I dare not tell you—no man could know it and live—Great God! I never dreamed of *this*!"

Stillness again, save for my now incoherent torrent of shuddering inquiry. Then the voice of Warren in a pitch of wilder consternation:

"Carter! for the love of God, put back the slab and get out of this if you can! Quick!—leave everything else and make for the outside—it's your only chance! Do as I say, and don't ask me to explain!"

I heard, yet was able only to repeat my frantic questions. Around me were the tombs and the darkness and the shadows; below me, some peril beyond the radius of the human imagination. But my friend was in greater danger than I, and through my fear I felt a vague resentment that he should deem me capable of deserting him under such circumstances. More clicking, and after a pause a piteous cry from Warren:

"Beat it! For God's sake, put back the slab and beat it, Carter!"

Something in the boyish slang of my evidently stricken companion unleashed my faculties. I formed and shouted a resolution, "Warren, brace up! I'm coming down!" But at this offer the tone of my auditor changed to a scream of utter despair:

"Don't! You can't understand! It's too late—and my own fault. Put back the slab and run—there's nothing else you or anyone can do now!"

The tone changed again, this time acquiring a softer quality, as of hopeless resignation. Yet it remained tense through anxiety for me.

"Quick—before it's too late!"

I tried not to heed him; tried to break through the paralysis which held me, and to fulfil my vow to rush down to his aid. But his next whisper found me still held inert in the chains of stark horror.

"Carter—hurry! It's no use—you must go—better one than two—the slab—"

A pause, more clicking, then the faint voice of Warren:

"Nearly over now—don't make it harder—cover up those damned steps and run for your life—you're losing time—so long, Carter—won't see you again."

Here Warren's whisper swelled into a cry; a cry that gradually rose to a shriek fraught with all the horror of the ages—

"Curse these hellish things—legions—My God! Beat it! *Beat it!* BEAT IT!"

After that was silence. I know not how many interminable aeons I sat stupefied; whispering, muttering, calling, screaming into that telephone. Over and over again through those aeons I whispered and muttered, called, shouted, and screamed, "Warren! Warren! Answer me—are you there!"

And then there came to me the crowning horror of all—the unbelievable, unthinkable, almost unmentionable thing. I have said that aeons seemed to elapse after Warren shrieked forth his last despairing warning, and that only my own cries now broke the hideous silence.

But after a while there was a further clicking in the receiver, and I strained my ears to listen. Again I called down, "Warren, are you there?" and in answer heard the *thing* which has brought this cloud over my mind. I do not try, gentlemen, to account for that *thing*—that voice—nor can I venture to describe it in detail, since the first words took away my consciousness and created a mental blank which reaches to the time of my awakening in the hospital. Shall I say that the voice was deep; hollow; gelatinous; remote; unearthly; inhuman; disembodied? What shall I say? It was the end of my experience, and is the end of my story. I heard it, and knew no more—heard it as I sat petrified in that unknown cemetery in the hollow, amidst the crumbling stones and the falling tombs, the rank vegetation and the miasmal vapours—heard it well up from the innermost depths of that damnable open sepulchre as I watched amorphous, necrophagous shadows dance beneath an accursed waning moon.

And this is what it said:

"You fool, Warren is DEAD!"

THE WIND IN THE WOODS

Bessie Kyffin-Taylor

Relatively little is known about the life of Liverpool-born Bessie Kyffin-Taylor (1880–1922), whose one known foray into the field of supernatural fiction was the 1920 collection *From Out of the Silence: Seven Strange Stories*, from which "The Wind in the Woods" is taken. In this tale we return to the theme of uncanny photography, now combined with the increased portability and ease of use offered by the hand-held Kodak camera. The first Kodak was marketed in 1888 by American entrepreneur George Eastman, putting photography into the hands of countless middle-class consumers (at $25, this early model was still beyond the means of many), and ushering in the age of the "snapshot". Kodak rolled out many other models in the years to come: the 1900 "Brownie", a small box camera going for only $1, had an impact on the spread of amateur photography perhaps second only to the introduction of Eastman's original model; others, such as the "Kodak's Vest Pocket" model, were folding cameras with accordion-like bellows connecting the lensboard to the camera's body. Most of these cameras were fixed-focus rather than focusing models; it is difficult to tell exactly what kind of Kodak Wilfred has, but it seems to be a fixed-focus type where "finding his focus" means calculating the proper distance from an object to take the picture, rather than adjusting a lens.

o say I was an artist would be giving myself too high-sounding a name, yet my days were spent in trying, and at times succeeding, in depicting scenes as I saw them—not people! I never attempted portraits, for the expression on human faces more often irritated me, than interested—every nine out of ten wore such a worried, harassed look, as if, in the race for gain, or pleasure, they had lost sight of all things conducive to rest or repose; I had no wish to paint such things, nor did I wish them to come and pose in their best garments, with a smile such as one and all would, I knew, adopt.

Fortunately for me, I was not dependent upon my efforts with brush and pencil, though I confess I made quite a nice income by them; but it was always joy to me to remember, if I did not want to paint, I need not, for my meals were forthcoming, whether I made the price of them or not.

I was the owner of a charming flat in London. This was my anchorage, and here I was looked after and cared for by an old family servant, a woman well on in years, who had been for long years a faithful friend and servant in my family, and now, in her later years, had constituted herself my factotum, ruling my small domain, and incidentally myself, with a firm hand, never by any chance seeming to realise that I really was grown up, but bestowing the same thought upon the changing of my socks on a wet day as she had done when I was nine or ten. Her name was "Merry"—Mrs. Merry. As children, we had all adored her; as a middle-aged man, I respected and looked up to her, glad to ask and take her wise advice on many issues of the day.

Mrs. Merry was well used to my vagabondish ways, though at times she was wont to say I should be much happier if I married and settled down! I always laughed at her, for my only love-story was buried fathoms deep in the dust-heap of forgotten things; and the very words "settle down" sent a cold shiver down my spine—it, the "settling down" process, would mean a wholesale giving up of all those ways I held so dear. No more sudden trêkings at a moment's notice, or coming home any day or any hour, as sure of welcome as I was sure of being safe from questions as to my doings. Mrs. Merry *never* questioned, though she was always delighted when told where I had been, or what I had done. Sometimes I had sketches to show to her, but as often I had none; in either case, she was convinced of my talent and ability, and her faith and loyalty never wavered.

It was early in July when a sudden desire for trees, rivers, and growing things caused me to drop the work I was on, call Mrs. Merry, and request a small Gladstone bag should be packed as quickly as possible, that I was going away. The old lady looked at me keenly, remarking—

"You don't look ill!"

I laughed.

"Nor am I," I said; "but it is hot in the town; also, I feel as if I must see trees instead of people for a while."

"That will mean strong boots and knickers, I suppose, sir?" was her next remark.

"Yes, Merry, dear, it will; also plenty of pipes, baccy, books, and a stick. I may paint, or I may not; in any case, expect me back a month from tomorrow, for sure, unless I send you word; and if you don't hear, why then," I added, laughing—"some one had better begin to look for me."

"I do wish you would settle down, Mr. Wilfred," was the old dame's parting shot, as she went out to do my behests.

Settle down, I mused, filling a much-used old briar, never, now, though my thoughts went back to those days of joy, when I and a sweet-faced girl with dark eyes and a little fair head just reaching to my shoulder, talked in twilight hours of a home that was to be. If she had passed to the "Great Beyond," I could have borne it better than the tale of treachery and cunning, which ended in my dark-eyed love leaving me on the morning, which should have been my wedding-day, merely announcing, by wire, that she had married my best chum, Kirk Compton, in London, that morning.

Trouble of that kind takes one of two lines, it either sends a man, or woman, to the bad—that is, to drink, gambling—anything of a wild, riotous kind of existence to, as they think, help them to forget—or it sends them into themselves, to more or less live a life of solitude, finding companionship in books or hobbies, fearful of making friends, lest they, too, should prove unfaithful; one's faith in goodness shattered, it is years, if ever, before one comes into one's own, realising that there is infinitely more in life than the shallow so-called love of one girl. And so, as I was not addicted to drink or cards, I became a recluse, or almost. I had a few friends, was voted a good chap, but a cynic, and gradually left to my own devices. I was happy as the years went on, finding my books and work all sufficient, while my fervent love of nature proved the healing of my sore, and I was content.

July 20th stared me in the face from a large lettered calendar, as I woke for my early cup of tea, on the day I was starting for a whole month, somewhere in Wales.

There is not any object in making a mystery of my destination, except the small fact that my chosen haunt was a very well-known district, within only an hour's journey from a large manufacturing town;

therefore, it is possible that there are people who might recognise and locate the district if I gave more than a mere hint of its place on the map. It has been for years a very favourite corner of mine; the hills which surround it are not so high as to be unclimbable, they are heather clad, though here and there one came upon an oasis of sprongy turf and golden bracken—what I call, in my own mind, "kind hills"—high enough to lift one up from life's little worries, but not high enough to be awe-inspiring, or to frown down upon us puny mortals. The rivers are fishable after rain, otherwise one can inspect the stones, which form the beds of these mountain streams, and decide among the dry stones which place might best conceal a trout, when the next rain comes; personally, I am quite willing to believe that once there were fish in plenty in the stream, but that lean years had driven the farm folks to catch them the best way they could.

Perhaps the chief beauty of the place lay in the charm of its many and varied woods—at least, this was to me the magnet which drew me here generally once or twice in a year.

Up on the hillsides the woods seemed to open out, one into another, ever revealing fresh beauties of trees, from the tender green of the sapling birch to the hoary old beech or oak of many years old; beneath their green arms, the ground was carpeted with soft tiny wild thyme, wild mint, and little flowers of many kinds whose names were unknown to me. Most of my hours were spent deep in the heart of these woods, which never failed to hold me entranced with their ever-varying lights and shades.

Below, nearer to the river, there were woods also, but of quite a different nature, there, high pine trees of sombre hue towered above you, each one seeming to say: "Let me stretch up to the blue sky and leave the gloom of this wood beneath me." For gloom there undoubtedly was, yet I have liked that gloom; sometimes, on a hot summer's day, I have enjoyed lying on a soft, dry heap of pine needles, listening to the gentle coo of wood-pigeons, nesting high above me. "Silent Wood," as I called it, was always sheltered from wind, for the pine trees were close together, and beyond a soft sighing wind in the tree tops I never remember feeling the wind from any quarter. The sunlight seldom penetrated the "Silent Wood," save only in single shafts between the pines, or, maybe, in some clear patch where a tree had fallen or been cut down; but, even lacking sunshine, it was always warm and dry.

One side of the wood was bounded by a path, the other side by the stream—at least in autumn and winter it was—for in summer it dried up or trickled away to reappear a mile or so further on, as if it had tumbled into some old mine shaft, and later, changed its course and returned.

"Silent Wood" was *not* my favourite, but it had a fascination for me, difficult to describe; and on this July morning, when I bid farewell to dear old Merry, and started for my holiday, "Silent Wood" was much in my mind as a quiet place to rest in, before I tackled longer, steeper walks, or began to think of taking canvas and paints with me.

My journey was long, also suffocatingly hot, dusty, and tedious; many people were travelling, and my compartment was well packed with bundles and packages, as well as people, so I hailed my last change with a sigh of relief, for soon the hills and trees would surround me instead of the bricks and mortar I had grown so tired of.

A broken-down trap, drawn by a fat Welsh pony, met me at my station; from thence we crawled up four long miles of hill ere I reached my favourite quarters, an old farmhouse in which I was always a welcome guest, and where two cheery rooms were always at my disposal. The peacefulness of that first evening will linger in my memory for many a day. To be able to gaze around, seeing nothing but hills, fields, trees, and sky, instead of houses, chimneys, motors, and people, was pure joy to me; and when, after a simple meal, I lit my pipe, I felt content to linger in the warm, hay-scented air indefinitely.

There are those to whom the contemplation of such a holiday, as the one I thought lay before me, would have been a dire penalty, those to whom solitude and nature would spell boredom and weariness; and I pity all those natures, for they know not what they miss.

I passed a gloriously restful night, and was up early, with a long day of golden sunshine ahead of me. I had never been here in July before, early spring or September had been my usual seasons; but to be here in July, in radiant warmth and beauty, was a treat I was prepared to revel in.

Day by day slipped away, in almost complete idleness, until a week had vanished, almost unnoticed by me, for calendars had been left behind me, and I, more often than not, forgot to wind up my watch—I had no use for time. I ate when I felt hungry, and slept when I was tired; but the end of this week found me thinking of brush and canvas, so I decided to take lunch in my pocket, trusting to luck for some tea if I desired it, and prepared for a long day's sketching.

"Which way do you think of going, sir?" asked my hostess, more, I fancy, from politeness than from any real interest in my goings and comings.

"Oh, I don't know," I answered, "but probably I shall wander to the woods."

"Which, sir?" she next enquired, a little to my surprise.

"Probably the shadiest," I replied, smiling, "the one below with the pine trees, and silence, is the one I most fancy today."

"The higher woods are nicer, sir, don't you think?" was her next remark.

"No, I don't," I said. "I like the pine woods, they are always so intensely silent; one never feels any wind there, and there is a breeze today."

"That is true, sir," said Mrs. Hughes. "There isn't any wind there—*as a rule*."

"As a rule?" I echoed. "Why, I've never felt it there, not even in autumn."

"No, sir, you wouldn't then, but you may now; and I'd go to the upper woods if I were you."

Now Mrs. Hughes had never, to my knowledge, taken the slightest interest in my doings previously, and her persistence this morning simply had the effect of making me feel perverse, as is the way of men; so, smilingly, I bade her good morning, determined, in my own mind, that "Silent Wood" should be my destination for that day. The good lady ventured no further remarks, but turned away to busy herself with farm duties, leaving me free to set off without further questioning.

There was a slight breeze, just enough to make walking more pleasant, but rather more than I liked for sketching purposes, so I was glad when I dipped down from the path by the river-side to the edge of my pet woods. They were, as ever, still, dark, and airless, just as I had pictured them many, many times as I smoked my pipe beside my studio fire while busy London surged on, beneath my windows.

In those woods, I have always felt as if I must tread softly. I do not remember ever to have sung or whistled there; yet, there was never anything to disturb, for I have never seen even a rabbit, it seemed too sombre a place for animal life; moreover, there was nothing but dry pine needles for them to eat. I don't remember ever *seeing* the wood-pigeons I occasionally heard above my head; so, lacking animal life, the place was even more silent than deep woods usually are.

It suited me in my present mood, however, and in the intense silence lay its greatest charm. Somewhere in the world there are a few kindred spirits, I have no doubt, to whom such perfect silence and freedom from every jar would appeal, as it appeals to me—those who often crave for just one hour's unbroken silence, and who find it one of the most difficult things to attain; those to whom the incessant opening and shutting of doors, clattering of things, ringing of bells, voices, and the coming and going of people have to be endured with a smile, though every nerve may be on edge, and the aching for quietness is almost more than can be borne—those people, and those only, will enter into and fully understand the intense charm to me of "Silent Wood."

I entered it, as usual, on this morning as on many previous ones, walking softly as if not wanting to disturb its peace by so much as a snap of a dry twig, and as I walked deeper and deeper into the shadows it seemed to grow stiller and more silent. The scent of the pines was soothing, and the warm, dry air seemed to draw it out and intensify it.

About the centre of the wood I paused to look and listen. Not a sound broke the stillness, save only the faintest cooing of the wood-pigeons; so there, in the patch of sunlight, I drew together heaps of pine needles to form a couch, stretching myself on it in complete enjoyment, canvas and brushes idle by my side.

The natural outcome of such an environment and such quiet calm was to fall soundly asleep—a glorious, restful sleep—knowing that there could not be any early knocking at my door, no engagements to keep, nothing, no one for whom I need wake until I had slept all I desired. I woke at long length, with the softest of breezes blowing gently on my face, so softly as to make me wonder, in my half-asleep state, if it also were part of my dreams; but no! there it was again, soft and cold, and this time a little stronger. I opened my eyes. Surely it must be night! I thought. How many hours had I slept? It seemed dark, yet high up between the pine-tree tops I could catch a glimpse of blue sky. Then it is not late, I thought, but how dark it is here under the trees. I must see the time, and shake myself into a more reasonable state of mind, for, truly, I feel almost nervy! So my thoughts ran as I raised myself from my pine-needle couch, and stood up.

I glanced round and could scarcely believe it was my beloved "Silent Wood," it seemed so chill and dark, not the soft gloom I was accustomed to there, but an eerie darkness as of a gathering storm; but ever and anon a little moaning wind swept past me, each just seeming more chill and dank.

"Horrible!" I murmured, fastening up my coat before preparing to pick up my little knapsack of odds and ends, "horrible! I never thought the place could be so chilly; I'll get out as speedily as I can for it must be late."

I peered at my watch, which was difficult to see in the gloom, to find I had, as usual, forgotten to wind it.

"It is probably about four!" I said aloud, "but it's like night!"

I spoke aloud, and my voice seemed to come back to me in mocking echo from the far side of the wood, "like night."

"I never knew there was an echo," I thought. "I'll try again tomorrow," I said clearly, and back from the distance came the echo— "tomorrow"—and a hoarse laugh came with it.

I started, I had not laughed! Then, who? "Oh, you idiot," I murmured, giving myself a shake, "it's some country yokel answering you back, making a fool of you; pull yourself together and get off home—you require your tea."

So, with a last look round, I turned my face towards home, and tea, but my feet seemed weighted, and seemed as if I could not leave the wood, eager as I was to reach the daylight.

I seemed to have already dragged myself double the distance I had to go ere I found myself at the edge of the wood, shivering in every limb, chilled to the bone, unnerved, as I could not believe possible, over—nothing at all! In the warmth of the sun I speedily recovered, and was ready to laugh at my own stupidity; to prove this to my own satisfaction, I gaily shook my fist at the woods behind me, calling back—"tomorrow," and, far away in the distant darkness, I fancied—for it could only have been fancy—I heard a mocking echo and a faint sound of laughter, as if the word "tomorrow" floated back to me; fancy or not, it served to hasten my steps, and the farm kitchen with its cheery tea-table, which I hurried to reach, quickly dispelled any lingering fear I might have felt.

For the first time, since my holiday began, I passed a restless night, burdened, when I slept at all, by dreams of mocking voice and laughter. My first thought on waking was one of dire vengeance, on some one, for causing me to lose a night's precious sleep. I would repay them, I vowed, as I sprang up, preparing to dress as rapidly as possible.

"Will you be in, sir, for lunch, or will you take it out?" asked my hostess, as soon as I had finished a wonderful breakfast of home-cured ham, fresh eggs, scones, and home-made jam.

"I will take it out, please, Mrs. Hughes," I replied. "Some of that fine ham, and some bread and butter, if you will be so good. Don't make it into those abominations called sandwiches though, it would utterly spoil both bread and ham. I never can enjoy food done up in that way, the bread tastes of ham and the ham only tastes of bread, and both are dry and worn out by the time you want your lunch; so separately, please—if you love me."

Mrs. Hughes eyed me as if uncertain whether to laugh or scold at what she termed my oddities—the laugh triumphed, and she went off chuckling over the ways of faddy men-folks. Presently, the good lady reappeared with a neat parcel, which she handed to me, with the remark—

"There you are, sir, *separately*, and I hope you will enjoy your lunch. Which way will you be going, sir?"

So again my destination seemed to be of interest to the worthy dame, but this time I wasn't going to let her off so easily.

"Why do you ask, Mrs. Hughes?" I enquired.

"Well, sir, it's Tommy, it's Tommy," she said hesitatingly. "Seems like the lad likes to be on the look-out for you, sir, and always pesters me to say which way you've gone, sir."

As the good lady was speaking she edged nearer and nearer the door, and her final words were uttered as the door closed between her and myself, leaving me looking rather blankly at the door, and quite unable to reconcile Tommy's present anxiety as to my whereabouts, seeing the lad had not apparently noticed my existence up to now.

However, they were none the wiser—no one, save myself, knew whither I was bound, and if I changed my mind, no one would know, or care.

I debated a few moments as to whether to burden myself with sketching materials or not, and, finally, a happy thought struck me, I would take my kodak, it was ready loaded with new and highly-sensitive films, so, if I liked, I could take special bits, and later, if I wished, sketch or enlarge from them in the quiet of my studio. So with my camera on my shoulder, my lunch in a handy pocket, I set off, prepared for another happy peaceful day in "Silent Wood." Yet now I had started, I wondered if it really would give me the pleasure I had anticipated to fulfil my vow of vengeance on Him, Her, or It, who had mocked me the previous day. I was *quite* determined, on one point, that I would discover the hiding place of my mocking friend, and rid myself of the disturber of my sanctuary. To begin with

I would not enter the woods by my usual path, I had a fancy to inspect the far side of it, which was as yet unknown to me, and which I had often thought of exploring, but so far had been too lazy to do so; it had been sufficient for me to get into the still warmth, and there to stay—resting, dreaming, or reading; but today I felt energetic, braced up, ready for anything, so instead of taking the lower path by the river to the woods, I struck off higher up, crossed a few fields and some tiresome fences, heavily loaded with barbed wire as if to keep out some invading enemy and not the three or four cows it guarded. My plan had led me higher than the woods, which now lay stretched below me in a large triangle, thick and dense, possibly half-a-mile in length, not more, I shouldn't think; looked at from where I stood it appeared quite an insignificant patch of dark trees surrounded by fields of waving corn, or haycocks, late in being carted home. Here and there, men and women were working in the fields; I could hear a reaper busy somewhere, and voices of children at play sounded clearly in the distance.

It was gloriously sunny, not a breath of wind stirred the leaves or grasses, yet, in spite of its beauty and brilliance, the dark trees lying below seemed to call me. I could see the waving branches of the pine trees, as if they were arms beckoning me to come, to rest in their shade. I knew I had to go; I knew in my heart I wanted to go, yet I lingered, drinking in the beauty of fields and sunshine as I strolled along, until, descending gradually, I found myself near the edge of the woods, at exactly the opposite corner from my usual point of entrance.

One more fence, a thick one of briars, thorns, and undergrowth, and I was in my beloved woods. It wasn't quite so dark on this side as the other, yet it felt more desolate, more cheerless somehow, possibly fewer people came this way, which might account for it; anyway, here I was, and now to explore. First, I quietly skirted the wood for a little way, but this proved uninteresting, so I struck in under the pines, and almost at once was conscious again of the warm scenty feeling of the air.

"Glorious," I murmured; "how peaceful, how still, but I will not rest yet, I want to look round first." Presently, I caught a glimpse of what appeared to be a building. Funny place for a house, I thought; I wonder if anyone lives there, if so, my friend of the mocking laughter is now unearthed; so, with a smile at my own smartness, I marched on until I reached the building, at least what I thought was a building—now, alas! a ruin. Two ends and one side were almost intact, the rest, except one chimney, was just piles of rough, grey stones. It had every appearance of having been deserted many years, for the tumbled-down stones were moss-grown, with here and there little ferns protruding between the crevices; the spot must once have been a lonely corner, though now it looked utter desolation.

Laying my camera and lunch down, I strolled to have a nearer inspection of the lonely ruin before I sat down. There was not any trace to be found of how many rooms the cottage had once contained, though probably three or four was the limit; what must once have been a fireplace faced me as I entered, and on one side, about two yards from the ground, were five stone stairs; evidently there had been a stone staircase or steps leading to an upper room or rooms, though no sign of any floor above remained now. I couldn't imagine a stone house falling to pieces so completely, it gave one the impression more of having been hurled down stone after stone, nothing else would have demolished it so utterly.

There being nothing more to inspect, I strolled back to my belongings, but the sight of my camera reminded me that, after all, I could get a picture of so battered a domicile without the fag of sketching it; it would be interesting, I thought, to have a photograph of those five curious stone steps, and battered walls, so I quickly found my focus, taking the picture from a little distance to get a big pine in as well. It was a curious tree, at least half of it had apparently been shattered at some time. I then went closer, focussing for the stone steps only. It was shady within the walls so I gave a little longer time, and hoped for success, though I felt sorry I had not even yet succeeded in getting exactly the point of view I wanted. I had one film left; I would wait until the sun lit up the far side, and would take that also. That was enough for now, and I had earned both lunch and rest.

Somehow, my moss cushion did not give me the comfort I liked, though to try to say why, was beyond me, apparently it left nothing to be desired, my back was against a pine as I faced the deeper shade of the woods in front of me. There was not any wind to disturb me, and no sound of any kind, all was quiet, serene, peaceful, and yet—

Again, and yet again, I found myself involuntarily turning to look over my shoulder at the heap of grey stones behind me. I didn't *want* to look at it, I had seen enough of it, yet turn I must and did, I was getting fanciful, for I could have sworn I saw a shadow of some person flit past the one-time doorway. Surely I had not missed a part of the place in my search, and there was someone hiding there. I would make sure. To this end I walked right round the place, looking well among the old bushes and holly trees—no sign of life—so I went back to my cushion and my rest.

One pipe I smoked, falling asleep ere I had finished it, to wake with a violent start, springing from my seat, sure, positive then, as I shall always be, that someone had laid a hand on my face. I tried to imagine a crawling thing had wandered over my face, I imagined a leaf falling, even tried the effect by closing my eyes and dropping a leaf on to my cheek, it was useless, no amount of thinking could make me believe that touch was aught but a hand.

Ghosts! I didn't believe in, I always looked on yarns of such things as the results of too heavy a supper, or a too vivid imagination, so was inclined to laugh at what I struggled so hard to minimise. I tried to whistle, but if you try to whistle with the corners of your mouth turned down, you will understand that effort ended in failure. I tried to hum a song, which resulted in a species of quavering dirge, I got up, I stamped, I beat the soft, unoffending turf with my stick, I did everything I could think of to shake off a creepy feeling that was fast getting a firmer hold of me, anything to avoid turning round as I felt impelled to do—all was useless, I might as well give in, but had now quite made up my mind I had had enough of the remains of the cottage, I would leave it to its solitude, first taking one more photo, then I would go on straight through the deep shades I loved, and out at the side I knew best. Just once, I admit it, I looked towards the fence and bank down which I had come, almost furtively, I glanced that way, as if in my heart I would rather have returned by the same path, but it was only momentary, for I knew that through "Silent Wood" was the way I should go.

I picked up my camera for my final snapshot, choosing the far side of the ruined place, now in the sunshine, and exposed my film. As the shutter clicked, the sunlight vanished, as if a heavy cloud had suddenly obscured it, and the camera in my hand shook, as if it had been hit—*my* hands were perfectly steady, I am positive of that, yet I had all but dropped my precious toy!

Someone must have thrown a stone I decided, but who the someone was, or where they were, I did not venture to look into, enough for me that I had got my pictures, and was ready to start through the woods, and so home to tea.

I was probably half-way, having long passed out of sight of the ruins, when I remembered my long forgotten ham and bread. I had better eat it, I supposed, so feeling happy again, now I was in the warm gloom of my favourite place, I made for myself another cosy seat, and proceeded with the now somewhat belated lunch. I was just about to bury the paper wrapping, as is my way, when it suddenly whisked away in a sudden gust of wind.

"Wind!" I ejaculated. "Here! Impossible!"

As I spoke, another little gust whirled past me, scattering the pine needles, and whirling a little crowd of dried bits round my feet. It really is most remarkable, I murmured to myself, the times without number I have been in these woods and never felt the smallest breath of wind until yesterday and today. I'd best be moving, it may rain, though I'll be dry enough here if it does, all the same I'll go. As I rose, another and another draught of cold air swept by me, and then a sudden quietness fell, and all around me seemed to be growing darker, and still darker, little whispering winds seemed chattering above my head, and colder and more chilly it seemed to grow.

I started off hurriedly, only to find, in the gathering darkness, I had missed my way. On and on I plunged, deeper and deeper the blackness grew, colder and colder the wind, now rising almost to a gale, anon, dying away with a moaning sound. Bravely I struggled, wildly endeavouring to locate one familiar tree or stone.

The wind, now icily cold, seemed to lash me, buffeting me, as if I, strong man as I was, had been but a weak puny child.

Suddenly I stopped, determined to find my bearings, determined I would *not* be driven along as I was. I raised my face; my eyes were streaming with water, in the smarting cold of the lashing wind.

Gloom, black gloom, met me on every side. Pines, once familiar, now seemed twice their original size, standing out rigid, gaunt, and black, no glimmer of light anywhere.

"My God, I am utterly lost," I said, aloud.

"Utterly lost," came back a voice from far away, and with the words, making my blood freeze and heart stand still, a shriek of hideous laughter.

With a valiant effort, I steadied my voice, and shouted aloud:

"Who are you? Come to my help."

"To my help," rang out the voice, and I shuddered as a shrill peal of laughter followed it.

"Won't you come?" I cried once more.

"You come," echoed the voice, and the laughter that came with it seemed of many voices—the gruff, hoarse laughter of a man, the shrill, cackling laugh of women, and even, I was sure, the laughter of children.

On, on, I plunged! gasping now for breath, praying, hoping for deliverance; lost, but blindly struggling to reach some haven of refuge. A more vicious bang of the tearing wind suddenly sent me forward, and I seemed to have reached grass at last. With a sob of relief, I raised my eyes, thinking to see the grass at the edge of the wood, but was frozen stiff with horror and amazement, to find myself on the clearing, with the ruined cottage before me.

"Ruined cottage," I called it, ruined no longer! To my amazed eyes it appeared intact: a door stood ajar, a window on each side of it, through each of which glimmered a faint light; two windows above, from one of which peered a white, tearful face—a man with an evil, sinister face, stood beneath the lone pine, holding a wailing child by its hair with one hand, and in the other—Oh God, the horror of it!—a long, sharp knife, which glistened as the glimmer from the windows struck it.

I didn't faint, I didn't fall, so rooted to the spot was I, I seemed as if made of stone. The wind had all but died away; and, but for the fact that, in my now frenzied brain, I *knew* I had seen the place desolate and ruined, I should have thought I was faced with a workman's dwelling, peopled by real beings. I *knew* it was NOT so. Fascinated, horrified, I gazed. The man moved, with a muttered curse, dragging the child with him up to the door; as he reached it, the wind redoubled its fury, howling, shrieking, like every evil let loose. I fell on my knees, powerless now to even pray; and hiding my face in my hands, I waited, for some awful thing, I knew, was to come.

It came, with a wild scream of awful horror, the scream from an upstairs window! and then a second, the shrill, awful scream of a child! Agonised, I knelt, and saw the man lurch through the door, reeling, join a group of waiting people hitherto unseen by me. As he came up to them, one of the women spoke to him, and then began to laugh. Oh God! the unspeakable horror of that laugh. One after another of the group spoke to the man, and each, as they moved off, laughed or chuckled, even two small boys who were with them burst into shrill laughter. I cannot describe it, save, only in one way, it sounded like fiends from Hell, so vile, so malicious, so diabolical were those awful sounds. As I knelt, unable to move, I struggled to keep a hold of myself, I found I was striving to explain away what I knew in my heart was totally inexplicable. I whispered to myself, "That laughter *is* real, *is* human, hideous as it is," but I knew it was neither real nor human. Always, to my dying day, it will ring in my ears, laughter such as no human creature could be responsible for.

Quite suddenly, there came a lull in the wind, a stillness in the air, the laughter died away. Could I, dare I move, rise, and venture to look? But even as I thought of it, the wind, with redoubled fury, broke forth again, causing me to crouch still lower as it swept over me. An awful crash sounded, a crash that echoed and re-echoed through the woods. The wind had seized and felled, as if with giant hand, the pine that had been standing at the far side of the cottage. So terrific was the blow that the end of the cottage, where it hit, fell like a house of cardboard! To demolish the rest of it seemed but child's play, as, with one whistling shriek, the wind tore beneath the now shattered roof, ripping it off, and almost the remainder of the walls, with a deafening roar, high above which rang out peal after peal of hideous laughter! until it, too, died away as now the wind was dying, dying fitfully, with an angry gust, and then a sobbing wail, until at length a long low wail seemed to pass through the woods and fade into silence, a long silence.

At last I moved, raised my head, looked, listened. Nothing, no sound broke the stillness; the ruined cottage was as I had first seen it, just a worn, weather-beaten heap of grey stones, a semblance of a fireplace, five stone stairs, that was all. I ventured nearer, trying to persuade myself I had dreamed the horrible scene. I must have dreamed it, for it had been dark, pitch dark, when the wind had begun to rise, and yet, by what light then had I witnessed this awful thing, for light of some kind there surely had been. Who were those people I had seen, from whom came that awful laughter? I was trembling yet, shaken, feeling desperately ill, no dream had brought me to this pass—then what?

Visitants from "Beyond"? But to what end, for they and their works were evil? I turned abruptly, with one thought in my head, to get out of the wood, and home. I glanced at my watch, having made a point this time of winding and setting it right—only five o'clock. I must be mad, I had gone through hours of dark night; how could it possibly be but five! I supposed, long afterwards, when I reviewed these hours, that it was the knowledge that it was only five o'clock, and not perhaps, as I expected, many hours later, that gave me the fillip of courage, which led me to linger still another moment near the ruins, and gaze, as if to print the thing on my mind. I stood possibly three yards from the ruined doorway, and said aloud "It was a murder!" Away through the woods came the mocking answer "A murder." "Oh God!" I gasped, "not again, for they are fiends from Hell!"—"From Hell!" came back the answer, and again the awful sound of laughter of many voices—

I turned and fled, holding my hands over my ears as I strove to run. I remember knocking violently against something, and falling, falling, falling, endlessly, or so it seemed, and then nothingness until I opened my eyes three weeks later, to find myself in bed in my quaint room at the farm, and beside my bed, placidly knitting, sat Mrs. Merry.

"Merry!" I whispered, and the sound, or want of sound, in my own voice startled me.

"Yes, it's me, sir," answered the dear soul, "and high time too; but we are not talking, sir, if *you* please, it is medicine time and then you'll sleep."

I only too gladly obeyed, unquestioningly, as I obeyed for many weeks, the quiet, though firm, commands of Mrs. Merry. I was far too weak to fight, even had it been of the slightest use; indeed, it was very little less than six weeks ere I was permitted to ask a question or have my own way in anything; but at length a day came when I was allowed to sit in a chair by the window, from which the view was something only expressed by colour, words could not do it. I gazed for a long time in silence, then said:

"I am well now, Merry, tell me what brought you, what has been wrong with me, where was I, everything—I must know."

She looked at me, then put her glasses on—she always did that if she meant to talk severely, then she said abruptly:

"You'd been missing for two days when they found you."

"Missing for two days?" I asked, incredulously, "But where was I?"

"You were at the bottom of an old lead mine," she answered, "on a big heap of dead leaves and ferns. Luckily, it wasn't one of the deep mines, and also the leaves and ferns saved you, though how they got there is a mystery," she added.

"But how on earth—" I began.

"Quite so, sir," she went on, "that's what we all want to know, how on earth, unless you were mooning along and wandered into a weak place in the ground above the mine. That's where you were, anyway, in one of the small shafts close to the old ruined cottage. You were quite unconscious; you must have had your camera in your hand, sir, because it was beside you, though how it wasn't broken is another mystery."

"Bring me my camera, Merry dear," I said.

"Very well, sir," she answered. "That can't do you no harm"; and off she went, to return presently, gingerly holding my kodak, as if fearful of it.

She was right. By some marvel it was unhurt; moreover the number of the film I had last turned to stood clearly forth. I would have them developed at once. I felt curious, but I had not yet asked all my questions:

"Who found me, Merry?" I next asked.

"Tommy Hughes, sir."

"Tommy Hughes!" I said. "What made him look for me?"

"Well, sir," answered the old lady, "they do say as he found another gentleman once in the same place, and when you didn't come home, he set off to look for you."

"Was the other chap hurt, Merry?" I asked.

"No, sir—at least not hurt, sir, because he was lying on ferns and leaves just the same. Oh no! he wasn't hurt, sir, not his body!"

"What do you mean?" I asked. "Tell me, please."

"Oh, dear sir, how you do worrit, and it's time for your soup, anyway."

"Tell me first, Merry," I said.

She glanced at me, to see if I was in earnest, and then, seemingly, decided that for the moment, at least, I was boss.

"His body was all right, sir, it was, his head, at least his wits, sir; he's been in a lunatic place ever since, so they say," she amended, with a sniff which, I knew, meant utter disbelief in gossip or village yarns.

I did *not* so entirely disbelieve, for, as the fragments of memory began to join together, I shuddered as I recalled my experience, and could only too readily believe that a very little weaker minded individual than I would very easily lose his reason if he went through all I had done. I would, however, leave further questioning until the next day, for I had observed the snap with which my dear old Merry had closed her lips.

The following day my doctor paid me a visit, one of his many, but this time he came in less professional manner, in fact he had every appearance of spoiling for a gossip, I could have wagered my last sou on it, so wasn't surprised when he accepted my offer of tea, and a smoke, with alacrity. The tea disposed of, he did not beat about the bush, but asked me if I could give him any light at all on my accident.

"I am curiously interested," he said, "because you are not my first case to have a very similar accident."

"Did your other patient make as good recovery, doctor?" I asked, instead of, as politeness demanded, answering his question.

"No, he did not," he replied. "He never recovered and never will in my opinion. He is mentally deranged, though all searching has failed to reveal a cause. He is quiet generally, and peaceable, but in a high wind he becomes frenzied, utterly distraught, his attendants are unable to cope with him, often he shrieks and yells, for the most part unintelligible rubbish. One night, in a furious gale, a man was blown over in the grounds, and the attendants were laughing about it when, without apparent reason, the poor insane chap fell on the luckless attendant and half-killed him, shouting all the time:

"'Stop laughing, will you!' It's always the same if the wind blows. They take him to a more sheltered room when it blows hard now.

"Tell me, will you, what preceded your fall—there must be some sort of link between the two, because, in your delirium, you raved of the wind, though we've had no wind to speak of since your arrival."

"I'll tell you the story, doctor, though you will be inclined to put me with your other patient, *unless* I can convince you, and this I may perhaps do, if my camera depicts what I saw."

I told him my experiences during two days in the woods I loved, I gave him every detail, even to the taking of the snapshots of the place, and he listened, silently puffing at his pipe, until I ended by telling him of how I struck something violently and fell, remembering nothing more until I found myself in my room.

There was a long pause as I finished, he seemed unable to speak, so I asked him how Mrs. Merry came upon the scene.

"She arrived after you had lain long unconscious, saying you had said if you were not home in a month to come and look for you—not hearing, she came and found you, as I have said, and has since nursed you devotedly."

"What does it all mean, doctor?" I then said.

His answer disconcerted me.

"I do not know, though I have heard strange stories told of the pine woods, which you are pleased to call 'Silent,' but I confess I have hitherto put them down to an extra glass or two of beer. Now, for the first time, I am bound to think more seriously of them, having on my hands first, the strange maniac, and then you, found in the same spot, under similar conditions, and—strangest of all—*on the same day* of the year!

"I don't know the tale, but no doubt your worthy host does, ask him, and, meanwhile, develop your snapshots, though I do not hope for much in the way of proofs from them.

"I will look in tomorrow, you had better rest now," and my matter-of-fact materialistic doctor picked up his hat and departed.

I sat at my window for a long time, thinking much, hearing again, in fancy, the roar of wind, the laughter of fiends, the crash of the tree. As it grew dark, I was possessed with the desire, at all costs, to develop those films, so, calling Mrs. Merry, I told her I was tired, and was going to bed, that there was nothing I required, so, bidding her "Good night," I made my rough and ready preparations, lacking all the essentials of a proper dark room, but in these days, tabloids of developers, a jugful of water, a candle-lamp, with a crimson silk scarf tied round it, would serve me very well.

The first negative came up beautifully, just an ordinary common or garden broken-down cottage.

The second was a different story, and I watched it fearfully. There was distinctly, unmistakably, a form of a man going into the doorway!

The third film, taken from the other side of the cottage, showed me a lower window, more or less unbroken, in the frame of which was the face of a man—so much I could see, but to me that meant much, for *I knew* that I was alone, horribly alone at that moment of taking the photo.

Next morning, I was up earlier than had been permitted for some time, and a very few minutes sufficed to print a rough print from each negative. I stared at them, stared, with my eyes nearly starting from my head. They were good photos, clear, sharply defined, no woolly-looking details, so easily mistaken for other than the actual things I intended to take, except the figure, and the face. Those I neither saw, nor intended to portray, yet there they were, and, as is so often the case, the camera lens depicted what the human eye did not see. The figure, tall, gaunt, seemed as if going into the house, but the face! the *face* in the frame of the window was unmistakably the face of the man who passed me, who entered the house, from which issued those screams of agony, the man who later joined the group of people to whom he spoke, the people who made the air hideous with their horrible laughter.

I kept my own counsel, hiding the photos also, until late in the afternoon, the doctor made his appearance. He studied them carefully, and then said:

"I should have laughed at your story, my friend, laughed at your photos of your so-called empty cottage, last evening, but tonight I cannot. I made a few enquiries after I left you, and the outline of what I gleaned was this:

"The cottage was built when the lead mines were working, for the use of the men, and was subsequently taken possession of by a foreman. He was a glum, taciturn brute, given to drink and gambling. He brought with him to the cottage, known as Leadmine Cottage, a very pretty young girl as his wife, though gossips say she was not. He seemed passionately attached to the girl, and also to a little child of three, said to be his niece's child. The man, by name Woodrow, led an almost double life, one half of which was spent with a gang of men and women, with whom he was said to drink and gamble, and who used to jeer at him for what they spoke of as his milksop life, in the company of his so-called wife. When with her, he was simply a devoted husband, and when sober always refused to associate with the gang who other times attracted him. Finally, the gang of criminals—I can call them nothing better—tried to embitter him against the girl, whom they thought was getting a firmer hold on him. One or other of them started to fill his mind with suspicions of the girl, telling him that chance visitors found Leadmine Cottage attractive. They used to follow him home, for the fiendish joke of hearing him abuse the girl and threaten her with worse things if she was untrue to him. These fiends finally plotted, and eventually sent a young doctor out there, saying someone was ill in the cottage. The unsuspecting doctor called late one evening, and Woodrow was persuaded to hide in the trees and watch. It was, I am told, a wild, stormy evening, one of those sudden storms that come in these mountain districts in summer, and break down corn, lash rivers to fury, and hurl trees and branches to the ground.

"Woodrow watched, and saw the doctor enter, saw him speak to the girl, saw her smile at him, and laughing, give him her hand as she might do to a doctor, who desired to feel her pulse; though this was apparently not the construction put upon her innocent action by her husband, goaded to madness by drink, as well as by his uncontrollable jealous nature. He waited until the doctor had gone, and then entered the cottage, murdered his wife and child, afterwards rejoining his fellow-criminals, whom, it is said, received his news with jest and laughter, glorying in the success of the vile plot which they guessed would give him wholly back to them and their evil ways.

"The cottage and all trace of the crime was effaced, so 'tis said, by the sudden rising of the wind, bringing down a tree, which fell athwart the house, shattering it to bits. The gang are believed to have fled the country, all but one, who later died in hospital after giving the story to a medical man there, whom, by a curious coincidence, if indeed there be such things, wrote it to a colleague of mine, whom I met last night at a dinner. It is a strange story, and one, in the light of your recent experience, not to be gainsaid. The story goes on to say, that in the same month every year, the murder takes place, with every detail complete, even to the rising wind; and that those who know the story and the wood, shun it as the plague, during that month. At any other time, I believe, it justifies your name for it of 'Silent Wood.'

"That is the story, my friend, make of it what you will. I have also taken the liberty of asking an aged miner to look in this evening. I want you to be good enough to start chatting casually of the wood, your fall, etc., and show him your photos. Don't give him any other lead. Now, I will see if he has come. He is very old, but can see pretty well. His little grandchild is bringing him to see me here, to save time, and the old boy wants a dose for a cough."

With this, the doctor vanished, to return almost at once, leading an old man by the arm.

They tell me folks live long up here, and surely it must be so if this is a specimen, for the old man looked ninety, and hale at that, though bent and withered. I gave him a chair and baccy, but instead of filling his pipe, he stared at me with clear, penetrating eyes, and mumbled:

"So you're the gent that fell down the mine."

"Yes," I said, "I'm that unfortunate man."

"Did you fall, or were yer put there?" he questioned, sniggering to himself.

"I don't know," I said.

"No, my boy, but I do," he wheezed, pointing a claw-like finger at me. "I do, yer were put there, my lad, put there, look you, and so will others be, if they do not keep away from the pines in July!"

"I took a picture of it," I said, after a pause.

"A picture—whatever—" answered the aged being, "show me the picture. I once worked there."

"Hurry," whispered the doctor, "he quickly fails."

I handed him the picture, holding a powerful magnifying glass over it as I did so.

"Aye, aye! there's Johnny Woodrow's house," he muttered, "all in a heap, all in a heap."

"This is another," I said.

"My God!" burst from his shaking lips. "My God, there's Johnny Woodrow, Johnny Woodrow, my old pal. Why, I thought him was dead, he is dead, I knows he's dead, how could he live after murdering his wife and little child—murdered them, he did, in the cottage by the pines, and them as interferes with the cottage, he'd put 'em down the mine—he said he would put 'em in the mine to starve, if they move a stone or meddle with wot 'e calls her grave. He told me he'd do it afore he went away, 'is very words were 'Living or dead, I'll do it, Bob,' and wot Johnny says he'll do, he *will* do."

His old head fell forward on his breast as he finished speaking, so we did not speak, save in a whisper.

"He sleeps," said the doctor. "Presently he will wake, but will not remember. We will leave him. Mary will take him home, and I'll send him some stuff in the morning. The old boy is nearly through," he added, "but I am glad he was here to give you what you wanted—proof!" though proof of what, or for what reason, I cannot pretend to fathom.

We parted a little later, my doctor and I—he to go on with his work for sick humanity; I, on the morrow, to return to my studio in London, back to the turmoil of town, back to live among the haunts of men, to leave the beauty of hills and rivers; but in some quiet hour in my studio, maybe during some winter night of wind and storm, I shall hear again the hideous laughter, shall dream of the scent of the pines—nay, perhaps I shall even try to forget the horror of all I went through, and may memory, sometimes kind, only recall the peace, the scent, the perfect still quietness of the woods I loved best, when I knew them only as

"SILENT WOOD."

THE NIGHT WIRE

H. F. Arnold

"The Night Wire", first published in *Weird Tales* in 1926, is one of only three stories attributed to "H. F. Arnold", who may have been Illinois-born Henry Ferris Arnold (1902–1963), though this is difficult to ascertain for certain. It is a tempting association to make, however, for if this is the same "Henry Ferris Arnold" mentioned in a 1938 press release (announcing that he has just been acquitted of a charge of battery after spanking his wife), then he was, at that time, a press agent working in Los Angeles. One might surmise, given the setting of this powerfully atmospheric story during the night shift in a West Coast news office, that he had been in a similar line of work for some years.

Technologically speaking, "The Night Wire" is situated at the intersection of two media—the typewriter and the electric telegraph—which had been brought together at the end of the nineteenth century to the great benefit of news agencies. The electric telegraph had been invented more or less simultaneously in the late 1830s by the American Samuel Morse and the Englishmen Charles Wheatstone and William Fothergill Cooke, and its value as a means of consolidating news reports was immediately obvious: in the mid-nineteenth century, regional wire services were created, and by century's end, newspapers relied heavily on a few international telegraph services for their information, giant agencies such as the London-based Reuters, the Associated Press (AP), and the United Press (UP) (which carried the

1938 news of the acquittal of the above-named Henry Ferris Arnold).
"The Night Wire" is full of the lingo of these services ("Flash",
"Bulletin", "New Lead", and so on); the "CP" agency transmitting
the weird report from Xebico seems to be a fictitious, Chicago-based
service, though it could conceivably refer to the real Canadian Press.
Interestingly, Arnold's tale of a preternaturally gifted human operator whose skill makes him seem almost an automaton was written
at the moment when such operators were being replaced by actual
machines—"tele-typewriters" (later, "teletype" machines, originally a
brand name) which cut out the need for any human telegraph operators, or a typist on the receiving end: you just needed someone at the
sending end who could use a typewriter.

A chilling precursor to the malevolent fogs conjured up later
by James Herbert, John Carpenter, and Stephen King, "The Night
Wire" is a minor pulp masterpiece which has achieved something
like cult status (there is even an underground hip-hop group called
"Radio Free Xebico").

"**N**ew York, September 30 CP FLASH

"Ambassador Holliwell died here today. The end came suddenly as the ambassador was alone in his study..."

There's something ungodly about these night wire jobs. You sit up here on the top floor of a skyscraper and listen in to the whispers of a civilisation. New York, London, Calcutta, Bombay, Singapore—they're your next-door neighbours after the street lights go dim and the world has gone to sleep.

Along in the quiet hours between 2 and 4, the receiving operators doze over their sounders and the news comes in. Fires and disasters and suicides. Murders, crowds, catastrophes. Sometimes an earthquake with a casualty list as long as your arm. The night wire man takes it down almost in his sleep, picking it off on his typewriter with one finger.

Once in a long time you prick up your ears and listen. You've heard of someone you knew in Singapore, Halifax or Paris, long ago. Maybe they've been promoted, but more probably they've been murdered or drowned. Perhaps they just decided to quit and took some bizarre way out. Made it interesting enough to get in the news.

But that doesn't happen often. Most of the time you sit and doze and tap, tap on your typewriter and wish you were home in bed.

Sometimes, though, queer things happen. One did the other night and I haven't got over it yet. I wish I could.

You see, I handle the night manager's desk in a western seaport town; what the name is, doesn't matter.

There is, or rather was, only one night operator on my staff, a fellow named John Morgan, about forty years of age, I should say, and a sober, hard-working sort.

He was one of the best operators I ever knew, what is known as a "double" man. That means he could handle two instruments at once and type the stories on different typewriters at the same time. He was one of the three men I ever knew who could do it consistently, hour after hour, and never make a mistake.

Generally, we used only one wire at night, but sometimes, when it was late and the news was coming fast, the Chicago and Denver stations would open a second wire and then Morgan would do his stuff. He was a wizard, a mechanical automatic wizard which functioned marvellously but was without imagination.

On the night of the sixteenth he complained of feeling tired. It was the first and last time I had ever heard him say a word about himself, and I had known him for three years.

It was at just 3 o'clock and we were running only one wire. I was nodding over reports at my desk and not paying much attention to him when he spoke.

"Jim," he said, "does it feel close in here to you?"

"Why, no, John," I answered, "but I'll open a window if you like."

"Never mind," he said, "I reckon I'm just a little tired."

That was all that was said and I went on working. Every ten minutes or so I would walk over and take a pile of copy that had stacked up neatly beside his typewriter as the messages were printed out in triplicate.

It must have been twenty minutes after he spoke that I noticed he had opened up the other wire and was using both typewriters. I thought it was a little unusual, as there was nothing very "hot" coming in. On my next trip I picked up the copy from both machines and took it back to my desk to sort out the duplicates.

The first wire was running out the usual sort of stuff and I just looked over it hurriedly. Then I turned to the second pile of copy. I remember it particularly because the story was from a town I had never heard of: "Xebico." Here is the dispatch. I saved a duplicate of it from our files:

"Xebico Sept. 16 CP BULLETIN

"The heaviest mist in the history of the city settled over the town at 4 o'clock yesterday afternoon. All traffic has stopped and the mist hangs like a pall over everything. Lights of ordinary intensity fail to pierce the fog, which is constantly growing heavier.

"Scientists here are unable to agree as to the cause, and the local weather bureau states that the like has never occurred before in the history of the city.

"At 7 p. m. last night municipal authorities—
(more)"

That was all there was. Nothing out of the ordinary at a bureau headquarters, but, as I say, I noticed the story because of the name of the town.

It must have been fifteen minutes later that I went over for another batch of copy. Morgan was slumped down in his chair and had switched his green electric light shade so that the gleam missed his eyes and hit only the top of the two typewriters.

Only the usual stuff was in the right hand pile, but the left hand batch carried another story from "Xebico". All press dispatches come in "takes," meaning that parts of many different stories are strung along together, perhaps with but a few paragraphs of each coming through at a time. This second story was marked "add fog." Here is the copy:

"At 7 p. m. the fog had increased noticeably. All lights were now invisible and the town was shrouded in pitch darkness.

"As a peculiarity of the phenomenon, the fog is accompanied by a sickly odour, comparable to nothing yet experienced here."

Below that in customary press fashion was the hour, 3:27, and the initials of the operator, JM.

There was only one other story in the pile from the second wire. Here it is:

"2nd add Xebico Fog

"Accounts as to the origin of the mist differ greatly. Among the most unusual is that of the sexton of the local church, who groped his way to headquarters in a hysterical condition and declared that the fog originated in the village churchyard.

"'It was first visible in the shape of a soft grey blanket clinging to the earth above the graves,' he stated. 'Then it began to rise, higher and higher. A subterranean breeze seemed to blow it in billows, which split up and then joined together again.

"'Fog phantoms, writhing in anguish, twisted the mist into queer forms and figures. And then—in the very thick midst of the mass—something moved.

"'I turned and ran from the accursed spot. Behind me I heard screams coming from the houses bordering on the graveyard.'

"Although the sexton's story is generally discredited, a party has left to investigate. Immediately after telling his story, the sexton collapsed and is now in a local hospital, unconscious."

Queer story, wasn't it? Not that we aren't used to it, for a lot of unusual stories come in over the wire. But for some reason or other, perhaps because it was so quiet that night, the report of the fog made a great impression on me.

It was almost with dread that I went over to the waiting piles of copy. Morgan did not move and the only sound in the room was the tap-tap of the sounders. It was ominous, nerve-racking.

There was another story from Xebico in the pile of copy. I seized on it anxiously.

"New Lead Xebico Fog CP

"The rescue party which went out at 11 p. m. to investigate a weird story of the origin of a fog which, since late yesterday, has shrouded the city in darkness, has failed to return. Another and larger party has been dispatched.

"Meanwhile, the fog has, if possible, grown heavier. It seeps through the cracks in the doors and fills the atmosphere with a terribly depressing odour of decay. It is oppressive, terrifying, bearing with it a subtle impression of things long dead.

"Residents of the city have left their homes and gathered in the local church, where the priests are holding services of prayer. The scene is beyond description. Grown folk and children are alike terrified and many are almost beside themselves with fear.

"Mid the wisps of vapour which partially veil the church auditorium, an old priest is praying for the welfare of his flock. The audience alternately wail and cross themselves.

"From the outskirts of the city may be heard cries of unknown voices. They echo through the fog in queer uncadenced minor keys. The sounds resemble nothing so much as wind whistling through a gigantic tunnel. But the night is calm and there is no wind. The second rescue party—(more)"

I am a calm man and never in a dozen years spent with the wires have been known to become excited, but despite myself I rose from my chair and walked to the window.

Could I be mistaken, or far down in the canyons of the city beneath me did I see a faint trace of fog? Pshaw! It was all imagination.

In the pressroom the click of the sounders seemed to have raised the tempo of their tune. Morgan alone had not stirred from his chair. His head sunk between his shoulders, he tapped the dispatches out on the typewriters with one finger of each hand.

He looked asleep. Maybe he was—but no, endlessly, efficiently, the two machines rattled off line after line, as relentless and effortless as death itself. There was something about the monotonous movement of the typewriter keys that fascinated me. I walked over and stood behind his chair reading over his shoulder the type as it came into being, word by word.

Ah, here was another:

"Flash Xebico CP

"There will be no more bulletins from this office. The impossible has happened. No messages have come into this room for twenty minutes. We are cut off from the outside and even the streets below us.

"I will stay with the wire until the end.

"It is the end, indeed. Since 4 p. m. yesterday the fog has hung over the city. Following reports from the sexton of the local church, two rescue parties were sent out to investigate conditions on the outskirts of the city. Neither party has ever returned nor was any word received from them. It is quite certain now that they will never return.

"From my instrument I can gaze down on the city beneath me. From the position of this room on the thirteenth floor, nearly the entire city can be seen. Now I can see only a thick blanket of blackness where customarily are lights and life.

"I fear greatly that the wailing cries heard constantly from the outskirts of the city are the death cries of the inhabitants. They are constantly increasing in volume and are approaching the centre of the city.

"The fog yet hangs over everything. If possible, it is even heavier than before. But the conditions have changed. Instead of an opaque, impenetrable wall of odorous vapour, now swirls and writhes a shapeless mass in contortions of almost human agony. Now and again the mass parts and I catch a brief glimpse of the streets below.

"People are running to and fro, screaming in despair. A vast bedlam of sound flies up to my window, and above all is the immense whistling of unseen and unfelt winds.

"The fog has again swept over the city and the whistling is coming closer and closer.

"It is now directly beneath me.

"God! An instant ago the mist opened and I caught a glimpse of the streets below.

"The fog is not simply vapour—it lives! By the side of each moaning and weeping human is a companion figure, an aura of strange and vari-coloured hues. How the shapes cling! Each to a living thing!

"The men and women are down. Flat on their faces. The fog figures caress them lovingly. They are kneeling beside them. They are—but I dare not tell it.

"The prone and writhing bodies have been stripped of their clothing. They are being consumed—piecemeal.

"A merciful wall of hot, steamy vapour has swept over the whole scene. I can see no more.

"Beneath me the wall of vapour is changing colours. It seems to be lighted by internal fires. No, it isn't. I have made a mistake. The colours are from above, reflections from the sky.

"Look up! Look up! The whole sky is in flames. Colours as yet unseen by man or demon. The flames are moving, they have started to intermix, the colours rearrange themselves. They are so brilliant that my eyes burn, yet they are a long way off.

"Now they have begun to swirl, to circle in and out, twisting in intricate designs and patterns. The lights are racing each with each, a kaleidoscope of unearthly brilliance.

"I have made a discovery. There is nothing harmful in the lights. They radiate force and friendliness, almost cheeriness. But by their very strength, they hurt.

"As I look they are swinging closer and closer, a million miles at each jump. Millions of miles with the speed of light. Aye, it is light, the quintessence of all light. Beneath it the fog melts into a jewelled mist, radiant, rainbow-coloured of a thousand varied spectrums.

"I can see the streets. Why, they are filled with people! The lights are coming closer. They are all around me. I am enveloped. I—"

The message stopped abruptly. The wire to Xebico was dead. Beneath my eyes in the narrow circle of light from under the green lampshade, the black printing no longer spun itself, letter by letter, across the page.

The room seemed filled with a solemn quiet, a silence vaguely impressive. Powerful.

I looked down at Morgan. His hands had dropped nervelessly at his sides while his body had hunched over peculiarly. I turned the lampshade back, throwing the light squarely in his face. His eyes were staring, fixed. Filled with a sudden foreboding, I stepped beside him and called Chicago on the wire. After a second the sounder clicked its answer.

Why? But there was something wrong. Chicago was reporting that Wire Two had not been used throughout the evening.

"Morgan!" I shouted. "Morgan! Wake up, it isn't true. Someone has been hoaxing us. Why—" In my eagerness I grasped him by the shoulder. It was only then that I understood.

The body was quite cold. Morgan had been dead for hours. Could it be that his sensitised brain and automatic fingers had continued to record impressions even after the end?

I shall never know, for I shall never again handle the night shift. Search in a world atlas discloses no town of Xebico. Whatever it was that killed John Morgan will forever remain a mystery.

SURPRISE ITEM

H. Russell Wakefield

Of the British writers producing ghost stories in the twilight of the genre's Golden Age, Herbert Russell Wakefield (1888–1964) was one of the most prolific and consistently excellent. His early collections *They Return at Evening* (1928) and *Old Man's Beard* (1929) invited comparisons to the work of M. R. James at his best; "Surprise Item" is taken from the second of these and, as the reader will immediately see, "Signor Marconi's magic box" has come a long way in the quarter century since Kipling's "'Wireless'" (Wakefield's story is set in 1926). In 1920, with the help of Marconi's Wireless Telegraph Company, a handful of enthusiasts were able to hear the voice of soprano Nellie Melba on their sets—the first public broadcast in Britain. (The BBC, mentioned in Wakefield's story, was formed two years after this, in 1922.)

he Haunted House Club was founded in 1923 by a group of persons who decided it was high time that the venerable controversy concerning the genuine or concocted, the subjective or objective reality (a loose term, as they knew, but sufficiently precise) of those phenomena, loosely comprised within the elastic definition "psychic," was decided. Quite possibly, this group agreed, no categorical decision could be made. At the same time—and with all due respect to the S.P.R.—it would inevitably be of value that a swift and pertinacious inquiry should be always made into the credentials of alleged haunted places. Therefore, when such alleged manifestations were published or came to their knowledge, it was decided that some member of the group should be ordered to the scene to examine the circumstances and report upon them. Then, if the investigator so recommended, the group should make a pilgrimage to the scene, institute such further inquiries as were feasible, and subsequently debate the case at the quarterly reunion.

The following is the report of Mr. Charles Baber into the Pevesham Wireless Case of April 14th, 1926—the sixth of the series:

In accordance with the instructions of the H.H.C., I journeyed down to Pevesham on June 15th. Pevesham is a medium-sized market town with 10,000 inhabitants. I called first on the local retailer of wireless sets and accessories. He informed me, rather diffidently and without enthusiasm, that there had been an unexplained case of "interruption" on April 14th. When more closely questioned, he stated that he himself had not been listening in on that evening, but he understood the trouble had only occurred over a four-mile radius from the Pevesham Town Hall. I should state that this area is served by the Daventry Station. He grudgingly owned that since the date of the "interruption" the demand for his stock and his services had appreciably diminished.

I then called on the editor of the local newspaper, who agreed to put a paragraph in his next issue stating that I was making this inquiry, and should be grateful for any assistance or information in furthering it. In response to this, I received a number of replies, the most important of which came from the local doctor, Mr. Stokes. Apparently, his son, aged sixteen, was in the habit of practising his shorthand by taking down the wireless talks, and he had an important record of what had occurred on April 14th.

I immediately went round to the doctor's house, and his son gave me a long-hand copy of what he had taken down between 9.15 and 9.40 on April 14th. Having absorbed the contents of this, I visited others who had replied to me, and found that they all agreed that something very closely resembling young Stokes's version had come through their ear-phones and loud-speakers on that occasion.

Young Stokes told me that the interruption had come in the middle of a talk on "Prospects for the Settler in Tasmania." It was broken into after about five minutes. He couldn't swear he had taken down every word of this interruption, as he was startled and perplexed, but he was convinced he had got most of it. The voice of the interrupter he judged to be that of an elderly person, "half-educated," he described it, "with the local twang." This person appeared to be in a condition of extreme agitation, though, of course, it might have been feigned. But he didn't think it was. He also said that many listeners in the neighbourhood had written strong protests to the B.B.C. about this most unpleasant and unnerving practical joke, as they supposed it to be. They had all received replies stating that the B.B.C. was quite at a loss to account for the interruption, but that the fullest inquiries would be made.

Here is the long-hand transcription of young Stokes's notes:

"Why is he here? They buried him deep. I'd sooner see him outright than just know he's there. He's been there since supper-time Thursday. He keeps between me and the door and I can't get past him. He stands there always, always facing me. I looked up just then and there he was. I'd sooner see him than just know he was there. I haven't had food or drink since tea-time Thursday, and that's days ago, three maybe. But there's food in the kitchen and a pitcher of water beside the tap in the scullery. Could I slip past him? Shove him aside? I might if his eyes weren't always on me. All on account of that little slut. As if I was the first—twenty-first more likely! What's he want with me? They buried him deep. I saw them lower him down and heard the dirt tap on his box. There's nothing there! I'll look up! Yes, he's there!

"Why couldn't I slip past him? All I've got to do is to walk straight forward and past him, through him, and eat and drink in the kitchen. Easy, isn't it! I'm getting weak; I should have done it in the beginning. I'll think about the window again. It's high but I might manage it. I'll keep my head down and put him off his guard, then run for it—that's what he did before, he's too quick for me. Didn't I drown you, you bastard? Didn't they bury you deep? Didn't they cover you up? That hot little piece! Always hanging round. She got what was coming to her. I wasn't the first, she told me that. Nor second, nor third. If he got that sort, it's his business if she gets into trouble. And then threatening me, asking me what I was going to do about it! Well, I showed him what I was going to do about it—and he swallowed some water. Water! By God, I want water! He's got to let me past.

Why is he here? They buried him deep. I'll see what he does if I get up and go towards him. I've tried that too many times. I know what he does. He always goes round with my eyes. All right, stare at me, you bastard! I drowned you, didn't I? You're down deep, aren't you? I'm getting weak. Water! Water!

"I didn't mean to shout out like that, for I've got to keep a head on me and get past him. Now, I'll think out a way of doing it. Suppose I make a move quickly towards the window, then he'll come over and get between it and me. Then if I dodge back and run for it, he'll be behind me. I might have done it on Thursday likely, but I'm weak and slow now. Now, you dead devil, I'm going for the window! And don't you watch me like that. Do you know what I'm planning? If I could see you plainer, I'd know. Yet you go round with my eyes. Supposing I stare one way and then make a dash the other. No, I've tried that. You're always there! I'll make it right for her if you'll let me past. You're dead! I saw the bubbles come up. I saw you buried deep... Suppose I pretend not to be up to anything and then make a dash for it! Or shall I make a show of going for the window? Then he'll come across and I might slip past him and get behind him—"

Young Stokes said that after this there was a moment's pause and then a muffled crash—and directly after the Wireless Symphony Orchestra came through with the selection from *Tosca*.

Now, I did not disguise from myself that this interruption might have been a hoax perpetrated by someone with a perverted sense of humour and a powerful "sending" set. But the phrasing of this monologue did not seem to me such as a hoaxer would employ. I therefore paid another visit to the local newspaper office and went through its files from the 14th of April till the end of the month.

My attention was caught by a paragraph in the issue of April 17th which stated that a farmer named Amos Willans had been found dead in his parlour the day before. He had been found lying on the floor and had apparently been dead for about three days. So I asked the editor if I could have a few words with the reporter who had "covered" the inquest. He is a lanky, inky, ambitious and thwarted young Scotsman, longing, of course, to get to Fleet Street, and with precious little chance of getting there. His name is Donald Paton. These "small rag" reporters have a disheartening existence, their hopes crushed and their style murdered by having to describe "cold collations," the minutiae of a stagnant local society, and the small, flat beer of a minor country town. Therefore, as Mr. Paton showed himself intelligent, and proved of good service to the Club, I should be pleased if his name could be mentioned in the report of the case we issue to the Press. This report invariably has a wide publicity and it may be the means of translating Donald Paton to that dubious paradise east of Temple Bar of which he dreams.

This is the gist of what he told me:

Old Willans—he was about sixty-four—had been a "character," and a very unpopular one. He had possessed a miserly temperament and an ungovernable temper. He had lived entirely alone, cooking for himself and only allowing a local charwoman to come in once a week to clean the place up. He had, however, sufficiently retained his vital forces to make himself somewhat of a problem to the better-looking young women of the neighbourhood. He was said to have had a certain "way" with him which had occasionally prevented his solicitations from receiving the rebuffs they merited. He seems to have been an original, if highly unpleasant, old person, capable of arousing heightened emotions towards himself—hate, fear, curiosity and a kind of grudging passion in the unwise and wantonly inclined local females.

Paton had obviously studied him with insight and understanding, so that he made the old devil stand starkly out before me as he described him to me. It was known that some time before his death he had been seen in company with the daughter of another farmer. She was a notorious young person, extremely promiscuous in her "love" affairs. She was seen leaving old Willans's farm late one night, and, not long after, suddenly went up to London and no news has been heard of her since. Her father had been found drowned in the River Axe, two miles from his farm. Since he was given to insobriety this caused little surprise.

To sum up, the facts are so vague and any coherent explanation of them would be so empirical and ill-substantiated that I do not think the Club would be justified in visiting the area. At the same time, a discussion of these events might be of interest.

Hoping that I shall be considered to have carried out my inquiry with zeal, if not with intelligence, I beg to subscribe myself,

Your obedient Investigator,

CHARLES BABER

(Number 5).

THE HAUNTED CINEMA

Louis Golding

The Manchester-born Louis Golding (1895–1958) was a poet, novelist, travel writer, and essayist whose strong sense of identity as a British Jew can be seen in such attacks on antisemitism as *A Letter to Adolf Hitler* (1932) and *The Jewish Problem* (1938), as well as the following tale, first published in Golding's 1934 collection *The Doomington Wanderer* ("Doomington" is Golding's stand-in for Manchester, though this tale's setting in an imagined community in Bessarabia points to Golding's family roots in Ukraine).

Cinema is, according to one definition, "a photographic projection of continuous images". Put another way, film as we know it can be thought of as a technological recipe with three main ingredients. One of these, photography, dates from the 1830s, while projected images had been exploited for entertainment and educational purposes for far longer, particularly in magic lantern shows and their shuddersome progeny, the Phantasmagoria. At the same time, Victorian toys such as the Zoetrope used sequenced pictures to generate the illusion of motion; the "chronophotographers" of the 1870s showed that such sequences could be harvested from real life. At the end of the nineteenth century two separate inventions, Thomas Edison's Kinetoscope and the Cinématograph of Auguste and Louis Lumière, put these elements together, and a new medium was born.

Golding's story was written at a time when sound films were rapidly supplanting silent ones in Hollywood (the first feature "talkie" was *The Jazz Singer* in 1927), and Kravest's new, invasively modernising *Grand Cinéma de Paris* seems to be quite *au courant* with the latest trends: we read that "Chaplin and Gable were the heroes of Kravest as they are the heroes of Los Angeles" (Clark Gable had become a major leading man two years previously, in the racy, pre-Code sound film *Red Dust*, while Chaplin's voice would not be heard for two more years, and then only minimally, in *Modern Times*).

HE INCIDENT I am about to relate concerning Kravest and the cinema there, and the Strange Thing that befell that cinema, I should not myself believe had it taken place outside the limits of the province of Bessarabia; had it taken place, in fact, anywhere but in Kravest itself. I should probably not have shaken off my drowsiness to listen to Reb Laibel at all, had not the sainted syllables of Kravest fallen from his lips.

It was the dusk of the Sabbath, when the greybeards gather in the side-room of the synagogue and tell stories of Eastern Europe, punctuating their memories with subtle quotation or complex analogy. And as Reb Laibel wound like a stream from meadow to meadow of his story, you would have thought that the country he had left three or four months ago was somehow immortally enwalled from our modern age. Until, with a pronunciation I dare not transcribe, he spoke of a cinema—spoke of it, moreover, with no less heat than his Hebrew compatriots must have spoken of Torquemada. And then it was that I heard the name of Kravest, Kravest and its sanctities, and I shook myself and listened.

For my father used frequently to speak of Kravest. It was to him a sort of Hesperides, and its golden apples were the Scrolls of the Law. The ear-locks of the old men in Kravest hung down to their jawbones. The wigs of the married women were prompt and lustrous. Little boys could repeat by heart the whole Pentateuch. Babes had insisted upon fasting throughout the Day of Atonement. It was stated—and my father, for one, would not contravert the report—that one year, when the festivities of Simchas Torah were completed, and Rabbi

Avrom, with his flock of revellers, trooped from the synagogue of the "Godly Brethren," he had ordered the moon to perform a circle four times round a certain star, once for each wall of Paradise—and the moon had obeyed him. So the whole company swore, and who dared question it? And such was the holiness of Kravest that even the Gentiles of that town had been touched with the surf of her holy tides. It was not unknown that certain of them had been seen, on the Feast of the Tabernacles, to shake the palm and reverse the citron as the old Jews passed with them on their way to the "Godly Brethren."

Such, then, was Kravest. Had a cinema come this way? O dolorous event! And this was how it came to pass, as I learned it from the lips of Reb Laibel. Reb Avrom—peace be upon him!—had gone to his rest, and though his successor at the "Godly Brethren," Reb Zcharyah, had as much erudition—if that were humanly possible—as he, he had not the same strength of character, the same faculty for prophetic invective against any least transgression of the Law. This it was which had given their chance to the three principal merchants of the town, Reb Yankel, Reb Shtrom, and Reb Ruven. There was no doubt that they had long been working subterraneously to get the synagogue into their own hands, but they had never dared to emerge into the awful light of Reb Avrom's eyes. One flicker of that inspired eyelid and you saw them scuttle into their burrows with a shaking of timid abdomen and a flash of white tail. But the combination of the weak amiability of Reb Zcharyah with a certain deal in roubles which was little to their credit and much to their profit gave them their opportunity. A bribed and hectored majority elected them to the three positions of office, and Reb Shtrom became the *parnass*, Reb Yankel and Reb Ruven the *gabboim*, of the synagogue.

Before very long rumours were abroad in Kravest that the new officers were convinced that the "Godly Brethren" was far too big and expensive a building for its purpose. It was stated that the upkeep of the establishment was robbing the children and widows. It was too near the centre of the town not to suffer a gentile corruption. It could not be doubted that the barn-like building near the river, on the outskirts of the town, would be more satisfactory as a synagogue from every point of view.

There is no time to enter into the historic battle that raged in Kravest. With a sinking of the heart I narrate only that the "Godly Brethren" removed to the river-side, and the old building itself was sold to an anonymous syndicate who converted it (if I am interpreting Reb Laibel's curious accent aright) into the "Grand Cinéma de Paris." The "Godly Brethren" became a shadow of itself; for, whilst Reb Zcharyah, with pale and haunted eyes, entrenched himself deeper and deeper into the fortresses of his intricate and unworldly scholarship, its three officers paid less and less attention to its physical organisation. Some of the most valued and venerable old men had not the energy to drag themselves there three times a day. Some of the young men set out for the "Godly Brethren," but were entrapped by the cinema *en route*. Ichabod! The glory was departed! And the material state of Reb Shtrom, Reb Yankel, and Reb Ruven, for no explicit reason, became more and more prosperous. They were not seen to be particularly industrious on the money-changing market. Reb Yankel gave up his flour-mill entirely. All three spent their mornings together drinking *Schnaps* and playing cards. Yet their fortunes seemed to expand as under a personal and private sun.

And then God intervened. So said Reb Laibel, drawing his fingers through the thickets of his long yellow beard. And so the others repeated as the miracle was unfolded in the thickening dusk. It must be understood that no special provision of films was made for the cinema at Kravest. Chaplin and Gable were the heroes of Kravest as they are the heroes of Los Angeles. A month or six weeks passed in which the transports of the degenerating Jewry of Kravest knew no intermission. Gallop and gallop went the horses over the prairies! Crackle and crash went the crockery in the ineffably comic restaurants! And then a calamitous film was displayed. The scene was a very expensive hotel in New York. The viands were of the most wealthy and the most profane order. But when none other than Reb Ruven was seen to be helping himself to a liberal share of milk-pudding after several courses of meats—damnable and most damnable juxtaposition!—conceive the state of mind of the audience at Kravest! There was no room for doubt. The familiar twisted nose of Reb Ruven, the scar below the lower lip, came nearer and nearer to the camera. A howl of execration was heard. But not so formidable as the howl which rent the roof of the cinema two weeks later, when Reb Yankel, in the costume of an English labourer, his corduroy trousers tied with string below the knees and stuffed into a monstrous pair of boots, was seen to be feeding a large sow in her sty and fondling one after another of her litter of sucklings. Walking-sticks hurtled through the air, seats groaned and split. In vain did Reb Yankel plead an alibi. In vain he urged that he never had set foot an inch beyond Kravest, as all the world knew. It was the hand of God, said Kravest, the hand of God!

The climax came a week later. The film displayed a scene which may well have been Hampstead Heath. Three pairs of figures, male and female, appeared on the horizon. Closer and closer they came— Reb Shtrom and Reb Yankel and Reb Ruven—and closer the Gentile hussies on their arms. (The crowd was roaring like a sea.) Then the three couples sat under the shade of a chestnut; then their lips...

But there was a sudden shrill cry, a hissing and whirring, and, at the moment that the cinematograph was flung to the ground, with a great rip the screen was torn from the beams. For the Above One, said Reb Laibel, who shall understand His ways?

And the "Godly Brethren" returned to their temple, after a solemn purification, and piety came back to Kravest, and as for Reb Shtrom, Reb Ruven, and Reb Yankel, may the Black Wind, said Reb Laibel, uproot their hair in tufts!

THEY FOUND MY GRAVE

Marjorie Bowen

Gabrielle Margaret Vere Campbell (1885–1952) wrote under many names, but she is known to posterity as "Marjorie Bowen", author of a great many novels (her first, the superb historical novel *The Viper of Milan*, inspired a young Graham Greene to pursue a literary career) and superlative ghost stories, the most anthologised being probably "The Crown Derby Plate" and "The Avenging of Ann Leete". "They Found My Grave" appeared under another of her pseudonyms, "Joseph Shearing", in the 1938 collection *Orange Blossoms*. The "old-fashioned gramophone" in this story is indeed a "Gramophone" proper (despite the term having come by this time to be used generically in Britain for any phonograph), in that it plays disc records… when, that is, it is not serving as an uncanny conduit to the world of the dead.

A note following the story in *Orange Blossoms* reads "with acknowledgements to Paul Joire's *Psychical and Supernormal Phenomena*. London 1916", which was a volume covering a range of experiments and observations on supernormal events. The episode which inspired this story is found in the chapter on "Typtology and Lucidity", terms which are referenced in Bowen's narrative.

da Trimble was bored with the sittings. She had been persuaded to attend against her better judgment, and the large dingy Bloomsbury house depressed and disgusted her; the atmosphere did not seem to her in the least spiritual and was always tainted with the smell of stale frying.

The medium named herself Astra Destiny. She was a big, loose woman with a massive face expressing power and cunning. Her garments were made of upholstery material and round her cropped yellowish curls she wore a tinsel belt. Her fat feet bulged through the straps of cheap gilt shoes.

She had written a large number of books on subjects she termed "esoteric" and talked more nonsense in half an hour than Ada Trimble had heard in a lifetime. Yet madame gave an impression of shrewd sense and considerable experience; a formidable and implacable spirit looked through her small grey eyes and defied anyone to pierce the cloud of humbug in which she chose to wrap herself.

"I think she is detestable," said Ada Trimble; but Helen Trent, the woman who had introduced her to the big Bloomsbury Temple insisted that, odious as the setting was, odd things did happen at the sittings.

"It sounds like hens," said Miss Trimble, "but *séances* are worse."

"Well, it is easy to make jokes. And I know it is pretty repulsive. But there are *unexplained* things. They puzzle me. I should like your opinion on them."

"I haven't seen anything yet I can't explain, the woman is a charlatan, making money out of fools. She suspects us and might get unpleasant, I think."

But Helen Trent insisted: "Well, if you'd been going as often as I have, and noticing carefully, like I've been noticing…"

"Helen—why *have* you been interested in this nonsense?"

The younger woman answered seriously: "Because I *do* think there is something in it."

Ada Trimble respected her friend's judgment; they were both intelligent, middle-aged, cheerful and independent in the sense that they had unearned incomes. Miss Trimble enjoyed every moment of her life and therefore grudged those spent in going from her Knightsbridge flat to the grubby Bloomsbury Temple. Not even Helen's persistency could induce Ada to continue the private sittings that wasted money as well as time. Besides, Miss Trimble really disliked being shut up in the stuffy, ugly room while Madame Destiny sat in a trance and the control, a Red Indian called Purple Stream babbled in her voice and in pidgin English about the New Atlantis, the brotherhood of man and a few catchphrases that could have been taken from any cheap handbook on philosophy or the religions of the world.

But Helen persuaded her to join in some experiments in what were termed typtology and lucidity that were being conducted by Madame Destiny and a circle of choice friends. These experiments proved to be what Ada Trimble had called in her youth "table turning." Five people were present, besides Ada and Madame Destiny. The table moved, gave raps and conversations with various spirits followed. A code was used, the raps corresponding in number to the letters of the alphabet, one for "a" and so on to twenty-six for "z." The method was tedious and nothing, Miss Trimble thought, could have been more dull. All manner of unlikely spirits appeared, a Fleming of the twelfth century, a President of a South American Republic, late nineteenth century, an Englishman who had been clerk to residency at Tonkin, and who had been killed by a tiger a few years before, a young schoolmaster who had thrown himself in front of a train in Devonshire, a murderer who announced in classic phrase that he had "perished on the scaffold," a factory hand who had died of drink in Manchester, and a retired schoolmistress recently "passed over."

The spirit of a postman and that of a young girl "badly brought up, who had learnt to swear," said the medium, also spoke through the rap code. These people gave short accounts of themselves and of their deaths and some vague generalisations about their present state. "I am happy." "I am unhappy." "It is wonderful here." "God does not die." "I remain a Christian." "When I first died it was as if I was stunned. Now I am used to it—" and so on.

They were never asked about the future, who would win the Derby, the results of the next election or anything of that kind. "It wouldn't be fair," smiled Madame Destiny. "Besides, they probably don't know."

The more important spirits were quickly identified by references to the National Dictionary of Biography for the English celebrities and Larousse for the foreign. The Temple provided potted editions of each work. These reliable tomes confirmed all that the spirits said as to their careers and ends. The obscure spirits if they gave dates and place names were traced by enquiries of Town Clerks and Registrars. This method always worked out, too.

Madame Destiny sometimes showed the letters that proved that the spirits had once had, as she hideously quoted "a local habitation and a name."

"I can't think why you are interested," said Ada Trimble to Helen Trent as they drove home together. "It is such an easy fraud. Clever, of course, but she has only to keep all the stuff in her head."

"You mean that she looks up the references first?"

"Of course." Ada Trimble was a little surprised that Helen should ask so simple a question. "And those postmen and servant girls could be got up, too, quite easily."

"It would be expensive. And she doesn't charge much."

"She makes a living out of it," said Ada Trimble sharply. "Between the lectures, the healings, the services, the sittings, the lending library and those ninepenny teas, I think the Temple of Eastern Psycho-Physiological Studies does pretty well…" She looked quickly at her companion and in a changed voice asked: "You're not getting—drawn in—are you, Helen?"

"Oh no! At least I don't think so, but last year, when you were in France, I was rather impressed—it was the direct voice. I wish it would happen again, I should like your opinion—" Helen Trent's voice faltered and stopped; it was a cold night, she drew her collar and scarf up more closely round her delicate face. The smart comfortable little car was passing over the bridge. The two women looked out at the street and ink-blue pattern of the Serpentine, the bare trees on the banks, the piled buildings beyond, stuck with vermilion and orange lights. The November wind struck icy across Ada Trimble's face.

"I don't know why I forgot the window," she said, rapidly closing it. "I suggest that we leave Madame Destiny alone, Helen. I don't believe that sort of thing is any good, it might easily get on one's nerves."

"Well," said Helen irrelevantly, "what are dreams, anyway?"

Ada remembered how little she knew of the early life of her cultured, elegant friend and how much she had forgotten of her own youthful experiences that had once seemed so warm, so important, so terrible.

"Come next Tuesday, at least," pleaded Helen as she left the car for the wet pavement. "She has promised the direct voice."

"I ought to go, because of Helen," thought Ada Trimble. "She is beginning to be affected by this nonsense. Those rogues know that she has money."

So on the Tuesday the two charming women in their rich, quiet clothes, with their tasteful veils, handbags, furs and posies of violets and gardenias were seated in the upper room in the Bloomsbury Temple with the queer shoddy folk who made up Madame Destiny's audience.

Ada Trimble settled into her chair; it was comfortable like all the chairs in the Temple and she amused herself by looking round the room. The Victorian wallpaper had been covered by dark serge, clumsily pinned up; dusty crimson chenille curtains concealed the tall windows. Worn linoleum was on the floor, the table stood in the centre of the room and on it was a small, old-fashioned gramophone with a horn. By it was a small red lamp; this, and the light from the cheerful gas fire, was the only illumination in the room.

A joss stick smouldered in a brass vase on the mantelpiece but this sickly perfume could not disguise the eternal smell of stew and onions that hung about the Temple.

'I suppose they live on a permanent hot-pot,' thought Ada Trimble vaguely as she looked round on the gathered company.

The medium lay sprawled in the largest chair; she appeared to be already in a trance; her head was sunk on her broad breast and her snorting breath disturbed the feather edging on her brocade robe. The cheap belt round her head, the cheap gilt shoes, exasperated Ada Trimble once more. "For a woman of *sense*—" she thought.

Near the medium was a husband, who called himself Lemoine. He was a turnip-coloured nondescript man, wearing a dirty collar and slippers; his manner hesitated between the shamefaced and the insolent. He was not very often seen, but Ada sometimes suspected him of being the leader of the whole concern.

She speculated with a shudder, and not for the first time, on the private lives of this repulsive couple. What were they like when they were alone together? What did they say when they dropped the gibberish and the posing? Were they ever quite sincere or quite clean? She had heard they lived in a "flat" at the top of the house and had turned a bleak Victorian bathroom into a kitchen and that they had "difficulties with servants."

Beside Mr. Lemoine was Essie Clark, a stringy, cheerful woman who was Madame Destiny's secretary, and as Ada Trimble supposed, maid-of-all-work, too. She had been "caught" sweeping the stairs and Ada thought that she mixed the permanent stew.

Essie's taste had stopped, dead as a smashed clock, in childhood and she wore straight gowns of faded green that fifty years before had been termed "artistic" by frustrated suburban spinsters, and bunches of little toys and posies made of nuts and leather.

The circle was completed by the people well known to Ada: a common overdressed little woman who called spiritualism her "hobby" and who was on intimate terms with the spirit of her late husband, and a damp, depressed man, Mr. Maple, who had very little to say for himself beyond an occasional admission that he was "investigating and couldn't be sure."

The little woman, Mrs. Penfleet, said cheerfully: "I am certain dear Arthur will come today. I dreamt of him last night," and she eyed the trumpet coyly.

"We don't know who will come, *if* anyone," objected Mr. Maple gloomily. "We've got to keep open minds."

Mr. Lemoine begged for silence and Miss Clark put on a disc that played "Rock of Ages."

Ada Trimble's mind flashed to the consumptive Calvinist who had written that hymn; she felt slightly sick and glanced at Helen, dreamy, elegant, sunk in her black velvet collar.

Ada looked at the trumpet, at the medium, and whispered "Ventriloquism" as she bent to drop and pick up her handkerchief, but Helen whispered back: "*Wait.*"

Essie Clark took off the record and returned to her chair with a smile of pleased expectancy. It was all in the day's work for her, like cheapening the food off the barrows in the Portobello Road. Ada Trimble kept her glance from the fire and the lamp, lest, comfortable and drowsy as she was, she should be hypnotised with delusions— "Though I don't think it likely here," she said to herself, "in these sordid surroundings."

There was a pause; the obviously dramatic prelude to the drama. Madame Destiny appeared to be unconscious. Ada thought: "There ought to be a doctor here to make sure." A humming sound came from the painted horn that had curled-back petals like a metallic flower. "Arthur!" came from Mrs. Penfleet and "Hush!" from Mr. Maple. Ada felt dull, a party to a cheap, ignoble fraud. "How dare they!" she thought indignantly, "fool with such things—supposing one of the dead *did* return." The gramophone was making incoherent noises, hummings and sighings.

"The psychic force is manifest," whispered Mr. Lemoine reverently in familiar phrase.

There was another pause; Ada Trimble's attention wandered to obtrusive details, the pattern of the braid encircling Madame Destiny's bent head, a dull yellow in the lamp's red glow, and the firmness with which her podgy fingers gripped the pad and pencil, even though she was supposed to be in a state of trance.

Suddenly a deep masculine voice said:

"*Beatus qui intelligit super egenum et pauperem.*"

Ada was utterly startled; she felt as if another personality was in the room, she sat forward and looked around; she felt Helen's cold

263

fingers clutch hers; she had not more than half understood the Latin; nor, it seemed, had anyone else. Only Mr. Lemoine remained cool, almost indifferent. Leaning forward he addressed the gramophone:

"That is a proverb or quotation?"

The deep voice replied:

"It is my epitaph."

"It is, perhaps, on your tomb?" asked Mr. Lemoine gently.

"Yes."

"Where is your tomb?"

"I do not choose to disclose." The voice was speaking with a marked accent. It now added in French: "Is there no one here that speaks my language?"

"Yes," said Ada Trimble, almost without her own volition. French was very familiar to her and she could not disregard the direct appeal.

"*Eh, bien!*" the voice which had always an arrogant, scornful tone, seemed gratified and ran on at once in French. "I have a very fine tomb—a monument, I should say, shaded with chestnut trees. Every year, on my anniversary, it is covered with wreaths."

"Who are you?" asked Ada Trimble faintly, but Mr. Lemoine gently interposed:

"As the other members of our circle don't speak French," he told the gramophone, "will you talk in English?"

"Any language is easy to me," boasted the voice in English, "but I prefer my own tongue."

"Thank you," said Mr. Lemoine. "The lady asked you who you were—will you tell us?"

"Gabriel Letourneau."

"Would you translate your epitaph?"

"Blessed is he who understands the poor and has pity on the unfortunate."

"What were you?"

"Many things."

"When did you die?"

"A hundred years ago. May 12th, 1837."

"Will you tell us something more about yourself?"

The voice was harsh and scornful.

"It would take a long time to relate my exploits. I was a professor, a peer, a philosopher, a man of action. I have left my many works behind me."

"Please give the titles." Mr. Lemoine, who had always been so effaced and who looked so incompetent was proving himself cool and skilful at this question and answer with the voice.

"There are too many."

"You had pupils?"

"Many famous men."

"Will you give the names?"

"You continually ask me to break your rules," scolded the voice.

"What rules?"

"The rules spirits have to obey."

"You are a Christian?"

"I have never been ashamed to call myself so."

"Where—in the Gospels—is the rule of which you speak?" asked Mr. Lemoine sharply. "There are special rules for spirits?"

"Yes."

So the dialogue went on, more or less on orthodox lines, but Ada Trimble was held and fascinated by the quality and accent of the voice. It was rough, harsh, intensely masculine, with a definite foreign accent. The tone was boastful and arrogant to an insufferable extent. Ada Trimble detested this pompous, insistent personality; she felt odd, a little dazed, a little confused; the orange glow of the gas fire, the red glow of the lamp, the metallic gleams on the horn fused into a fiery pattern before her eyes. She felt as if she were being drawn into a void in which nothing existed but the voice.

Even Mr. Lemoine's thin tones, faintly questioning, seemed a long way off, a thread of sound compared to the deep boom of the voice. The conversation was like a ball being deftly thrown to and fro. Mr. Lemoine asked: "What do you understand by faith?" And the voice, steadily rising to a roar, replied: "The Faith as taught by the Gospel."

"Does not the Gospel contain moral precepts rather than dogma?"

"Why that remark?"

"Because narrow or puerile practices have been built on this basis."

"A clear conscience sees further than practices."

"I see that you are a believer," said Mr. Lemoine placidly. "What is your present situation?"

"Explain!" shouted the voice.

"Are you in Heaven, Hell or purgatory?" rapped out Mr. Lemoine.

"I am in Heaven!"

"How is it that you are in Heaven and here at the same time?"

"You are a fool," said the voice stridently. "Visit my grave and you will understand more about me."

"Once more, where is your grave?"

The horn gave a groan of derision and was silent; Mr. Lemoine repeated his question, there was no answer; he then wiped his forehead and turned to his wife who was heaving back to consciousness.

"That is all for today," he smiled round the little circle; no one save Ada and Helen seemed affected by the experience; Mr. Maple made some gloomy sceptical remarks; Mrs. Penfleet complained because Arthur had not spoken and Essie Clark indifferently and efficiently put away the gramophone and the records.

When the red lamp was extinguished and the light switched on, Ada looked at Madame Destiny who was rubbing her eyes and smiling with an exasperating shrewd blandness.

"It was Gabriel Letourneau," her husband told her mildly. "You remember I told you he came some months ago?" He glanced at Ada. "The medium never knows what spirit speaks."

Ada glanced at Helen who sat quiet and downcast, then mechanically gathered up her gloves and handbag.

"Did you find this person in Larousse?" she asked.

"No. We tried other sources too, but never could discover anything. Very likely he is a liar, quite a number of them are, you know. I always ask him the same questions, but as you heard, there is no satisfaction to be got."

"He always boasts so," complained Mr. Maple, "and particularly about his grave."

"Oh," smiled Mr. Lemoine rising to indicate that the sitting was at an end. "He is a common type, a snob. When he was alive he boasted about his distinctions, visits to court and so on; now he is dead he boasts of having seen God, being in Heaven and the marvels of his grave."

When they were out in the wind-swept evening Helen clasped Ada's arm.

"Now, what do you make of *that*? Ventriloquism? It is a personality."

"It is odd, certainly. I was watching the woman. Her lips didn't move—save just for snorting or groaning now and then."

"Oh, I dare say it *could* be done," said Helen impatiently. "But I don't think it is a trick. I can't feel that it is. Can you? That is what I wanted you to hear. There have been other queer things, but this is the queerest. What do *you* think?"

"Oh, Helen, dear, I don't know!" Ada was slightly trembling. "I never thought that I could be moved by anything like this."

"That is it, isn't it?" interrupted Helen, clinging to her as they passed along the cold street. "*Moved*—and what by?"

"Intense dislike—the man is loathsome!"

"There! You said *man*. It was a voice only!"

"Oh, Helen!"

They walked in silence to the waiting car and when inside began to talk again in low tones, pressed together. No, there was no explanation possible, any attempt at one landed you in a bog of difficulties.

"He spoke to me," sighed Ada Trimble, "and, you know I quite forgot that he wasn't *there*—I wish that I could have gone on talking to him, I feel that I should have been sufficiently insistent—"

"To—what, Ada?"

"To make him say something definite about himself—"

"It's crazy, Ada! It lets loose all kinds of dreadful thoughts. He might be here now, riding with us."

"Well, he can't talk without the trumpet." Then both women laughed uneasily.

"My dear, we are getting foolish!" said Helen, and Ada answered: "Yes. Foolish either way—to talk of it all if we think it was a fraud—and not to be more serious if we don't think it a fraud."

But as people usually will when in this kind of dilemma, they compromised; they discussed the thing and decided to put it to the test once again.

They became frequent visitors to the Bloomsbury Temple and began to pay to have private sittings with the direct voice.

Busy as they were, Madame Destiny and Mr. Lemoine "fitted in" a good number of these and the harsh voice that called itself Gabriel Letourneau usually spoke, though there were annoying occasions when Persian sages, Polish revolutionaries and feeble-minded girls of unknown nationality, insisted on expounding colourless views.

By the spring the personality of Gabriel Letourneau was complete to Ada and Helen. They had been able to build him up, partly from details he had supplied himself and partly out of their own uneasy imaginations. He had been—or was now, but they dare not speculate upon his present shape—a tall, dark, gaunt Frenchman, with side whiskers and a blue chin, the kind of brown eyes known as "piercing" and a fanatical, grim expression.

Ada had often spoken to him in French but she could never penetrate his identity. A professor, a peer in the reign of Louis Philippe? It was impossible for her to attempt to trace so elusive a person. At first she did not try; she told herself that she had other things to do and she tried to keep the thing out of her mind, or at least to keep it reduced to proper proportions. But this soon proved impossible and sensible, charming, broad-minded Ada Trimble at length found herself in the grip of an obsession.

The voice and her hatred of the voice. It was useless for her to tell herself, as she frequently did, that the voice was only that of the woman who called herself Astra Destiny and not a personality at all. This was hopeless, she *believed* in Gabriel Letourneau. He had, she was sure, a bad effect on her character and on that of Helen. But opposite effects. Whereas Helen became limp, distracted, nervous and talked vaguely of being "Haunted," Ada felt as if active evil was clouding her soul.

Why should she hate the voice? She had always been afraid of hatred. She knew that the person who hates, not the person who is hated, is the one who is destroyed. When she disliked a person or a thing she had always avoided it, making exceptions only in the cases of cruelty and fanaticism. There she had allowed hate to impel her to exertions foreign to her reserved nature. And now there was hatred of Gabriel Letourneau possessing her like a poison. He hated her, too. When she spoke to him he told her in his rapid French that

Helen could not follow, his scornful opinion of her; he called her an "ageing woman"; he said she was pretentious, facile, a silly little atheist while "I am in Heaven."

He made acid comments on her carefully chosen clothes, on her charmingly arranged hair, her little armoury of wit and culture, on her delicate illusions and vague, romantic hopes. She felt stripped and defaced after one of these dialogues in which she could not hold her own. Sometimes she tried to shake herself out of "this nonsense." She would look sharply at the entranced medium; Ada had never made the mistake of undervaluing the intelligence of Astra Destiny and surely the conversation of Gabriel Letourneau was flavoured with feminine malice?

Out in the street with Helen she would say: "We really *are* fools! It is only an out-of-date gramophone."

"Is it?" asked Helen bleakly. "And ventriloquism?" Then she added: "Where does she—that awful woman—get that fluent French?"

"Oh, when you begin asking questions!" cried Ada.

She examined the subject from all angles, she went to people who, she thought, "ought to know," but she could get no satisfaction; it was a matter on which the wisest said the least.

"If only he wouldn't keep boasting!" she complained to Helen. "His grave—that now—he says it is a marvellous monument and that people keep putting wreaths on it, that they make pilgrimages to it—and Helen, why should I *mind*? I ought to be pleased that he has that satisfaction or—at least, be indifferent—but I'm not."

"He's been hateful to you, to us," said Helen simply. "I loathe him, too—let us try to get away from him."

"I can't."

Helen went; she drifted out of Ada's life with a shivering reluctance to leave her, but with a definite inability to face the situation created by Gabriel Letourneau. She wrote from Cairo and presently did not write at all. Ada, left alone with her obsession, no longer struggled against it; she pitted herself deliberately against the voice. Sometimes, as she came and went in the Bloomsbury Temple, she would catch a glint in the dull eyes of Mr. Lemoine or the flinty eyes of Madame Destiny that made her reflect how many guineas she had paid them. But even these flashes of conviction that she was being the worst type of fool did not save her; she had reached the point when she had to give rein to her fortune.

In September she went to France; countless friends helped her to search archives; there was no member of the Chamber of Peers under Louis Philippe named Letourneau. She wrote to the keepers of the famous cemeteries, she visited these repulsive places herself; there were Letourneaus, not a few, but none with prename Gabriel, or with the inscription quoted by the voice. Nor was there anywhere an imposing monument, covered with wreaths and visited by pilgrims, to a professor peer who had died in 1837.

"Fraud," she kept telling herself, "that wretched couple just practised a very clever fraud on me. But why? What an odd personality for people like that to invent! And the deep masculine voice and the idiomatic French—*clever* is hardly the word. I suppose they got the data from Larousse." The courteous friends helped her to make enquiries at the Sorbonne. No professors of that name there, or at any of the other big universities.

Ada Trimble believed that she was relieved from her burden of credulity and hate; perhaps if she kept away from the Bloomsbury Temple the thing would pass out of her mind. She was in this mood when she received an answer to a letter she had written to the keeper of the cemetery at Sceaux. She had written to so many officials and it had been so long since she had written to Sceaux and she had such little expectation of any result from her enquiries that she scarcely took much interest in opening the letter.

It read thus:

> *Madame, In reply to your letter of November 30th, I have the honour to inform you that I have made a search for the Letourneau tomb which fortunately I found and I have copied the epitaph cut on the tomb.*

> *Gabriel Letourneau*
> *Man of Letters*
> *Died at Sceaux June 10th 1858.*
> *Beatus qui intelligit*
> *Super egenum et pauperem.*

> *This neglected grave was in a miserable condition covered by weeds; in order to send you the above information it was necessary to undertake cleaning that occupied an hour, and this merely on the portion that bears the inscription. According to the registry this Letourneau was a poor tutor; his eccentric habits are still remembered in the quarter where he lived. He has become a legend—and "he boasts like a Gabriel Letourneau," is often said of a braggart. He has left no descendants and no one has visited his grave. He left a small sum of money to pay for the epitaph.*

> *(signed) Robert, Keeper of the Cemetery*
> *at Sceaux. 231 Rue Louis le Grand,*
> *Sceaux (Seine).*

Ada Trimble went at once to Sceaux. She arrived there on a day of chill, small rain, similar to that on which she had first heard the voice in the Bloomsbury Temple. There was a large, black cemetery, a row of bare chestnut-trees overlooking the walls, an ornate gate. The conscientious keeper, M. Robert, conducted her to the abandoned grave in the corner of the large graveyard; the rotting, dank rubbish of last year's weeds had been cut away above the inscription that Ada had first heard in the Bloomsbury Temple a year ago.

She gazed and went away, full of strange terror, What was the solution of the miserable problem? There were many ways in which the Lemoine couple might have chanced to hear of the poor tutor of Sceaux, but how had they come to know of the epitaph for years concealed behind ivy, bramble and moss? M. Robert, who was so evidently honest, declared that he never remembered anyone making enquiries about the Letourneau grave and he had been years in this post. He doubted, he said, whether even the people to whom the name of the eccentric was a proverb knew of the existence of his grave. Then, the shuffling of the dates, 1858 instead of 1837, the lies about the state of the grave and the position that Letourneau had held while in life.

Ada had a sickly qualm when she reflected how this fitted in with the character she had been given of a slightly unhinged braggart with egomania. A peerage, the Sorbonne, the monument—all lies?

Ada returned to England and asked Madame Destiny to arrange another sitting for her with the direct voice. She also asked for as large a circle as possible to be invited, all the people who had ever heard Gabriel Letourneau.

"Oh, that will be a large number," said Madame Destiny quickly, "he is one of the spirits who visits us most frequently."

"Never mind, the large room, please, and I will pay all expenses. I think I have found out something about that gentleman."

"How interesting," said Madame Destiny, with civil blankness.

"Can she possibly know where I have been?" thought Ada Trimble, but it seemed absurd to suppose that this hard-up couple, existing by shifts, should have the means to employ spies and detectives. The meeting was arranged and as all the seats were free, the room was full.

The gramophone was on a raised platform; it was placed on a table beside which sat Madame Destiny to the right and her husband to the left. The red lamp was in place. A dark curtain, badly pinned up, formed the back cloth. Save for the gas fire, the room—a large Victorian *salon*—was in darkness. Ada Trimble sat on one of the Bentwood chairs in the front row. "He won't come," she thought. "I shall never hear the voice again. And the whole absurdity will be over."

But the medium was no sooner twitching in a trance than the voice came rushing from the tin horn. It spoke directly to Ada Trimble and she felt her heart heave with horror as she heard the cringing tone.

"Good evening, madame, and how charming you are tonight! Your travels have improved you—you recall my little jokes, my quips? Only to test your wit, dear lady, I have always admired you so much—"

Ada could not reply, the one thought beat in her mind, half paralysing her, "He knows what I found out—he is trying to flatter me so that I don't give him away."

The voice's opening remarks had been in French and for this Mr. Lemoine called him to order; the usual verbal duel followed, Lemoine pressing the spirit to give proof of his identity, the spirit arrogantly defending his secrets. The audience that had heard this parrying between Lemoine and Letourneau before so often was not interested and Ada Trimble did not hear anything, she was fiercely concerned with her own terror and bewilderment. Then the voice, impatiently breaking off the bitter sparring, addressed her directly in oily, flattering accents.

"What a pleasure that we meet again, how charming to see you here! The time has been very long since I saw you last."

Ada roused herself; she began to speak in a thick voice that she could scarcely have recognised as her own.

"Yes, one is drawn to what one dislikes as surely as towards what one hates. I have been too much concerned with you, I hope now that I shall be free."

"Miss Trimble," protested Mr. Lemoine, "there are others present, pray speak in English. I think you said that you had been able to identify this spirit quite precisely."

In French the gramophone harshly whispered: "Take care."

"Well," said Mr. Lemoine briskly, "this lady says she found your grave, what have you to say to that?"

"I beg the lady not to talk of my private affairs"; voice and accent were alike thick, with agitation, perhaps despair.

"But you have often spoken of your tomb, the wreaths, the pilgrimages, you have talked of your peerage, your professorship, your pupils. As you would never give us corroborative details, this lady took the trouble to find them out."

"Let her give them," said the voice, "when we are alone—she and I."

"What would be the sense of that?" demanded Mr. Lemoine. "All these people know you well, they are interested—now Miss Trimble."

"I found the grave in Sceaux cemetery," began Ada. The voice interrupted her furiously: "You are doing a very foolish thing!"

"I see," said Mr. Lemoine coolly, "you are still an earthbound spirit. You are afraid that something hurtful to your vanity is about to be revealed..."

"You should be free from this material delusion. We," added the turnip-faced man pompously, "are neither noble nor learned. We shall not think the less of you if it is true you have boasted."

"I am not a boaster!" stormed the voice.

"Your grave is in the cemetery at Sceaux," said Ada Trimble rapidly. "You died in 1857, not 1837; you were neither peer nor professor—no one visits your grave. It is miserable, neglected, covered with weeds. It took the keeper an hour's work even to cut away the rubbish sufficiently to see your epitaph."

"Now we know that," said Mr. Lemoine smoothly, "we can help you to shake off these earthly chains."

"These are lies." The voice rose to a hum like the sound of a spinning top. "Lies—"

"No," cried Ada. "You have lied, you have never seen God, either."

"You may," suggested Mr. Lemoine, "have seen a fluid personage in a bright illumination, but how could you have been sure it was God?"

The humming sound grew louder, then the horn flew over, as if wrenched off and toppled on to the table, then on to the floor. Mr. Lemoine crossed the platform and switched on the light.

"An evil spirit," he said in his routine voice, "now that he has been exposed I don't suppose that he will trouble us again." And he congratulated Ada on her shrewd and careful investigations, though the stare he gave her through his glasses seemed to express a mild wonder as to why she had taken so much trouble. The meeting broke up; there was coffee for a few chosen guests upstairs in the room lined with books on the "occult"; no one seemed impressed by the meeting; they talked of other things, only Ada Trimble was profoundly moved.

This was the first time she had come to these banal coffee-drinkings. Hardly knowing what she did she had come upstairs with these queer, self-possessed people who seemed to own something she had not got. They were neither obsessed nor afraid. Was she afraid? Had not Gabriel Letourneau vanished for ever? Had he not broken the means of communication between them? Undoubtedly she had exorcised him, she would be free now of this miserable, humiliating and expensive obsession. She tried to feel triumphant, released, but her spirit would not soar. In the back of her mind surged self-contempt. "Why did I do it? There was no need. His lies hurt no one. To impress these people was his one pleasure—perhaps he is in hell, and that was his one freedom from torment—but I must think sanely."

This was not easy to do; she seemed to have lost all will-power, all judgment. "I wish Helen had not escaped," she used the last word unconsciously; her fingers were cold round the thick cup, her face in the dingy mirror above the fireplace looked blurred and odd. She tried to steady herself by staring at the complacent features of Astra Destiny, who was being distantly gracious to a circle of admirers, and then by talking to commonplace Mr. Lemoine whose indifference was certainly soothing. "Oh, yes," he said politely, "we get a good deal of that sort of thing. Malicious spirits—evil influences—"

"Aren't you afraid?" asked Ada faintly.

"Afraid?" asked Mr. Lemoine as if he did not know what the word meant. "Oh, dear no, we are quite safe—" he added, then said: "Of course, if one was afraid, if one didn't quite believe, there might be danger. Any weakness on one's own part always gives the spirits a certain power over one—"

All this was, Ada knew, merely "patter"; she had heard it, and similar talk, often enough and never paid much attention to it; now it seemed to trickle through her inner consciousness like a flow of icy water. She was afraid, she didn't quite believe; yet how could she even but think that? Now she must believe. Astra Destiny could not have "faked" Gabriel Letourneau. Well, then, he was a real person—a real spirit? Ada Trimble's mind that once had been so cool and composed, so neat and tidy, now throbbed in confusion.

"Where do they go?" she asked childishly. "These evil spirits? I mean—today—will he come again?"

"I don't suppose so, not here. He will try to do all he can elsewhere. Perhaps he will try to impose on other people. I'm afraid he has wasted a good deal of our time."

"How can you say 'wasted!'" whispered Ada Trimble bleakly. "He *proves* that the dead return."

"We don't need such proof," said Mr. Lemoine, meekly confident and palely smiling.

"I had better go home now," said Ada; she longed to escape and yet dreaded to leave the warmth, the light, the company; perhaps these people were protected and so were safe from the loathed, prowling, outcast spirit. She said good-bye to Madame Destiny who was pleasant, as usual, without being effusive, and then to the others. She could not resist saying to Essie Clark: "Do you think that I did right?"

"Right?" the overworked woman smiled mechanically, the chipped green coffee-pot suspended in her hand.

"In exposing—the voice—the spirit?"

"Oh, *that*! Of course. You couldn't have done anything else, could you?" And Miss Clark poured her coffee and handed the cup, with a tired pleasantry, to a tall Indian who was the only elegant looking person present. Ada Trimble went out on to the landing; the smell of frying, of stew, filled the gaunt stairway; evidently one of the transient servants was in residence; through the half-open door behind her, Ada could hear the babble of voices, then another voice, deep, harsh, that whispered in her ear: "*Canaille!*"

She started forward, missed her foot-hold and fell.

Mr. Lemoine, always efficient, was the first to reach the foot of the stairs. Ada Trimble had broken her neck.

"A pure accident," said Astra Destiny, pale, but mistress of the situation. "Everyone is witness that she was quite alone at the time. She has been very nervous lately and those high heels..."

UNCLE PHIL ON TV

J. B. Priestley

A well-known public figure for much of the twentieth century, John Boynton Priestley (1894–1984) wrote so much, and so variously (novels, essays, journalism, plays, movie scripts), that his relatively small output of supernatural (and supernatural-adjacent) stories can easily get lost in the shuffle. Appearing in 1953 in the British monthly magazine *Lilliput* as well as Priestley's collection *The Other Place and Other Stories of the Same Sort*, "Uncle Phil on TV" features perhaps *the* defining technology of a century chock-full of new technologies. As is the case with so many inventions, a number of important pioneers might be invoked here—particularly Paul Julius Gottlieb Nipkow, John Logie Baird, and Vladimir Zworykin—but the lion's share of credit—or blame—for all-electronic television goes to the American Philo Taylor Farnsworth, who transmitted his first images in 1927. The BBC, which we have already encountered in connection with "Surprise Item", began television broadcasts in the 1930s, but it would be some years before TV became a central feature of life throughout Britain. As John Baxendale notes, Priestley here gives us a wonderful snapshot of this transitional time, capturing such concerns as "the high cost of the set (£120 in 1952 is over £2500 in today's money); uncertainty about how you watch it (in solemn silence like in a theatre, or as a continuous background to domestic life); [and] how and when you invite the neighbours in to watch (a common quandary for early adopters)".

ncle Phil's insurance money came to a hundred and fifty pounds, so that night the Grigsons had a family conference about it, in the big front room above the shop. They were all there—Mum and Dad, Ernest, Una and George her husband (Fleming was their name, but of course Una was a Grigson and George helped Dad in the shop), and even Joyce and young Steve, who were usually off and out and stayed out, as Mum said, till all hours. As a matter of fact Mum, who had let herself cool down and had tidied her hair for once, looked very proud and happy to see them all together like that, just as if it was Christmas though it was only October and her feet weren't so bad as they always were at Christmas. It was nice, even though Uncle Phil had been Mum's elder brother and now he was dead and this hundred and fifty pounds was his insurance.

"It's mine by rights of course," said Mum, referring to the money, "but I think—and so does Dad—it ought to be spent on something for the family."

"Had him to keep," said Dad darkly, "and had to put up with him."

"I'll say," cried young Steve.

"You be quiet," said Mum. "I won't say you hadn't to put up with him, but he did pay his share—"

"Not lately he didn't," said Dad. "Worked out all right at first, when prices weren't so bad, but not lately it didn't. Not at twenty-three shillings a week."

"That's right," said Ernest, who was a railway clerk and very steady, so steady that sometimes he hardly seemed alive at all. "Some of us had him to keep. I'm not saying we oughtn't to have. I'm just making the point, that's all."

"I wish somebody'd come to the point," cried Joyce, who of course wanted to be off again. "If there *is* one."

"That'll do, you saucy monkey," said Mum, who soon lost her temper with Joyce. "Just remember this was Uncle Phil's money in a way. And now he's Passed On." And then she could have bit her tongue off, saying a silly thing like that. For now a shadow settled over the family gathering.

The doctor, an impatient and overworked man, had been very angry about Uncle Phil's passing on, which ought not to have happened when it did. Uncle Phil had had a very bad heart, and the doctor had warned Mum and Dad that the things Uncle Phil had to take, when he felt an attack coming on, had to be within easy reach. But that Tuesday morning somebody had put Uncle Phil's box of things up on the mantelpiece, where he couldn't reach them when his last fatal attack had come on. A lot of questions had been asked, of course, but nobody could remember putting it up there; and it had been all very awkward and even downright nasty. It hadn't been done on purpose, even the doctor didn't suggest that, but somebody in the family had been very careless. And there was no getting away from the fact that for various good reasons they were all glad, or at least relieved, that Uncle Phil was no longer with them. He hadn't liked them any more than they'd liked him. Even Mum had never been really fond of him. Dad had tried to put up with him, you couldn't say more than that. And the younger members of the family had always disliked and feared the sarcastic old man, with his long sharp nose and sharper tongue, his slow movements, his determined refusal to leave the fireside even when they were entertaining friends and hated to have him there watching them. Before he had come to them, he had worked for some Loan Company, nothing but moneylenders really, in Birmingham, and perhaps this job had made him very hard and cynical, you might say nasty-minded. Also, some accident he'd had made him carry his head on one side, so that he always looked as if he was trying to see round a corner; and even this, to say nothing of the rest of him, got on their nerves. So naturally it was a relief to know that never again would they see him coming in to dinner, so deliberate and slow, his head on one side, his long nose seeming to sniff at them and their doings, a hard old man all ready to make some cutting remark. But at the same time it was awkward because of those things that were up on the mantelpiece when they ought to have been on the little table by his chair. So while Mum was telling herself what a daft donkey she'd been, everybody else was silent.

Then Mum for once was glad George Fleming was such a brassy sort of chap. "Here, we've had the funeral once, we don't want it again," cried George. "He's gone, and that's that. And I'm not going to pretend I'm sorry. He never liked me and I never liked him. If you ask me, he looked like a pain in the neck, and he was one—"

"Every time, George," young Steve shouted.

"I couldn't agree more," cried Joyce, who picked up a lot of fancy talk at work even if she didn't pick up much money there.

"Let me finish," said George, frowning at the young Grigsons, for whom he was more than a match. "You've got this hundred and fifty quid, Ma. And you don't know what to do with it—right? Well, I got an idea. Something we could all enjoy."

This was more like it. Mum gave him an encouraging smile. "And what would that be, George?"

"Television set," replied George, looking round in triumph.

Then everybody began talking at once, but George, who didn't look like a bull for nothing, managed to shout them down. "Now listen, listen! We've got TV here in Smallbridge at last, and comes over good too. What more d'you want? Gives you everything. Sport for me and Dad and Steve. Plays and games and all that for you women. Dancing and fashion shows too. Variety turns we'd all like. Serious stuff for Ernest. Ask your friends in to enjoy it."

That was what clinched it for Mum, who had several friends who certainly wouldn't be able to afford a set of their own for some time; she saw herself bringing them in and telling them what was in store. So she made herself heard above the babble that broke out again. "What would a nice set cost, George?"

"You could get a beauty," replied George, who always knew the price of everything, "for a hundred and twenty quid. Saw one at Stocks's the other day. Might get a bit of discount from Alf Stocks too."

Dad and Ernest nodded a grave assent to this. Una, who wouldn't have dared do anything else, supported her husband. Joyce hinted that a home with a good television set might be more popular with herself and girl and boy friends. Young Steve was all for it, of course. So it was agreed that George should take advantage of the first slack half-hour in the shop the next day and go along to Stocks's to bargain for the hundred-and-twenty-pound beauty. Then there was much excited happy talk about TV programmes and who could be asked in to see them and who couldn't; and clearly there was a general feeling, although even George dared not openly express it, that fate had been kind in exchanging Uncle Phil, whom nobody wanted, for this new wonder of the world.

Two days later, before Dad and George had come up from the shop and the others had returned from work, the television set, with aerial and everything in order, was there in the front sitting-room, looking a beauty indeed. Alf Stocks himself showed Mum and Una how to work it, and wouldn't leave until he'd seen each of them turn it on and off properly, which took some time because Mum was flustered. As soon as Alf Stocks had gone, Mum and Una looked at one another, and though it was nearly time to be getting a meal ready for Joyce and the men, they decided to have a look by themselves for ten minutes or so. Una turned it on, not having any trouble at all, and it began showing them a film that looked like an oldish cowboy film, which wasn't exactly their style, still it was wonderful having it in the sitting-room like that. The people were small and not always easy to see and their voices were loud enough for giants, which made it a bit confusing; but they watched it for quarter of an hour, and then Mum said they'd have to be getting the meal ready or there'd be trouble. Una wanted to keep it on, but Mum said that would be wasting it. So they turned it off, just after the Sheriff had been getting some evidence about the rustlers from Drywash Peter the Old-timer.

They didn't say anything for a minute or two, while Una was starting to lay the table and Mum began doing the haddock. Then Mum popped out of the kitchen, and looked at Una as if she had something rather important to say but didn't know how to start. And Una looked at her too, not saying anything either. Then finally Mum said: "Una, did you happen to notice that other little man who was there—you know in that last bit we saw—with the Sheriff?"

"What about him?" asked Una, who had now started cutting bread.

"Well, did you notice anything?"

"Seeing that you're asking—I did." But she went on cutting bread.

"What, then?"

"I thought, just for a sec," said Una, sawing away at the loaf and sounding very calm, "he looked just like Uncle Phil. Is that what you mean?"

"Yes it is," said Mum, "and it gave me quite a turn."

"Just a what's-it—coincidence," said Una. "There—that ought to do."

"Plenty," said Mum. "It's only getting stale if you cut too much. There's some of that sponge in the tin. I'll get it. Yes, of course—as you say—just a coincidence. Nearly made me catch my breath, though. I wouldn't say anything to the others, Una. They'd only laugh."

"George included. And then he'd tell me he'd had quite enough of Uncle Phil. So I won't say anything." Una waited a moment. "Who you having in tonight to look at it?"

"We'll settle that when they all come in," replied Mum rather proudly.

There was a bit of trouble, as Mum guessed there would be, when they all did come in. Joyce and Steve, with some timid backing by Una, were in favour of what amounted to a continuous performance by the set. Dad and Ernest were dead against this idea, which they thought wasteful and silly. They wanted to make a sort of theatre of it, with everybody sitting in position a few minutes before the chosen programme was ready to start, and then lights turned off and *Quiet, please!* and all that. George Fleming thought that was going too far but he was against the continuous touch too. One thing they had to decide, he pointed out, was how many people could sit in comfort and see the set properly. So he and Steve went and worked it out and after some argument agreed that you could manage a dozen, that is, if you brought up the old settee as a sort of dress circle. Meanwhile an argument had broken out among the women about who ought to be invited for this first evening, until Dad, with some moral support from Ernest, put his foot down, as he said, and declared that tonight it would be family only. Ernest, who was inclined to look on the dark side, said they needed at least one evening of it to make sure the set worked properly and didn't make them look silly.

Mum had been disappointed at first but after they had washed up and tidied, and Joyce, staying in for once, and Steve had arranged the chairs in front of the set, she felt it was nice and cosy to have a television show just for themselves. George, who had had a technical session with Alf Stocks in the shop, took charge of the set in his masterful way, so that Dad, who had a bit too much of George at times, whispered to Mum that they ought not to have let him buy the set for them, because now you'd think he owned it. However, there they all were, Dad and Ernest with their pipes going, Una and Joyce eating toffee-de-luxe, and the set winking brightly at them. There was some argument about how much light there ought to be in the room, and this was settled finally by switching off the bowl lamps in the centre and leaving on the standard on the other side. Then the television picture looked bright, sharp and lovely.

The first item, dullish for the Grigsons, was about how men trained for various sports. Mum and Una were bored with it until near the end, when there was a scene of boxers in a gymnasium. Not that they cared about that of course, but the point was that some men who weren't boxers appeared in this scene, carrying things about or just looking in, and among these men—just seen in a flash, that's all—was a little elderly man who carried his head to one side and seemed to have a long nose. Steve, who was always quick, spotted him and sang out that a little chap had just gone past who looked like old Uncle Phil. The others didn't notice or didn't bother to say anything; but Mum and Una gave each other a look, and, as they said afterwards, felt quite peculiar, because, after all, this was the second time.

Well, next was a snooty lady talking about clothes, with some models helping her, and of course this was all right because no men came into it at all. But the only one who liked it much was Joyce, who thought about nothing but clothes and boys. However, it didn't last long.

Then—and this was when the bother really started—there was a sort of game, about telling where you were born, a very popular programme that had had a lot of write-ups in the papers. A lovely actress was in it, as well as that man who was always in these shows just because at any minute he might be very rude and have to apologise afterwards. But there was also a sort of jury, who didn't do much but just sit there and see fair play. Ten of them altogether—four women and six men; and you never saw them long, just a glimpse now and then, and it was specially hard to get a good look at the end man farthest away. Which was a pity so far as the others were concerned, because then they might have understood at once. But Mum, beginning to shake, didn't think this time it was somebody who looked like Uncle Phil, she knew very well it *was* Uncle Phil. In fact, she couldn't be certain he hadn't given her one of his nasty looks.

"Una, just a minute," she said shakily, as soon as the newsreel started, and off she went into the back room, trusting that Una would have sense enough to follow her. The next minute they were staring at one another, out of sight and sound of the others, and Mum knew at once that Una was as worried as she was.

"You saw him at the end there, didn't you, Una?" she asked, after giving herself time to catch her breath.

"Yes, and this time I thought it really *was* him," said Una.

"I *know* it was. I'll take my dying oath it was."

"Oh—Mum—how could it be?"

"Don't ask me how it could be," cried Mum, nearly losing her temper. "How should I know? But there he was—yes, and I'm not sure he didn't give me one of his looks."

"Oh—dear!" Una whispered, her eyes nearly out of her head. "I was hoping you wouldn't say that, Mum. Because I thought he did too, then I thought I must have been making it up."

"Una, that's three times already," said Mum, not sharp now but almost ready to cry. "I'm certain of it now. That was him in the film. That was him in the boxing. Don't tell me it's a what's-it—just accidental. He's there."

"Where?"

"Now don't start acting stupid, Una. How do I know where? But already we've seen him three times, and if I know him this is only his first try. It'll be a lot worse soon, you'll see. It's just like him trying to spoil our pleasure."

"Oh—Mum—how could he? Listen, I believe we were thinking about him—"

"It wasn't thinking about him—"

"I expect you were and you didn't know it," Una continued with some determination. "Same with me. Then we think we see him—"

"I *know* I saw him," cried Mum, exasperated. "How many times have I to keep telling you?"

"You'll see—it'll wear off."

"Wear off! You'll get no wearing off from him. I tell you, he's there, just to spite us, and he's staying there. You watch!"

While they were staring at one another, not knowing what to say next, Steve popped his head in. "Come on, you two. Bathing show next. Boy—oh boy!" Then he vanished.

"You go, Una," said Mum, her voice trembling. "It'll look funny if neither of us goes, and I can't face him again tonight. I'm going to make myself a cup of tea. Honestly, I'd give the show away if I went."

"Well," said Una, hesitating, "I suppose I ought. I can't see how he could be there—and I believe it's all our fancy. But if I did see him again, I'd scream—couldn't stop myself." And she went off rather slowly to the front room.

Mum was just pouring out her tea when she heard the scream. The next moment Una came flying in, followed by her husband, who looked annoyed. "Mum, he was there again."

"What's the idea?" George demanded, like a policeman.

"I'll tell him," cried Mum. "You sit down and drink that tea, Una dear. Now then, George Fleming, you needn't look at me like that. Just listen for once. Una's upset because she must have seen Uncle Phil again. We'd seen him three times before—and that must have been the fourth. He was there again, wasn't he, Una? Yes, well I'm not surprised." She looked severely at George, daring him to laugh. "He was there, wasn't he? Tell me the truth now, George."

"Why should I lie?" said George, not even smiling. "I'll admit it's quite a coincidence. Twice I noticed a chap who looked very like Uncle Phil—"

"Four times I've seen him now," cried Una, sitting with her cup of tea. "Honestly I have, George."

"And you can't explain it, can you?" And now George *was* smiling, as he looked from one harassed woman to the other.

"How can anybody explain it?" said Mum crossly. "He's there, that's all."

"Come off it, Ma," said George. "You'll be telling me next he's haunting us. Couldn't be done. Let's have a bit of common. I can explain it."

"Oh—George—can you?" Una was all relief, gratitude and devotion.

"Certainly." George waited a moment, enjoying himself. Mum could have slapped him. "Look—they have to have a lot of chaps round when they're doing these scenes—chaps with the cameras, lights and all that. Well, it just happens that one of 'em—who keeps getting into the picture when he oughtn't—looks like Uncle Phil—head on one side and so forth. And this set reminds you of Uncle Phil—bought with his money—so every time you see this chap you tell yourself it must be him, though of course it couldn't be—stands to reason."

"That's it, George," cried Una. "Must be. Mum—we were just being silly."

But Mum, who could be very obstinate at times, wasn't so easily persuaded. "I see what you mean, George. But I don't know. I can't believe these television chaps are as old as that. And what about that look he gave me?"

"Oh—come off it," said George, losing his patience. "You imagined that. How could the chap take a look at you? He was just looking at the camera, that's all. Now let's pack this up and go back and enjoy ourselves. Come on—some variety turns next. You don't want to spoil it for everybody, do you?"

This artful appeal was too strong even for Mum's misgivings, and George triumphantly escorted them to the front room. The variety show was about to begin; already a band was playing a lively tune. Mum found herself looking round with satisfaction at the expectant faces of her family. This was more like it, what she'd hoped for from a television set.

Three girls did a singing and dancing turn, to start off with, and it wasn't bad. Ernest, who was sitting next to Mum, breathed hard at them, but whether out of approval or disapproval, she didn't know. Since that dark fancy girl at the confectioner's had given him up, Ernest had seemed to be off women, but of course you could never tell, steady as he was. Next turn was a nice-looking young chap who played an accordion, and Mum felt secretly in agreement with Joyce who loudly declared he was 'smashing'. He finished off with some nice old panto songs that they all began to sing. Now at last Mum felt really happy with the set. And of course just after that was when it had to happen.

A conjurer appeared, a big comical fellow who pretended to be very nervous. George told them he was the top turn of the show, very popular. He did one silly trick and then pretended to do another and make a mess of it, which made them all laugh a lot. Then he said he'd have to have somebody from the audience, though there wasn't any audience to be seen. As soon as he said that, as Mum told them afterwards, she suddenly felt nervous. And then there he was, giving them a nasty sideways grin—Uncle Phil.

"I won't have it," Mum screamed, jumping up. "Turn it off, turn it off." But before anyone could stop her, she had turned it off herself. As they gaped at her, she stood in front of the set and stared at them defiantly.

"What's the matter with you?" cried Dad, looking at her as if she'd gone mad. And as the others all began talking, he turned on them: "Now you be quiet. I'm asking Mum a question. We can't all talk at once."

Joyce started giggling and Steve gave a loud guffaw, as boys of that silly age always do.

"Do you mean to say, Fred Grigson," said Mum, glaring at him, "that you haven't noticed him yet? Five times—counting the one I didn't see but Una did—he's turned up already, and this is only the first night we've had it. Five times!"

"What you talking about?" asked Dad angrily. "Five times what? Who's turned up?"

"Uncle Phil," said Una quickly, and then burst into tears. "I've seen him every time." And she went stumbling out of the room, with George, who was a good husband for all his faults, hurrying after her.

Dad was flabbergasted. "What's the matter with her? I wish you'd talk sense. What's this about Uncle Phil?"

"Oh—don't be such a silly donkey," cried Mum. "He keeps coming into these television pictures. Haven't you got any eyes?"

"Eyes? What's eyes got to do with it?" Dad shouted, thoroughly annoyed now. "I've got some sense, haven't I? Phil's dead and buried."

"I know he is," said Mum, nearly crying. "That's what makes it so awful. He's doing it on purpose, just to spoil it for us."

"Spoil it for us?" Dad thundered. "You'll have me out of my mind in a minute. Here, Ernest, did you see anybody that looked like Uncle Phil?"

Later, round the supper table, they sorted it out. Una and Mum were certain they had seen Uncle Phil himself five and four times respectively. George said he had seen a camera man, or somebody who looked like Uncle Phil, three times. After maddening deliberation, Ernest agreed with George. Joyce said she had twice seen somebody who looked the spit image of Uncle Phil. Steve kept changing his mind, sometimes agreeing with his mother and Una, sometimes joining the Coincidence School. Dad from first to last maintained that he had seen nobody that even reminded him of Uncle Phil and that everybody else had Uncle Phil on the brain.

"Now you just listen to me, Dad," said Mum finally. "I know what I saw and so does Una. And never mind about any coincidences. They wouldn't make me jump every time like that. Besides I know that look of his, couldn't miss it."

"How on earth—" Dad began, but she wouldn't let him go on.

"Never mind about *how on earth*," Mum shouted. "Because I don't know and you don't know and nobody does. What I'm telling you is that he's got into that set somehow and there'll be no getting him out. It'll get worse and worse, you mark my words. And if we've any sense we'll ask Alf Stocks to take that set away and give us our money back."

This roused George, who made himself heard above the others. "Oh—come off it, Ma. Alf Stocks would never stop laughing if we told him he'd have to take that set back because Uncle Phil's haunting it. Now—be reasonable. You and Una got excited and started imagining things. Everything'll be okay tomorrow night, you'll see."

"Oh—will it? That's what you say."

"Of course it's what I say. It's what we all say."

"Have it your own way," said Mum darkly. "Just keep on with it. But don't say I didn't warn you. He's there—and he's staying there—and if you ask me, this is only the start of it. He'll get worse before he gets better. Wherever he is, he's made up his mind we shan't enjoy a television set bought with his insurance money. You'll see."

In the middle of the following afternoon, when Mum and Una had the place to themselves and usually enjoyed a quiet sensible time together, they were both restless. They had gone into the front room, to sit near the windows and keep an eye on the street below, but it was obvious that they would never settle down. There in its corner was the TV set with its screen that looked like an enormous blind eye. For some minutes they pretended not to notice it. Finally, Una said: "I looked in the *Radio Times* and there's a programme for women this afternoon."

"I know," said Mum rather grimly. "I looked too."

"We'd be all right with that, surely? In any case—"

"In any case—what?" Mum still sounded rather grim.

"Well," said Una timidly, "don't you think we might have got a bit worked up last night—and—imagined things?"

"No, I don't," said Mum. Then, after a moment: "Still, if you want to turn it on—turn it on. If it's a women's programme—middle of the afternoon too—perhaps he won't show up. He used always to have a sleep in the afternoon."

"But—listen, Mum. As George says—"

"Never mind what George says. George doesn't know it all even though you'd sometimes think he does. But go on—turn it on, if you want to."

Una walked across and rather gingerly manipulated the switches. With an absent-minded air, Mum arrived in front of the set and sat down in a chair facing it. The next minute they were looking at and listening to the matron of a girls' hostel, a woman so determinedly refined that she sounded quite foreign.

"You see, it's all right," said Una, when the matron had been followed by two girls playing the violin and piano.

"So far," said Mum, "but give him time. Still—this is very nice, I must say."

After the music a man came on to talk about buried treasure. He was a youngish chap, schoolmaster type, very nervous and sweating something terrible. "You'd be surprised at what some of us have found," he told them. "And now I want to show you a few things—genuine treasure trove." He beckoned anxiously to somebody off the screen, saying: "If you don't mind—thank you so much."

It was Uncle Phil who walked on, carrying some of the things, and as soon as he was plainly in view he turned that twisted neck of his, looked straight out at Mum and Una, and said: "Talk about treasure! You Grigsons haven't done so bad with that hundred-and-fifty quid of mine."

"You see—talking to us now," screamed Mum as she dashed forward. "But I'll turn him off." And as she did, she added firmly:

"And that's the last time he does that to me. I'll not give him another chance. God knows what he'll be saying soon!" She pointed an accusing finger at Una, who was still trembling in her chair, and went on: "I suppose we're still a bit worked up and just imagined *that*. Now, Una—you saw him, you heard him—didn't you? Right, then. No going back on it this time."

And Mum marched out and made for the kitchen, where she clattered and banged until it was time for a cup of tea. Steve, who worked in an auctioneer's office and kept odd hours there, was the first home that day, and without saying a word to his mother and sister he hurried straight through into the front room, obviously making for the television set. The two women, who were in the back room, preparing the evening meal, said nothing to him. This, as Una guessed at once, was Mum's new line; no more protesting, no more trying to convince the others; just a grim dark silence, waiting for the final din and flare of 'I told you so'. As they laid the table, they could hear voices from the set but no actual words. Five minutes, ten minutes, passed.

Then abruptly the voices from the front room stopped. There was a silence that lasted perhaps half a minute, and then Steve, looking quite peculiar, came slowly into the back room. He tried to avoid meeting the questioning stares of the two women. He sat down and looked at the dining-table. "Nearly ready?" he enquired, in a small choked voice.

"No it isn't nearly ready," said Mum. "You're very early today. Why did you switch that set off like that?"

"Oh—well," said Steve, wriggling, "didn't seem much point in bothering with a dreary old flick."

This wretched performance hadn't a chance even with Una, and of course Mum could read him as if he were a theatre poster. "Stop that silly nonsense," said Mum. "You saw him, didn't you?"

"Saw who?"

"You know very well who—your Uncle Phil. Didn't you?"

"Well, yes, I thought I did," said Steve carefully.

"Thought you did! You saw him nearly as plain as you can see me, didn't you?"

"No—but I did see him." Steve was clearly embarrassed.

"Did he say anything—I mean, to you?"

"Now, Mum, how *could* he—"

"Stop that," shouted Mum. "I'm having no more of that nonsense. And just you tell your mother the honest truth, Steve. Now—did he say anything to *you*? And if so—what?"

The youth swayed from side to side and looked utterly miserable. "He said I took two shillings of his."

The women gasped. "Now isn't that just like him?" cried Mum. "And you never took two shillings of his, did you?"

"Yes, I did," Steve bellowed unhappily, and then charged out, so that he seemed to be pounding down the stairs before they had time to raise any protest.

"Just what I thought," said Mum before going into her terrible grim silence again. "It'll get worse, like I said."

Sometimes it was nice when the men came up from the shop like boys out of school, hearty and boisterous; and then at other times it wasn't. This was one of the other times. And unfortunately they had decided that the idea of Uncle Phil appearing on television programmes was Humorous Topic Number One, and roared round the place making bad jokes about it. With her lips almost folded away, Mum heard them in the grimmest of silences. Una caught George's eye once or twice, but there was no stopping him. How much was the B.B.C. paying Uncle Phil? Had he got his Union card yet? Would they be starring him in a show soon? And couldn't Ma take a joke these days?

"We haven't all got the same sense of humour, George Fleming," she told him. "And now I'm going out. I promised to go and see Mrs. Pringle."

Una looked dubious. It was the first she had heard of any visit to Mrs. Pringle, and Mum liked to discuss her social engagements well in advance. "Shall I come too?" she asked nervously.

"No reason why you shouldn't, Una dear," Mum replied grandly. "We can leave these men to have a nice evening of television. And I hope they enjoy it." And off she went, with Una trailing behind.

A little later, when he had his pipe going, Dad said to George: "Well, that's how they are, and always will be, I expect. Moody. One day they're all for a television set, must have it. Next day, just because of some silly nonsense, won't look at it. Hello!"—this was to Joyce, who came hurrying in—"where've you been, girl?"

"Where d'you think?" cried Joyce. "Working. No, I don't want anything to eat. I'll have something in the Empire caffy. We're going there."

"What's the use of spending all this money on a television set," Dad shouted as she ran upstairs, "if you're going to waste more money at the Empire?"

She stopped long enough to shout down: "You've not talked to Steve, have you?"

"No, haven't seen him yet."

"Well, I have," she cried triumphantly. And that was the last of her.

Dad and George did not wait for Ernest, for they knew he would be late, this being his night for attending his Spanish class. (Nobody knew why he was learning Spanish; perhaps it helped to keep him steady.) So after clearing the table and doing a bit of slapdash washing up (just to show Mum), they moved luxuriously, in a cloud of tobacco smoke, into the front room. They were, as they knew, just in time for

Television Sports Magazine, a sensible programme they could enjoy all the better for not having a pack of impatient bored women with them.

The first chap to be interviewed for this *Sports Magazine* was a racing cyclist, who could pedal like mad but was no great shakes at being interviewed, being a melancholy youth apparently suffering from adenoids. However, Dad and George had a good laugh at him, legs and all.

"And now for a chat with a typical old sportsman," said the Sporting Interviewer, all cast-iron geniality, "the sort of man who's been watching cricket and football matches and other sporting events for the last sixty years or so. Welcome to Television, Mr. Porritt!"

Mr. Porritt, who came strolling into the picture, was small, old, bent. He carried his head to one side. He had a long and rather frayed nose, and an evil little eye. And without any shadow of doubt he was Uncle Phil.

"No," cried Dad, "it can't be."

"Let's hear what he says," cried George. "Then we'll know for certain."

"Now, Mr. Porritt, you've been watching sport for a good long time, haven't you?" said the Interviewer.

"That's right," said Uncle Phil, grinning and giving Dad and George a wicked look. "Saw a lot o' sport, I did, right up to the time when I had the bad luck to go and live at Smallbridge, with a family by the name of Grigson. That finished me for sport—and for nearly everything else."

"How d'you mean?" shouted Dad, jumping up.

"Shop-keeping people," Uncle Phil continued, "in a petty little way—frightened o' spending a shilling or two—"

"No, don't turn him off," shouted George, almost going into a wrestling match with his father-in-law. "Let's hear what he has to say."

"If you think I'm going to sit here listening to slurs and insults," Dad bellowed. "Take your hands off me."

"Listen—listen—look—look!" And George succeeded in holding Dad and keeping him quiet for a few moments.

"Yes, indeed," Mr. Porritt was saying, in rather a haw-haw voice, "the first Test match I ever attended—dear me—this is going back a long time—"

"It's not him now," Dad gasped. "Quite different." Which was true, for the Mr. Porritt they saw and heard now was not at all like Uncle Phil. After a moment or two, Dad said quietly: "Now, never mind Test matches, George. Turn it off. We've got to have a talk about this."

Even though the screen was dark and silent, they both instinctively moved away from it and sat down by the fireplace. "Now then, George," Dad began, with great solemnity, "we've got to get this straight. Now did you or did you not think that Mr. Porritt, when he first started, was Uncle Phil?"

"I was almost certain he was," replied George, who had lost his usual self-confidence. "Last night, I'll admit, I thought it was some B.B.C. chap who happened to look a bit like him—"

"Never mind about last night," said Dad hurriedly. "And did you or did you not hear him talk about us—very nasty of course?"

"I did," said George, who began to feel he was in a witness box.

"So did I," said Dad, and then, perhaps realising that this bald statement was something of an anticlimax, he raised his voice: "And it don't make sense. Couldn't happen. Here's a man who's dead and buried—"

"I know, Dad, I know," cried George hastily. "And I agree—it couldn't happen—"

"Yes, but it *is* happening—"

"Not really," said George, looking very profound.

"How d'you mean—*not really*?" cried Dad, nettled. "Saw and heard for yourself, didn't you?"

"If you ask me," said George slowly and weightily, "it's like this. Uncle Phil's not in there, couldn't possibly be. He's on our minds, in our heads, so we just *think* he's there. And of course," he continued, brisker now, "that's what was the matter with Una and Mum. They kept seeing him last night, like they said, and you can bet your boots they saw and heard him—or thought they did—today, before we came up from the shop. And I'll tell you another thing, Dad. Young Steve dashed out again, before we were back, didn't he? And Joyce said she'd talked to him."

"You think they got mixed up in it, do you?"

"Young Steve was, I'll bet you anything. And whatever it was he saw and heard, it sent him out sharp and upset Mum and Una—see?"

Dad re-lit his pipe but performed this familiar operation rather shakily. His voice had a tremble in it too. "This is a nice thing to happen to decent respectable people. Can't amuse themselves quietly with a TV set—hundred-and-twenty-pound set too—without seeing a kind of ghost—who starts insulting 'em. Here, George, do you think all the other people hear what he says?"

"No, of course they don't. They just hear Mr. Porritt."

"But it isn't Mr. Porritt all the time."

"I know—but I mean, whoever it ought to be. Don't you see," and George leant forward and tapped Dad on the knee, "we only imagine he's there."

This annoyed Dad. "But why should I imagine he's there? I'll tell you straight, George, I'd had more than enough of Brother Phil when he was alive, without any imagining. All I wanted tonight was a *Sports*

Magazine—not any insults from that miserable old sinner. I call this downright blue misery."

They were still arguing about it, without taking another look at the set, when Ernest came in. "Hello," he said, "aren't we having any television tonight?"

"No," said Dad, and was about to explain why when George gave him a sharp nudge.

"Just having an argument about something we heard on it earlier," said George. "You turn it on whenever you like, Ernest."

Ernest said he would as soon as he had put on his slippers and old coat, which was something he always made a point of doing when he came home in the evening. And while Ernest was outside, George explained to Dad why he had given him that nudge. "Let's see what Ernest makes of it."

"I don't see Ernest imagining anything," said Dad. "If Ernest sees Uncle Phil, then Uncle Phil's there all right."

"Now then," said Ernest, a few minutes later, as he looked at the *Radio Times*, "—ah—yes—*Current Conference*—a discussion programme, I believe. That should be interesting—and we're just in time for it." He sounded like somebody, the ideal stooge, taking part in a dull programme.

When the set came to life, George and Dad rather stealthily moved nearer. Ernest had planked himself dead in front of it, looking as if TV had been invented specially for him. The screen showed them some chaps sitting round a table, looking pleased with themselves. The room was immediately filled with the sound of their voices, loud and blustering in argument. The camera moved around the table, and sometimes went in for a close-up. These politicians and editors seemed to be arguing about the present state of the British People, about which they all apparently knew a great deal. A shuffling at the door made Dad turn round, and then he saw that Mum and Una had returned and were risking another peep. They ignored him, so he pretended he hadn't seen them. Meanwhile, the experts on the British People were all hard at it.

"And now, Dr. Harris," cried the Chairman, "you've a good deal of specialised knowledge—and must have been thinking hard—so what have you to say?"

A new face appeared on the screen, and it belonged to a head that was held on one side and had a long nose and the same old wicked look. Dr. Harris nothing! It was the best view of Uncle Phil they had had yet.

"What have I to say?" Uncle Phil snarled. "Zombies. Country's full o' zombies now. Can't call 'em anything else. Don't know whether they're alive or dead—and don't care. Zombies. And if you want an example, just take Ernest Grigson of Smallbridge—"

"Stop it," screamed Mum from the doorway. "He gets worse every time."

George had the set switched off in three and a half seconds, probably a record so far.

Ernest looked dazed. "I must have dropped off," he explained to them all, "because I seemed to see Uncle Phil and thought he mentioned my name—"

"And so he did, you pie-can," roared Dad. Then he turned to George: "I suppose you're going to say now we all imagined that together. Urrr!"

"It's just his wicked devilment," cried Mum, coming in and joining them now. "Is this his first go tonight?"

"Not likely, Ma," said George, and explained what had happened to the *Sports Magazine*.

"Personal slurs and insults every time now," said Dad bitterly.

"But wait a minute," said Ernest, looking more dazed than ever and speaking very carefully. "Even if he was alive, they wouldn't have Uncle Phil on that *Current Conference* programme. I mean to say, they only have—"

"Oh—for goodness sake, Ernest!" cried Una. "What's the use of talking like that? I'll scream in a minute."

Mum looked severely at the men. "Now you'll perhaps believe me when I tell you what happened when Una and me turned it on earlier—yes, and what happened to poor Steve." And they had to listen to a very full account of Uncle Phil's earlier appearances, together with some references to his antics on the screen the previous night. This led to a further and still noisier argument between George and Dad, on metaphysical lines, turning on whether Uncle Phil was really there or was being projected into the screen by their imagination. Just when it was becoming unbearably complicated, it was sharply interrupted.

A little procession of young people marched into the room. Steve had a youth his own age with him, and Joyce, looking pale but determined, was accompanied by two watery-eyed spluttering girl friends and a scared-looking boy friend.

"Now what's the idea, you two?" cried Dad, annoyed at being silenced.

"We've been talking," said Joyce, who had a will of her own, "and now I'm going to turn that set on, just to see for myself, and nobody's going to stop me." She looked so fierce that nobody attempted to stop her. "What's supposed to be on now?"

"One of those pieces about crime not paying," George told her as she went across to the switches.

They all looked and listened in silence. A rather dolled-up woman appeared on the screen, and was saying: "Well, that's one point of view. And now for another. What do you think, Inspector Ferguson?"

"Here we go," muttered George. "I'll bet you a quid."

There was a gasp from all the Grigsons. This time Uncle Phil's horrible sharp face filled the whole screen, and his voice, when it came, was louder than they had ever heard it before. This time even Mum had to listen.

"Take the case of an elderly man with heart disease," said Uncle Phil, already with a gleam in his eye. "When an attack comes on, he has to crush some pill things in his mouth—or he's a goner. And suppose somebody—just a young niece perhaps—deliberately puts those life-savers out of his reach—so when he has an attack he'll finish himself trying to get to them—it's a kind of murder—"

"Not on purpose I didn't—you dirty lying old weasel!" Joyce screamed, and then threw the stool at the screen.

Next morning, Alf Stocks was there, shaking his head at Mum. "No use telling me it's brand-new and priced at a hundred-and-twenty. Tube's done in, see—that's the trouble. I'm taking a chance offering you twenty-five for it. Yes, I dare say it was an accident, but then some accidents—" and then, as Mum said afterwards, he gave her a sharp, sideways, old-fashioned look—"are very expensive."

THE TELEPHONE

Mary Treadgold

Author, editor, and producer for the BBC, Mary Treadgold (1910–2005) wrote fifteen novels—notably a series of children's equestrian stories—and a single ghostly tale, which appeared in Lady Cynthia Asquith's *Third Ghost Book* (1955). Among those who must surely have wished that Treadgold had written more in this vein was fellow children's author Roald Dahl, who included "The Telephone" in his personal selection of the best ghost stories of all time, alongside tales by Robert Aickman, E. F. Benson, Sheridan Le Fanu, and Edith Wharton—select company indeed.

Unlike the telegraph and railway (and in contrast to its reception in America), the telephone was slow to take root in Britain, possibly because it was too invasive, intrusive, and... loud: George Bernard Shaw, who worked as a young man for Edison's Telephone Company in London, wrote of the "stentorian efficiency [with which] it bellowed your most private communications all over the house instead of whispering them with some sort of discretion. This was not what the British stockbroker wanted...". By the 1950s, however, the technology was as much a part of the social and cultural fabric there as anywhere else—and as Treadgold's story demonstrates, hearing whispered phone conversations in your home can be far more disturbing than any stentorian bellowing.

"I f you would catch the spleen and laugh yourselves into stitches, follow me," I called to Sir Toby—and as I ran across the stage caught the eye of the white-haired man in the V.I.P.'s row. The light from the stage streamed out over the darkened theatre. He was leaning forward, amused, laughing—and as Sir Toby chased after me I laughed back. I had fallen in love with him at sight—there, from the middle of the stage at an end-of-term Dramatic School performance of *Twelfth Night*.

We met at the party after the show—and met again—and again—and then we began to meet in backstreet Soho restaurants, and then in my tiny London flat. I loved him desperately. I had never been in love before, and Allan had not been in love for over thirty years—not since he had married Katherine, he told me, in some queer little snowbound Canadian township. "I never meant this to happen. I've never felt like this about any woman before. I don't understand myself," he said restlessly.

All through that winter I clung to Allan. We kept the long secret winter afternoons and evenings together. There was so much that he wanted to give me—the things that I wanted for myself, more than wanted, believed that I must have. "I want to give you kindness—and shelter—and love," he said. He and Katherine had had no children.

But it could not go on like that. Every time he came to my flat the conflict in him deepened. It was like the deepening rift splitting a tree-trunk down to its roots. He would turn wearily towards me. "How can I hurt her?" he would ask me. "Katherine and I—we've been together all these years. Long before you were even born. Why,

I knew her when she was a school girl—a child. Look at what we've done together—look at our work."

I tried to understand. But I seemed to see only a grey ghostly marriage, a kind of deadly, intellectual middle-aged companionship stretching back down the years. There was nothing there, I thought, that should be preserved. It would be so different for *us*, I thought, and I clung the more desperately. "I cannot live without you," I said, believing that I could not.

Our dilemma, Allan's agony, was resolved by Katherine finding out. There was no drama, no scenes. During the next few months I never knew what passed between them. I dared not ask. I felt like a child whose parents are gravely discussing in the next room portents beyond its comprehension. But presently Katherine went unobtrusively back to Canada without Allan...

Allan shut up the house in Hampstead, and talked of selling it. We neither of us wanted to live there. Immediately after our marriage we came up to this cottage in the Western Highlands which we rented through an advertisement in the *Times*. That year Scotland had one of its rare perfect summers. We bathed and fished, and the long halcyon days passed over us with scarcely a break in the weather. I was blissfully happy. Free from the conflicts and indecisions of the past months, we turned again to each other, discovering new releases, a new and deepening absorption. Our cottage lay by the shore in a curve of the hills, and whenever I remember that summer it seems as if the falling tides of the Atlantic were always in our ears, and as if the white sands were always warm under our bare feet.

But again, it could not last. One scorching day in early September I came round the cottage at lunchtime, carrying a pot-roast over to the table under our rowan-tree. I found Allan sitting staring down at an open airmail letter that the postman had just delivered. He looked up as I put the pot-roast down. His face was dazed, and his hands were shaking.

"Katherine is dead," he said incredulously. "Dead... This letter's from her sister in Toronto... She says—" and he stared again at the letter as though they were lying words, "she says—heart failure. Very peacefully, she says."

His eyes went past mine to the open sea. Then he got up and went into the house, while I—I stayed, pleating the gingham cloth between my fingers. Once more I felt like the child who had inadvertently witnessed a parent's distress—shocked yes, but horribly embarrassed. Then I followed Allan into the cottage, and I put my arms round him. All that day I watched over him in my heart as he moved about the place. But we did not mention Katherine—nor the next day—and, although I waited for Allan to speak, her name never passed our lips during the next three weeks.

Three weeks later to the day, among other letters forwarded from London by the Post Office, arrived the telephone bill for the Hampstead house—the second demand. We had forgotten about the first.

"Damn," said Allan—we were once again eating our lunch in the garden—"damn, I ought to have had the thing disconnected before we ever left London."

I picked up the envelope and looked at the date of forwarding. "They'll probably have cut you off themselves by now," I said. But Allan was already crossing the grass to collect the pudding from the kitchen oven. "Go in by the hall," I called after him. "You can find out if it's still connected by ringing the number. If you hear it ringing away at the London end you'll know it's still on."

And I lay back in my deck-chair, staring up at the scarlet rowan-berries against the sky and thinking that Allan was beginning to hump his shoulders like an old man, and that his skin looked somehow as if the sea-salt were drying it out...

"Well?" I said. "Still connected?" Perhaps I invented the slight pause before Allan carefully set down the apple-pie, and replied, "Yes—still connected."

That evening I went up to bed alone, because Allan said he wanted to trim the lamps in the kitchen. I was sitting in the window in the late Highland dusk, brushing my hair and looking out over the sea, when I heard a light tinkle in the hall below. I turned my head. But the house lay silent. I went over to the door.

"Hampstead 96843." Allan's voice—low—strained—came up the stairs.

There was a long silence. And then my heart turned over, for I heard his voice again, whispering:

"Oh, my dear—my dear—"

But the words broke off—and from the dark well of the hall came a low sob. I suppose I moved, and a floorboard creaked. Because I heard the receiver laid down, and I saw Allan's shadow move heavily across the wall at the foot of the stairs.

We lay side by side that night, and we never spoke. But I know that it was daybreak before Allan slept.

During the next few days I became terribly afraid. I began to watch over Allan with new eyes, those of a mother. For the first time I knew a quite different tenderness, one that nearly choked me with its burden of grief and fear for him as he moved about the cottage like a sleepwalker, trying pathetically to keep up appearances before me, his face, as it seemed, ageing hourly in its weariness. I became frightened, too, for myself. I kept telling myself that nothing—nothing—had happened. But in the daytime I avoided looking at the dead black telephone inert on its old-fashioned stand in the hall. At night

I lay awake, trying not to picture that telephone wire running tautly underground away from our cottage, running steadily south, straight down through the border hills, down through England... During that week I tried never to leave Allan's side. But once I had to go off unexpectedly to the village shop. When I returned I had to pretend that I hadn't seen him through the half-open door, gently laying down the receiver. And twice more in the evening—and there must have been other times—when I was cooking our supper, he slipped out of the kitchen, and I heard that faint solitary tinkle in the hall...

I could have rung up the telephone people, and begged them to cut off the Hampstead number. But with what excuse? I could have taken pliers and wrenched our own telephone out of its socket. I knew that nothing would be solved with pliers. But by the weekend I did know what I could try to do, for sanity's sake, to prevent us from going down into the solitudes of our guilt.

On Friday afternoon—after tea—my opportunity came. It was a glorious evening—golden, with the sand blowing lightly along the shore, and a racing tide. I persuaded Allan to take the boat out to troll for mackerel on the turn. I watched him go off from the doorway. I waited until I actually saw him push the boat off from our small jetty. Then I turned back into the cottage, and closed the door behind me. I had shut out all the evening sunlight so that I could hardly see the telephone. But I walked over to it. I took it up in both my hands. I drew a long deep breath, and I gave the Hampstead number. All that I had been told of Katherine during those bad months in London had been of kindness and gentleness and goodness—nothing of revenge. To this I clung, and upon it I was banking. My teeth were chattering, and I was shaking all over when the bell down in London began to ring. I suppose at that moment I lost my head. I thought—I could have sworn—I heard the receiver softly raised at the far end. But I suppose I should have waited instead of bursting into words. Now I shall never *know*. And they were not even the words I'd planned. I suppose I reverted, being so frightened, to the kind of prayer one blurts out in childhood:

"Please—please—" I said down the mouthpiece. "Please let me have him now. I know everything I've done's been wrong. It's too late about that. But I won't be a child anymore. I'll look after him, like you've always done," I said. "Only please let me have him now. I'll be a wife to him. I promise you—if that's what you are wanting. I can get him right again, and I'll take care of him. Now and forever more," I said.

And I banged the receiver down, and fled upstairs to our bedroom. Through the window I could see the little boat bobbing about on the sea. I sat down in the window in the full evening sun, and I shook all over, and I cried and cried...

In the small hours of the morning came the crisis. I woke—it must have been about half past four. The bed was empty. In an instant I was wide awake, because down in the hall I could hear the insistent tinkle of the telephone receiver, struck over and over again, and above it, mingled with it, Allan's voice. Somehow I got the lamp lighted. The shadows tilted all over the ceiling and I could hear the paraffin sloshing round the bowl as I stumbled out to the head of the stairs.

"Katherine—Katherine—"

He was shaking the receiver, and babbling down the mouthpiece when my light from the staircase fell upon him. He let the receiver drop, and stood looking up at me.

"I can't get her," he said. "I wanted her to forgive me. But she doesn't answer. I can't reach her."

I brought him up the stairs. I can remember shivering with the little dawn sea-wind blowing through my cotton nightdress from the open window. I made him tea, while he sat in the window, staring up at the grey clouds of the morning. At last he said:

"You must book yourself a room at one of the hotels in Oban. Only for a couple of nights. I'll come back—probably tomorrow, or the next day. You see—" and he began to explain carefully, politely as if to a foreigner, "you see, I've got to find Katherine, and so I have to go down unexpectedly to London—"

From our remote part of the Highlands there are only two trains a day. Allan went on the early morning one. I had, of course, no intention of going to any hotel. I knew where my promise to Katherine lay, where lay my love. I said "Yes—yes" to everything Allan said, and stayed in the cottage all that day. And then I caught the evening train.

There was no chance of a sleeper. I huddled in the corner of a carriage packed with returning holidaymakers, my face turned first to the twilight, and then to the darkness rushing past the window. In the dead cold hours, when the other passengers sprawled and snored, the terror for Allan nearly throttled me. Once I dozed off, and woke, biting back a scream because I thought I saw the telephone wire running alongside the train, stretched and singing, "You'll never *know*. You'll never *know*…"

Euston in the morning loomed gaunt and monstrous. The London streets were dripping with autumn rain. I told the taxi-man to drive as fast as possible up to Hampstead. When he pulled up in Allan's road before a gate set in a high wall, I was already half out of the taxi. I pushed the fare at him, slapped open the gate, and ran up the short drive. I just had time to notice that the white Regency house was more or less what I had pictured, before I was up the flight of steps and tugging at the iron bell-pull. I was tired—deadly tired, deadly afraid. What courage I had ever had seemed to have fled. "I promise. I promise. Oh, if you've ever really been here, please have gone," I gabbled, while the London rain poured over me, and the bell reverberated through the house.

At last I heard a movement inside the house, and then footsteps slowly drawing towards the door. For a second Allan and I stood gazing at each other. Then—suddenly—I was over the threshold, and in his arms. While the door swung gently to behind us, I drew him over to the staircase, drew him down, knelt beside him as he sat there on the second stair. He turned his face against my shoulder, and heaved a sigh.

After a little while, I raised my head and looked about me. We were in a large white-panelled hall, with a window through which I could see a plane-tree, its quiet branches stroking the glass. The only thing in common with our hall up in Scotland was the telephone, standing on a mahogany table against the wall. For some moments I gazed at it. My terror was wholly gone—like a dream at morning. But I became aware of a new emotion—disquieting, faintly discreditable. I looked suspiciously down at Allan, I wanted to *know*. Cautiously I began to frame my question. He was so still that I wondered if he had fallen asleep. But just then he stirred, and I took his head between my hands and, as he smiled at me, turned his face searchingly towards the light. It was calm as though washed by tidal waters. I knew that I could never ask my question.

At that moment the front door bell began to peal. We both jumped, and got to our feet.

"You go," said Allan, disappearing into the back of the house.

The sharp-nosed young man in the dripping mackintosh was aggrieved. "Been sent to cut you off," he said. "Bill unpaid—nothing done—"

I turned back into the hall. About me, above me, the house lay quiet. Only against the window the boughs of the plane-tree clamoured in a sudden flurry of wind and rain. The question I could never ask—the answer never to be given—surely both were irrelevant? For all the tranquillity of the house, I felt my panic begin again to stir. There was only one thing that mattered to me—to us.

"Allan—" I called—and I tried not to let my voice quaver—"It's about the telephone. Do you—do you *want* it cut off?"

I held my breath. The reply came immediately.

"Why—darling—we're going back to Scotland tonight, out of this damnable climate. We don't want to pay for what we aren't going to need anymore. Tell them they can disconnect it at once."

MORE TALES OF THE WEIRD TITLES
FROM BRITISH LIBRARY PUBLISHING

We welcome any suggestions, corrections or feedback you may have, and will aim to respond to all items addressed to the following:

> The Editor (Tales of the Weird), British Library Publishing,
> The British Library, 96 Euston Road, London NW1 2DB

We also welcome enquiries through our Twitter account, @BL_Publishing.